Y0-BSN-030
3 3455 02689 5331

BREAKING NEWS

Center Point
Large Print

Also by Susan Page Davis and available from Center Point Large Print:

The Priority Unit
Fort Point
Found Art
Heartbreaker Hero: Eddie's Story
The House Next Door
The Labor Day Challenge
Ransom of the Heart

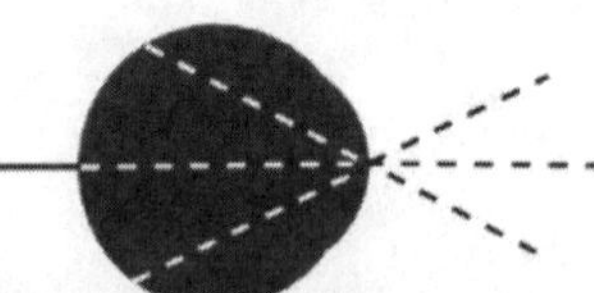

BREAKING NEWS

Susan Page Davis

Center Point Large Print
Thorndike, Maine

This Center Point Large Print edition is published in the year 2019 by arrangement with the author.

The text of this Large Print edition is unabridged.
In other aspects, this book may vary from the original edition.
Printed in the United States of America on permanent paper.
Set in 16-point Times New Roman type.

ISBN: 978-1-64358-363-1

The Library of Congress has cataloged this record under Library of Congress Control Number: 2019944736

Prologue—1968

Elwood Fairmont drove toward home a bit late. Olivia would make the children wait for their supper until he arrived, and no one would be happy. Sometimes he dreaded walking through the door.

He approached the gravel road that led to their lakeside house and braked only enough to make the turn safely. Too late he saw the dark blue sedan racing up the narrow lane. He swerved as his adrenaline surged, but it wasn't enough. Metal crunched metal.

The impact was inevitable, but not too severe. Both cars stopped, and dust filled the air. Elwood's hands shook as he shut off the engine and opened his door. His brain registered that the erratic driver of the other car was Thomas Jacobs, his summertime neighbor of many years. But that was impossible. He couldn't be here now.

"Senator Jacobs! I can't believe it."

The gray-haired man stared at him through his side window and slowly opened his car door.

"Elwood, it's you."

"Are you all right, sir?" Elwood's pulse still

pounded, but he reached to help the senator. Jacobs and his family owned the summer cottage across the road from the Fairmont house, and while they weren't close friends or social equals, they were on good terms.

"I—Yes, I—" Jacobs looked back down the dirt road, then toward the paved highway. "Elwood, you've got to help me."

"But, sir, what happened to you? They said you disappeared from your office in Washington two weeks ago. The papers have talked about nothing else. Everyone thinks you're dead."

Jacobs reached toward him with a placating desperation. "That's what I need right now, Elwood. You mustn't tell anyone you saw me. Not anyone."

"But, sir, your car!" Elwood looked pointedly at the smashed fender and headlight, and Jacobs followed his gaze.

"Most unfortunate."

"Are you sure you're all right?" Elwood asked.

"Yes, yes." Jacobs ran a hand through his hair. "Can you help me?"

"Of course. What do you want me to do?"

The senator hesitated. Another car approached along the main road. Jacobs turned his back to it and ducked below the open door of his sedan.

"I've got to get out of here," he said when it had passed. "I'm so sorry, Elwood. Here." Jacobs pulled a wad of folded bills from his pants pocket and counted off four fifty-dollar bills, thrusting them into Elwood's hand.

"What's this for?"

"The damage to your car."

"My insurance—"

"Fine, but you can't tell them who the other driver was. Tell them it was a hit and run. Please, Elwood. I'm begging you."

The back of Elwood's neck prickled. How would he explain this to Olivia and not tell her he'd seen Thomas Jacobs?

"Sir, does your family know you're alive? I just don't get it."

Jacobs leaned into his car and pulled out a briefcase. "I apologize for the trouble I've caused you, Elwood, but it has to be this way for now. If everything goes right, in a short time you'll hear the news that I've been found alive and well. Meanwhile, no one, and I mean *no one,* can know that I've been in Maine, or even that I'm still in this world. Do you understand?"

"I . . . I think so."

"Good. Now, take this for me." Jacobs handed Elwood the briefcase. "If you can just keep this safe for a few days, it would be an enormous help to me."

"Well, I guess I can do that."

"Thank you. I plan to come back for it very soon, but it's better if I'm not carrying it around tonight. And I have some things in the trunk. Do you mind?"

"Well, I guess not."

They transferred two cardboard boxes sealed with packing tape to Elwood's trunk. The brief-case went in beside them.

"There." Jacobs wiped his brow. "I have to get away from here as quickly as possible. I have a place to stay for a short time. Just put those things in a safe, inconspicuous place until I ask you for them."

"When will that be, sir?"

Jacobs frowned. "It should be within the week, but if you don't hear from me personally within thirty days, destroy those papers."

"All of it?"

"Yes. If I haven't returned by then, it will only bring you trouble."

Elwood drew a deep breath, but Jacobs was already in his car, backing it away from Elwood's.

He watched Jacobs turn onto the main road and drive away, then he looked down at the ground. Broken glass glittered in the twilight. He'd better clean it up. Olivia would be furious when he got home. Not only was he late, but the car was smashed, and he had no good explanation. He couldn't lie to her. But he'd promised.

Thirty days, he told himself. He'd made a promise, and he had to keep it for thirty days.

He stooped and picked up the fragments of

glass, wrapping them in his handkerchief. Probably the senator would be back sooner than that, and everything would be cleared up. He hoped so. As he straightened and opened his car door, a black Mercedes rolled down the main road. It slowed as it approached the road to the lake, and the man in the passenger seat stared at Elwood. He found it hard to draw a breath. He was glad they couldn't see his crumpled fender from their angle of approach. The car went on, disappearing around a curve on the road to Belgrade Lakes.

Elwood shivered. His relief in learning that Senator Jacobs was alive was dampened by the awkward events of the last ten minutes. *What have I gotten into?*

He got behind the wheel, tucked the handkerchief and the glass into the litter bag hanging from the cigarette lighter, and started the car.

Chapter 1

Forty Years Later

Janet Borden stepped onto the front porch of the old farmhouse and gave a firm knock on the barn red door, so that her elderly neighbor, Elwood Fairmont, would hear. He was a bit deaf, a condition which his hearing aids failed to remedy entirely.

A cool breeze came off the lake, ruffling her shoulder-length hair, and she shivered, wishing she had pulled on a jacket. September in Maine was unpredictable, and she had guessed wrong when she saw the brilliant sunlight glimmering on the water. After waiting a minute, she shifted the plastic carrier on her arm, careful not to tilt the strawberry-rhubarb pie. She brushed back the lock of hair that hung in her eyes and knocked again, a bit harder. Perhaps he was napping. She hated to disturb him, but he would be disappointed if he missed her visit.

Several seconds passed, and Janet began to feel uneasy. She looked around. Far out on the lake, a motorboat puttered toward the marina. There was no traffic on the gravel road. The Bordens' house and Elwood's were the only year-round homes on the dirt lane. All of the other structures were summer cottages, on the side of the road nearer the water. The seasonal residents, who paid dearly for their strips of lake frontage, had left at the end of August. The last of them, Mr. and Mrs. Pike, had pulled out on Labor Day afternoon, stopping at Janet's to be sure she had their phone number in Massachusetts, in case there was storm damage to their cottage during the winter.

Where could Elwood be? Maybe a friend took him out for a drive. Janet's concern outweighed her slight misgivings, and she tried the doorknob. It turned, and the heavy door swung inward.

"Elwood?" She put a smile in her voice as she stepped inside. "Elwood, hello! It's Janet."

Silence greeted her. She set the pie on the dining table and glanced into the kitchen, but it was empty. As she turned back toward the dining room, a small sound caught her attention, and she hurried on into the living room, or "parlor" as Elwood called it.

He lay on the floor, breathing raggedly, one hand reaching toward her across the woolen braided rug. His glasses had fallen beside him, and his thinning gray hair was rumpled.

Janet rushed to kneel beside him.

"Elwood, are you ill?"

Panic filled his eyes as he stared up at her, gasping with a choppy desperation.

"Lie still," she said. "I'm calling the ambulance."

The phone was in the dining room, she knew, on the windowsill. Janet and her husband, Kurt, had urged Elwood to get a signal button he could wear around his neck in case of emergency, but the old man had dismissed the suggestion with a wave of his hand. "My sister had one, and she set it off every time she coughed," he had said.

Janet punched in 911, straining to hear any sound from Elwood in the next room, and wishing she'd brought her cell phone. Her reflection in the mirror over the buffet didn't comfort her. Her rounded face was pale, and her dark hair was tousled beyond casual. "I can't stay on the line with you and be near him," she told the dispatcher. After describing Elwood's condition and making sure they had the location right, she went back to his side.

His eyes were closed, but he was still breathing. She kept watching and saw his chest take a slight jump every few seconds.

"They're on their way." She stroked his hand and began to pray silently, urgently.

Elwood moaned.

"Hold on, dear friend."

"Kids," Elwood managed to squeeze out.

"Kids?" asked Janet. "You want me to call your children?"

He shook his head.

"Take it easy," she said. "We'll talk later."

But he reached up and grasped her wrist. "Tell them . . ."

"Tell them what?"

He took several erratic breaths, and Janet heard the faint wail of a siren.

"I shouldn't have . . ."

She leaned closer, not sure she had understood. "What is it, Elwood?"

"I never told them." She could barely make out the words, and it seemed a huge effort for him. His facial muscles skewed as he labored to speak. *A stroke,* she thought.

"You'll have a chance to tell them whatever you want soon, Elwood. First you need to get well. We'll get you to the hospital." The siren screamed louder.

"No, no."

"It's all right, Elwood." She patted his wrinkled cheek, sensing his frustration as he groped for the words he wanted. The siren cut off, and wheels crunched the gravel on the drive. Janet squeezed his hand. "Help is here. I'm going to bring them to you."

She recognized one of the EMTs. The young woman had come around to collect for new equipment for the fire department, after the voters had turned down the warrant article at the town meeting. Property taxes were so high in the lakeside community that the residents hated to see anything new added to the budget, but Janet thought they had been shortsighted. Defibrillators and thermal imaging cameras would save lives. She had put a twenty-dollar bill in the EMT's envelope and chatted with her for a few minutes about the need for cutting edge health care.

She opened the door wider as the two EMTs came up onto the porch. "Serena, I'm glad you got here so fast. Mr. Fairmont is very ill, I'm afraid. A stroke, maybe. He spoke to me once, but it was a struggle."

They hurried to the parlor, and Serena's partner, a stocky man whose name tag said "Garrett," followed.

"There, Mr. Fairmont," Serena said as she knelt beside him. "Can you hear me?" Her bleached hair was held back by a fat fabric ring. She bent low over Elwood's still form.

His eyes opened in his ashen face and focused on Serena. He took in one of those tortured gasps that sent fear rushing through Janet's veins. "I—I—"

Garrett opened a bag, handed Serena a stethoscope, and asked Janet, "How old is he?"

"Nearly eighty."

Garrett made radio contact with the dispatcher. "Eighty-year-old male, patient is lethargic, weak, unable to get up off the floor, exhibiting facial droop and slurred speech . . ."

Elwood reached toward Janet, his fingers closing just short of her sleeve.

"What is it?" she asked, leaning close to his ear.

"I shouldn't have kept it." He pulled in a raspy breath. "Tell them—tell—"

"Don't try to talk, sir," Serena said, placing the end of the stethoscope on his chest.

"You must," Elwood choked.

His agitation made Janet throw Serena an apologetic glance. She leaned down again. "Must what, Elwood?"

"I should have done what he told me."

"What who told you?" Janet asked, stroking his hand.

"I'm so . . . sorry." He closed his eyes once more and took a deep, shuddering breath.

Janet tried in bewilderment to analyze what he had said. She and Elwood had formed a friendship during the three years the Bordens had lived next door to him, and Janet liked the old man. Their frequent conversations over the past few months had touched on many topics, including art, local politics, and the meaning of life. She knew Elwood and his children were not on the best of terms, but he had never expressed such deep regret or remorse.

She took his hand. "You don't need to worry about that now. Just rest and let these people help you."

"No, no!" He struggled, pushing against the rug

with his elbows, and Janet looked at the EMTs in alarm.

Garrett held on to the frail man's shoulders. "Lie back, sir. Take it easy. Just relax."

"Tell them!" Elwood insisted, his eyes homing in on Janet. "You have to tell them I'm so—so—."

"I will," she said, more to put him at ease than out of conviction that she could do as he wished.

He sank back on the floor and sighed. "You tell them . . ."

Janet glanced at Serena, and saw a veiled look pass between her and Garrett.

Elwood drew in another shaky breath, and his eyelids fluttered against the papery skin of his cheek. They all waited, and Serena listened to his chest.

"We're losing him!" Serena cried, and Janet realized Elwood had not reached for the next breath.

"Get back!" Garrett snapped at her, and Janet catapulted away, giving them room to work. As they went into the frantic but steady routine of CPR, she watched with a sense of unreality.

Elwood was dying. There was something she had to tell his children, but she didn't know what.

Janet swallowed hard and turned away, a panicky prayer for her friend skipping from her mind toward heaven.

• • •

"You did all you could," Kurt said. He let Janet refill his coffee cup but declined dessert—the neglected strawberry-rhubarb pie. Janet had carried it home after watching the ambulance pull out of Elwood's driveway late that morning.

She ought to have known Kurt wouldn't eat the pie. He ran three times a week and was proud of the thirteen pounds he had lost over the summer. He was in such good shape that Janet felt downright inferior if she let herself dwell on it. If it hadn't been for the touch of gray at his temples and the crinkles at the corners of his eyes, he could have passed for a decade younger than his fifty-two years.

Unfortunately, after she'd called Kurt at the newspaper office and told him of Elwood's illness, and after she'd called Elwood's youngest daughter and had a good cry, she had sat down and eaten two pieces of the pie. Now she couldn't give it someone else, and Kurt wouldn't eat the rest. She'd been hoping to drop a size this summer, but somehow her dieting plans always failed.

"They say he's lingering." She shook her head. "Sharon is driving up here. Maybe she's at the hospital by now."

"I've been praying all afternoon that she'd make it in time," Kurt said.

Fresh tears welled in Janet's eyes. Kurt was steady and predictable. For almost thirty years he had kept her anchored in reality. She needed that, although at times his very dependability annoyed her.

She scowled at him. "I wish you'd eat that pie."

"It's full of sugar. You know I love pie, but—"

"Yes, I know." She turned away and set the coffeepot back on its base then deliberately covered the pie with foil and put it as far back in the refrigerator as it would go. She wondered how long it would take her to get it out.

"Elwood's children will be comforted to know that you were there with him." Kurt sipped his coffee and sat back to look at her.

Janet almost asked him why he didn't give up coffee if he was so determined to outlive her, but she didn't. It wasn't like her, and she realized that the stress of the day drove her behavior.

"Maybe I could have done more." She looked to Kurt for confirmation of her own doubts, but he shook his head and reached for her hand, drawing her back to her chair.

"No. Just think, Janet. If you hadn't gone over, no one would have known he needed help. You found him and got help for him, and he was able to speak to you, to ask you to let his children know he was thinking of them. That will mean a lot to them."

She looked into his compassionate blue eyes and sighed. "Maybe I should have done something—you know—medical."

"Like what?"

"I don't know. Aspirin, maybe?"

Kurt shrugged. "When you're not sure what the problem is, that can be dangerous."

She knew it was true. "But what about his so-called urgent message? I don't know what to make of it."

"It sounds as though he did something that he regrets, and he wants the children to know he's sorry."

"Yes, but what was it?"

"Does it matter?"

Janet frowned. "I guess not. But . . . well, he seemed so intent, Kurt. It was extremely important to him that his kids knew this . . . whatever it was."

"Kids." Kurt laughed, and Janet smiled, too. The youngest of Elwood's four children was nearly her age.

"Yes, well, if it's regrets for their disagreements in the past, I hope he has a chance to apologize to them in person."

"You think it was that bad between them?"

She sipped her tea and set the mug down. "He's told me a little bit. Just hints, really." She reflected on her many visits with her widowed neighbor. Since she and Kurt had bought the house down the road from Elwood's, they had adopted him. Kurt went over occasionally and helped him with seasonal chores around the yard and the old Greek Revival farmhouse. Janet took him goodies once a week or so and sat with him to listen to his stories. "I know his two sons are very bitter toward him. Paul, the younger one, hasn't spoken to him in years. Not even a Christmas card."

"That's a shame." Kurt drained his coffee mug. "Maybe that's it. He's ready to patch things up and wishes he'd done it sooner."

Janet looked up at him, trying to remember every word Elwood had gasped out that morning. "There was something in particular that was bothering him. He said, *I shouldn't have kept it. I should have done what he told me.*"

"And you've no idea to whom he was referring?"

Janet couldn't help smiling. Kurt was city editor at the newspaper in Waterville, the small city fifteen miles away, and he talked like an editor. His grammar was always impeccable. Even last year, when their older daughter Anne's husband had called with the happy news of their first grandchild's birth, Kurt had kept his deadpan demeanor.

"At first he just laid there looking like a rubber doll, and then he took a big breath and screamed bloody murder," their son-in-law, B.J., had said, laughing with joy. "He's got a great set of lungs."

Kurt had smiled at Janet and murmured into the phone, "Lay there."

"What's that?" B.J. asked. Janet could hear his excitement, although she was six feet from the telephone receiver.

"He just lay there," Kurt said gently. "That's great news, B.J. We'll come down this weekend to see him."

Now she shook her head, thinking about Elwood's garbled speech. "No. He didn't say much more. Just that he was sorry, and I must tell the children." Janet scowled, wishing she had a piece of pie in front of her. "When they took him away in the ambulance, I found Elwood's address book and called Sharon."

"Is she the one who was here in July?" Kurt asked.

"Yes. She seemed quite nice when I met her, so I picked her of the four children. Her married name's Schlesser. She remembered me. She said she would come right up and stay at her father's house. And she'll tell the others. I suppose they'll come, too."

"Do you think so? If the boys dislike him so much, I mean."

Janet was less dubious. "He's likely to die, Kurt. Surely they'll come."

"I hope you're right."

"I made up the bed in one of the spare rooms

at Elwood's for Sharon. She said she'd call me when she gets here."

Kurt nodded. "You're a good neighbor, Janet. You did everything you could."

She looked down at her hands, clasped on the brown woven tablecloth.

"You did," Kurt insisted, "but if it will make you feel better, bake more pies. No doubt they'll have a full house over there, and if Elwood dies, they'll have folks over after the funeral. They'll need lots of food. Isn't that the usual custom in these parts?"

"Yes. I'll make butter tarts and little muffins."

"There you go," Kurt said.

"Will you eat that pie?"

"Save it for the Fairmonts."

"It's got two pieces missing."

"I see."

She winced, but his tender smile soothed her.

Kurt stood and pulled her to her feet, slipping his arms around her. "I love you," he said.

Chapter 2

Kurt headed down the corridor to his small private office, glad the tense meeting with his boss was over. He spent most of his working hours in the bustling newsroom, at the center of the action, but retreated to the tiny box-like room allotted to him when he needed some quiet time.

The head photographer, Wally Reed, came toward him down the hall, swinging his camera bag and whistling. Kurt could smell the cigarette smoke that clung to the graying man's clothes from ten paces away.

"Where you headed, Wally?" Kurt asked.

"Colby College, for the soccer team practice. They've got some hotshot freshman from Argentina, and Sports is doing a spread. Then I have to go take leaf pictures for Special Sections. Leaf pictures." Wally shook his head in disgust, and Kurt figured that if they'd been outside he would have spat on the ground.

"What's wrong with pretty leaves?" he asked. Wally had the finesse to make a mud puppy look good on film, but he always found something to complain about.

"They've hardly started turning yet. They want color for an 'Autumn in Maine' section that's going to be published two weeks from now. I'm sorry, but it's only the seventh of September, and the color won't peak for another month."

Kurt smiled. "I know you, Wally. You'll find some red leaves."

"Ha. Sickly orange, maybe." But Wally's grimace slid into a smile as he punched the elevator button. "Never should have started putting color in newspapers."

Kurt entered his office, and the weight of the task he was facing hit him again. He needed a few minutes of quiet time, out of view of his subordinates, to prepare himself. He closed the blind on the window between him and the hallway, then opened the top desk drawer and lifted a small book. He turned to the Psalms and sat quietly for several minutes, reading and thinking. His mind kept drifting to the unwelcome job he had to do.

This was the hard part of being in management. He loved his position and rarely missed the grind of the reporter's job. Over the years he'd had plenty of that—facing down a tough politician during an interview that became a confrontation, or dashing out at midnight to the scene of a car wreck and coming back charged up with adrenaline, yet at the same time sickened. Seeing his byline over a story and knowing he had written it well no longer satisfied him.

Now he oversaw the total operation in the newsroom, deciding which reporter would cover each breaking story, and what headline would smack the readers in the face the next morning. Each evening when he left the office, he was determined not to think about the job again until morning. Now and then the evening editor called him at home over some glitch that needed Kurt's expertise, but in general he refused to think about the paper at night. Janet made home a quiet retreat, and he appreciated that.

He got up each morning and fetched the paper from the driveway, to dissect over breakfast. There was no sense being blindsided with surprises when he got to the office. He scrutinized each page and made sure the night crew had put the package together right. Then Kurt would talk to Janet, lighthearted, about their plans for the weekend or the latest news from the kids.

Janet suited him, and he never stopped thanking God for her. She might be a bit of a worrier, and she struggled with her weight, but she was the perfect wife for him. Her tenderness and caring heart were the antidote Kurt needed to the harsh, violent news that filled his days. Her analytical mind often surprised him. Janet had worked as a bank teller in Connecticut, before they moved to Maine, helping pay the kids' college tuition, but Kurt was sure she could have been a lawyer or a physicist if she'd wanted to. Sometimes it scared him, the possibilities Janet had given up to be with him.

Today was different from most days. Instead of concentrating on making the paper better than it was yesterday, today he had to delve into personnel matters, and that was the most distasteful part of his job.

He started to rise, to go out and summon Mick Tyler, but decided to avoid the chance of embarrassing Mick in front of the other people in the newsroom. He reached for the phone instead, punched in the senior reporter's extension, and waited. It rang three times. Had Mick left his desk? At last his voice came, impatient and annoyed.

"What?"

"Mick, this is Kurt. I'd like you to step down the hall to see me for a minute, please."

"I'm right in the middle of something."

"The city council story?"

There was a pause, then Mick said, "No, actually. Something else."

Kurt frowned. Mick should have filed the city council article before noon, and it was already two o'clock.

"I won't keep you long." There was a click, and Kurt replaced the receiver. Mick's rudeness had incited several complaints to the management over the last few months, and Kurt had a strong impression that the publisher only put up with

Mick's temper and his increasing slackness about assignments and deadlines because of his past successes as a writer. He'd pulled in a lot of awards for the paper. His forceful style and ruthless research techniques no doubt expanded the readership, and perhaps even the advertising contracts. But last year's investigative triumph wouldn't sell papers tomorrow.

"What's up?" Mick stood in the doorway, leaning against the jamb. He slumped as though relaxed, but his dark brown eyes smoldered with suspicion.

"Sit down." Kurt stood and closed the door, edging past Mick to get back to his chair. He ought to have told Mick to meet him in the conference room. You could hardly move in here, it was so cramped. "Grant Engstrom asked me to speak to you."

"This can't be good." Mick yawned and fumbled in his breast pocket.

"You're right." Kurt sat back and watched him, but Mick refused to make eye contact.

He took out a container of mints and popped several into his mouth. "All right, let me have it."

Kurt sat forward and picked up his pen. Mick watched his hands, but still didn't meet his gaze.

"Engstrom thinks you need to improve in a few areas."

"Is this my evaluation? I thought we did that last spring."

"Yes, we did. You might recall that I pointed out several categories where you'd let things slide a bit."

Mick shrugged.

"Mick, I haven't seen any improvement. In fact, I haven't even seen any effort on your part to improve. Now Engstrom's on my case to get results from you."

Mick curled his upper lip in disdain. "Engstrom's so out of touch he wouldn't know a hot tip if it singed the seat of his pants."

Kurt knew there was a bit of truth in that. Engstrom's lack of news sense had often exasperated him. "Perhaps, but Grant Engstrom is still the publisher of this newspaper, which means people call him when they're unhappy with what they read in it."

"Somebody's complaining about me?"

"He's had several calls recently. Your coverage of the incident at the junior high school was sketchy at best, and Representative Morton found your piece about him, and I quote, *reprehensible and erroneous.*"

"He's reprehensible and pompous."

"The reporter's appraisal of the subject shouldn't be obvious to the reader."

Mick stuck the package of mints back in his pocket. "You let it go to press."

Kurt eyed him for a long moment. "As a matter of fact, I didn't. You were supposed to give me that piece a week ago Friday, but you didn't. You apparently filed it at the last minute Sunday night, and the editor barely had time to read it and slap it on the page. I didn't see it until Monday morning, and by then it was too late. I admit I wondered at the time—"

"What? If I handed it in late on purpose?"

"You know I wouldn't have run it the way it was. No matter how you feel about the representative, that was a scathing piece. And what about the city council story?"

"Which one?"

"The one from last night's meeting."

"You haven't seen it yet."

"That's right. You were supposed to get it to me by noon. When precisely do you expect I'll have a chance to read it?"

Mick fidgeted just a bit, and Kurt felt for the first time that he was gaining ground.

"I'll have it for you within an hour."

"Good." Kurt sat back with a sigh. "Mick, you're an excellent writer, but then, you know that. Maybe people have praised you too much. There's a problem with being good at your craft, you know. People expect you to go on delivering. You can't be excellent one day and lax the next."

"Well, thanks for the pep talk." Mick started to rise.

"We're not finished."

Mick clenched his teeth. "Do you want that city council story or not?"

"Sit." Kurt stared until Mick sat. "Engstrom wants you to take a leave of absence."

"A *what?*" Mick's incredulity was almost comical.

"Take some time off. Maybe get away for a few weeks and relax. No deadlines, no phones, no editors on your back."

Mick stared at him.

"Life's too short," Kurt said. "You've had a good career here. You don't want to completely blow it, Mick."

"You're talking like my job's in jeopardy."

Kurt laid his pen down carefully. "Grant Engstrom cares about the bottom line. That means he cares about the feelings of his advertisers."

"Oh, right. But he doesn't care about the feelings of his staff."

"Take some time off, Mick. Come back fresh."

Mick stared at the bare oak floor, shaking his head. "I can't believe this. I could have gone to Boston three or four years ago, you know. They offered me big bucks. Man, I should have gone."

Kurt said nothing, and Mick looked him in the eye at last.

"You'd like that, wouldn't you? You want me to leave."

"No," Kurt said decisively. "But you're burnt out, Mick. I don't know what's done it, whether it's boredom, or the stress of the job, or something personal, but sometimes a reporter needs a change. It happened to me, and I went into a different job. For you, maybe all you need is a little time and a fresh perspective."

Mick nodded slowly. "There's a lot going on."

"At home?"

Mick laughed, a short, hollow sound. "I'd say yes, if I were still living at home. Callie tossed me out a month ago."

"I'm sorry."

"Yeah, right."

"Where are you staying?"

"Does it matter?"

"Yes."

"With a friend."

Mick obviously had revealed as much as he wanted Kurt to know. "All right. But you know this is affecting your work. You need to straighten things out."

"Yeah, yeah, you said that. *Life is too short.*"

Kurt nodded, thinking of Elwood Fairmont lying on the braided rug in his living room and wheezing out his regrets to Janet.

"What are you thinking?" Mick asked.

Kurt smiled and shook his head. "I was just remembering our neighbor. He had a stroke yesterday."

"Ah. The sweet old neighbor. A touching illustration of the brevity of life."

Kurt inhaled sharply, trying to stifle the annoyance Mick roused in him. "He's a nice man. But he has a lot of regrets."

"Is this where you tell me I should learn my lessons the easy way and not end up like your neighbor?"

"I sincerely hope you don't, Mick."

"The old geezer's probably overdue at the undertaker's."

Kurt winced.

"Hey, you live out in Belgrade, don't you?" Mick asked suddenly, as though the turn of the conversation had sparked an absorbing new train of thought.

"That's right. On Pine Lane, near the lake."

Mick leaned toward him. "That's near where Senator Jacobs lived, right?"

"Who?"

Mick gestured impatiently, as though Kurt were sluggish. "Thomas Jacobs. You know. He disappeared in the spring of '68."

Kurt blinked and let his brain toss that around. "That was before my time, I guess, but I do seem to recall . . ."

"Right," Mick said, pouncing on his vague acknowledgment. "There was a huge scandal. The senator disappeared, and there was a big to-do about it. Something about some money, a federal payroll or something, I forget what exactly. But then a month or so later, Bobby

Kennedy was assassinated, and everyone just forgot about Jacobs. It wasn't news anymore."

Kurt thought hard, pulling out scraps of articles he had read in the past. "Jacobs. Didn't he disappear from the Capitol building in Washington?"

"That's right. The Democratic Senator from Maine. His house was in your neighborhood."

"Is that right? I didn't know that."

"Sure. He and his family used to come every summer. I remember Charlotte, his daughter. She was the snootiest girl I ever knew. Wouldn't socialize with us locals. Of course, she was older than me, but I remember she used to make her father's chauffeur drive her out to the country club in Waterville for dances. Wouldn't go to the townfolk's dances at the gym."

Kurt watched Mick and realized his eyes were animated for the first time in months. His voice had taken on the excitement Kurt had heard three years ago, when he first met Mick. The reporter's adrenaline had cranked up like this when he was about to start covering a big story, but Kurt hadn't seen him show more than a marginal interest in a new project for a long time.

He strove for a casual note as he opened his desk drawer and took out a pad of sticky notes. "Say, Mick, why don't you do a feature on Senator Jacobs?"

Mick jerked back and looked at him in amazement. "That story's almost as old as you are."

"But it has this local angle. Does the family still live in the area?"

"No. His wife never came back here after he disappeared."

Kurt nodded, thinking. "Still, there must be a lot of people in the area who remember Senator Jacobs and his family. Nostalgia. You know."

"Probably wouldn't turn up anything new," Mick said.

"But older people like to read about things that happened when they were young. You could ask them what they think about the scandal, too."

"Well, sure. Everybody probably has a theory about what happened to the senator in '68."

"Do you?"

"I was just a kid then." Mick's enigmatic smile made Kurt wonder what that kid had thought so long ago.

"I think you should do it." Kurt scribbled on the note pad. "Go out to Belgrade tomorrow. Visit the town office, find out if the house is still standing and who owns it now. Talk to neighbors and any old-timers you can find. I don't expect you to solve Senator Jacobs's disappearance or anything, just poke around a little and ask those nosy questions you're so good at. If you think there's a feature in it, I'll detail a photographer for you, and he can get some photos of the house. We'll run it in the Sunday edition. A full page spread."

"You really think so?"

"Sure. The readers will love it. I'll alert Advertising. Maybe they can sell a whole page of ads to Belgrade businesses. If we work together on this and you do it right, Grant Engstrom will love it."

Mick stood up slowly but didn't move toward the door. Kurt tore off the memo sheet and stuck it on the flat surface of the desk. "You'll need, what, a week or so to do the research? I'll still need that city council piece today, though."

"Sure," Mick said. "But what about the leave of absence?"

Kurt let it hang in the air for a moment, then smiled up at Mick. "Sometimes a fresh lead is as good as a vacation."

Mick laughed and was out the door. Kurt sat back and exhaled. He hoped he was doing the right thing. Mick was so close to the edge.

The phone rang, and he picked up the receiver. "Kurt Borden."

"Did you talk to Mick Tyler?"

Kurt smiled in chagrin. Speaking of rudeness, the publisher could use a few lessons in etiquette. "Yes, Grant, I did."

"Is he going to take some time off? Because I was thinking we might be able to get an intern in cheap for a few weeks, until we see if Tyler's going to shape up."

"No, actually we're going to try something different. I'm getting him off the city hall beat for a week or two and putting him on a new project. I think you'll like it." Kurt swiveled his chair so that he faced the window overlooking the Kennebec River and prepared to make his case and soothe the irate publisher.

Chapter 3

Sharon Fairmont Schlesser sat in Janet's sunny kitchen the next day, drinking Canadian tea. Janet smiled in delight when she accepted a piece of pie. After eyeing Sharon's petite figure, Janet had feared she wouldn't eat anything laced with carbohydrates.

"I really shouldn't," Sharon said with a guilty shake of her head. She was the youngest of Elwood's four children, and Janet thought she wore her fifty years well. Her shoulder-length, light brown hair had a natural wave, and she played up her lovely eyes with understated makeup. Even in her designer jeans and forest green turtleneck, she looked stylish.

"I was taking this to your father when I found him." Janet cut two generous slices and lifted them onto the Fostoria dessert plates she seldom used. "He told me several times how your mother had gout and couldn't eat rhubarb, so she never cooked it. But he loved it, so once in a while I would make it for him."

"That's Dad for you." Sharon picked up her fork. "You and your husband have been wonderful. I've felt so much easier about Dad being alone here, knowing he had good neighbors."

"He's easy to like." Janet smiled, remembering how eager Elwood had been to talk to her. Mrs. Fairmont had died the winter after the Bordens moved in next door, and Janet had made Elwood her personal project. Her own father lived three hundred miles away, but Elwood was so accessible, and so paternal. He could be gruff at times, but he was witty and appreciative of her efforts. Kurt took to him, too, and insisted on putting up the cumbersome, old-fashioned storm windows each fall for Elwood, after Janet had washed them.

"I'm glad you knew that side of him. He spoke of you and your husband often." Sharon took a bite of the pie, and her eyes flared in surprised pleasure. "Oh, Janet, this is superb! You've absolutely got to give me the recipe."

Janet smiled. "It's simple. I'll write it out for you." She went to the cupboard where she kept her recipe box. She might feel dowdy next to Sharon—Janet hardly ever wore makeup anymore, since she had stopped working outside the home, and she stuck with casual dress most of the time—but she knew her cooking could stand up to anyone else's. As she fished for a pen in her junk drawer, she glanced at Sharon, wondering how to bring up the words Elwood had spoken the day before. "There's something I want to tell you, but it's a bit odd."

"Oh? Does it have to do with Dad?" Sharon took another generous bite of pie.

"Yes. It's something he said yesterday, before the ambulance took him away."

Sharon laid down her fork and waited, a slight frown creasing her brow.

Janet located a pen at last and brought it with the recipe box to the table. "It may be nothing, but at the time he seemed quite agitated about it. He asked me to tell you and your brothers and sister something."

"What?"

Janet pressed her lips together. "I don't know. I mean, he said a couple of times that he was sorry, but I don't know what he meant by that—whether he was sorry for a particular incident, or for the general state of his relationship with you kids, or what." She smiled an apology at Sharon. "This isn't very helpful, is it? I hesitated to say anything, because I'm sure it raises a lot of questions in your mind."

"Well . . ." Sharon lifted her teacup and took a sip, staring off toward the side window. "You say he was excited?"

"Upset, I think, but he was in great physical distress. I'm not sure how much that had to do with what he said."

"What did he say exactly?"

Janet paused, wanting to get it right. "He said he was sorry. That was clear. And there was something he was worried about, something he'd kept that he shouldn't have." She shrugged. "A promise, maybe?"

Sharon shook her head, her face a blank.

"Well, anyway, he also mentioned that someone had told him to do something. He said, *I should have done it,* or something like that. He regretted not having done what someone asked him to."

"Probably Mother. She always complained that he didn't listen to her." Sharon cut the rest of her pie into four neat pieces. "I'll have to walk five miles to work this off, but it's worth it."

Janet smiled and pulled a fresh recipe card from the pack in the front of the box. She wrote "Strawberry-Rhubarb Pie" on the top line. "I wouldn't have mentioned it, except he seemed so very urgent about it. And I didn't want to be like him, having regrets for not fulfilling someone's request, so I'm telling you. But I did assure him he'd soon feel better and have a chance to tell you himself, whatever it was he wanted you to know."

Sharon nodded. "Thank you. I hope it turns out that way. We've all had our run-ins with Dad, especially the boys, but I believe he truly loved us and cared about us, even though he didn't spend a lot of time with us. I hope he recovers and has a chance to get whatever it is off his chest."

Janet copied the ingredients for the pie quickly and handed the card to Sharon. "There. Use your usual recipe for the crust."

"Thanks. My husband will go wild over this."

"Is he coming up?"

"Not unless Dad dies." Sharon winced. "I don't mean to sound callous. When you called, it sounded as though Dad was at death's door, but the doctors have some hope. Anyway, Vic needed to work today. He said that if I need him, he'll drive up tomorrow. If not, he'll stay in Massachusetts. But my daughter, Tory, called last night. When I told her about Dad, she suggested she might drive up and join me if I end up staying more than a few days."

"That's great. And the others are coming tomorrow, you said?"

"Yes, my sister, Geneva, is driving up from Camden, and my brothers are flying." Sharon stood with the recipe card in her hand. "I'd better get going. I want to get their rooms ready, and I plan on going back to the hospital around four."

Janet rose to see her to the door. "Let me come over and help you make the beds. I brought some of Elwood's linens over here to air. I hope you don't mind."

"Thank you so much! I noticed that the upstairs rooms had been closed off and smelled a bit musty. I threw all the windows open before I ran over here."

"Great. Let me just grab those things off the line out back." Halfway across the kitchen, Janet stopped and wheeled toward Sharon. *"I should have done what he told me."*

Sharon blinked twice. "I beg your pardon?"

"Those were your father's exact words. *I should have done what he told me.*"

Sharon frowned. "So he couldn't have meant Mother."

"No, I guess not."

Kurt looked up when the back door to the newsroom opened. Mick Tyler strode into the newsroom and headed straight to his desk.

"Excuse me, Dave," Kurt said to the rookie reporter. "We'll talk about this later. Just finish up that advance on the lecture series."

"Will do."

Kurt shoved his hands in his pockets and ambled over to Mick's desk.

"Been to Belgrade?"

"Yup." Mick glanced up at him but kept on pulling items from his battered briefcase: a small, spiral-bound notebook, a voice-activated tape recorder, a few loose sheets of paper, and a silver pen. Kurt noted with approval that he seemed sober and purposeful.

"Find out anything about the Jacobs house?"

Mick laughed. “Boss, you’re gonna love this. You know where Pine Lane is, don’tcha?”

Kurt nodded. “I live there. But you knew that.”

Mick’s grin spread over his entire face. “That’s right. Know who else lives on Pine Lane?”

“Well . . .” Kurt decided to play along. “My neighbor, Mr. Fairmont, for one.”

“He the guy who had the stroke?”

“Yes.”

Mick nodded. “That’s too bad. I didn’t put it together yesterday when you told me about it, but I know him.”

“You do?” Kurt sat down on the edge of Mick’s desk.

“Sure. His son and I were friends in school. I didn’t know the old man well, but I met him a few times, say about forty-five years ago.”

“And?”

Mick opened his desk drawer and rifled the tray in it, flinging paper clips and pencils onto the carpet. “Nothing. That’s irrelevant to my story. Although there’s a station wagon with Massachusetts plates in his yard today.”

“That must be his daughter,” Kurt said.

“Could be. Well, anyway, who lives in the house directly across from Fairmont?”

“It’s a summer home. The Hillmans own it, but they live out of state. They usually come up weekends from Memorial Day to Labor Day, and they stay two or three weeks in July.”

Mick nodded, still grinning. "You're absolutely right. That's the name the town office gave me for the current owner."

"Current owner?" Kurt eyed him, waiting for the punch line. "I guess this means you were researching the former owners."

"Bingo. That's the house."

"Senator Jacobs's house?"

"Yup. I was pretty sure, but I checked the old tax maps to be absolutely certain. Thomas Jacobs owned it from 1946 to 1969. Or actually, 1968, because that's when he disappeared. His wife sold it in '69."

"So, you think there's a story in it?"

"You gonna give me a photographer? I want to tell him exactly what shots I need."

"Sure. Wally can meet you there Monday."

Mick sobered. "Kurt, thanks. I mean it."

"I'm sure you'll do a great job. And the city council story you did yesterday was good, by the way. Engstrom thinks so, too."

"Well, this beats being forced to take a leave, for sure." Mick smiled at him. "This story's gonna be great, and I'll get it to you on time. I promise."

Kurt stood up, feeling easier about Mick's outlook than he had in months. "Terrific. I can't wait to read it."

"Just you wait." Mick picked up the notebook. "You'll have it next Friday, and I guarantee, you won't want to bury this in the D section. It's gonna be a killer story."

"How long are we going to keep up the death watch?" Paul Fairmont paced back and forth at the end of his father's hospital bed, from the window to the door of the bathroom and back. His nervous energy made Sharon uneasy. Paul's attention seemed to dart here and there, never resting on one thing long. He was fifty-two, but the dark circles beneath his eyes and the extra thirty pounds he carried made him look older. He was a couple of inches shorter than his brother, Andrew, and had never lost his resentment for that. "I can't stay here more than a few days," he said.

"I, for one, have to be back at work Wednesday," said Geneva Dale, the oldest of the four. She pulled an emery board from her purse and began to file her nails. She was a top-selling real estate agent in Camden, an upscale village on the coast, and she made sure everyone knew how essential her presence was in the office.

"What if he's still comatose by then?" Paul whipped the curtain back and stared out at the rain and the vast parking lot below.

"He's not comatose!" Sharon sank onto one of the chairs the nurses had provided.

"Well, he can't hear us," Andrew said. Sharon had tried to get him to shoulder some of the responsibility of the arrangements for their father's care, since he was the oldest son, but Andrew seemed happy to leave all of the details to her and Geneva.

"How do you know that? Just because he can't respond to us doesn't mean he's deaf." Tears filled Sharon's eyes, and she blinked hard. Her older siblings had always made fun of her tendency to cry easily, but she couldn't help it. Her emotions were never far below the surface.

Geneva nodded. "The nurses seem to think he can hear when he's not asleep."

Paul bent and stared unceremoniously at his father's partly-closed eyelids. "Do you think he's asleep?"

"No, I don't. Get out of his face." Geneva pulled at Paul's sleeve. Her younger brother glared at her, and Sharon thought how alike their expressions were, though Geneva's cheeks were thin. They had the melting brown eyes all the Fairmont siblings inherited from their mother, and the same soft brown hair, although Sharon was sure Geneva had covered her gray.

"He doesn't even have his hearing aids in," Paul said. "You know he can't hear without them." He resumed his pacing.

Andrew remained seated in the corner and let out a deep sigh. "We've been here two days."

Paul gave a bark of laughter. "As if we didn't all know that. I ought to be back at my desk

Monday. I think I'll go call the airline and see if they can get me to Independence tomorrow."

Andrew stretched his legs out in front of him. "Why don't you do that? I'm sure the insurance company will fold if you're not there."

"I suppose you'll stay here until he breathes his last or makes a miraculous recovery in time to see his children keeping loving vigil."

"Paul!" Geneva frowned. "I know you boys were never close to Dad, and you're frustrated by all this waiting, but you could show a little respect."

"Paul, why don't you go out for a walk?" Sharon asked. "If there's any change, we'll come get you."

A nurse entered the room. "Excuse me. I just need to check Mr. Fairmont's condition."

"I thought that's what all the machines are for." Andrew pulled his long legs in so she wouldn't trip over his feet.

"It is, but we can't rely only on the monitors. We come in every now and then to be sure the data we're getting accurately reflects his condition."

"Where have you been?" Geneva scowled at Andrew. "They've been doing that all along." She dropped the emery board into her leather tote bag and pulled out an *Architectural Digest*.

"I didn't know what they were doing." Andrew stood up. "If you'll excuse me, I'm meeting Mick

Tyler for supper. I'll probably go right to the house afterward."

"Mick Tyler?" Sharon arched her eyebrows. "I haven't seen him since your graduation."

Andrew shrugged. "I call him now and again, when I'm in Maine."

"Is he still working at the paper?" Geneva asked.

"Yes, he's their star reporter, or at least that's the way Mick tells it."

"He always thought too much of himself," Geneva muttered.

"Say hello from all of us," Sharon said. "We'll see you back at the house."

Andrew headed out the door, and Paul followed.

"Where are you going?" Sharon called.

"To call the airline." Paul didn't look back.

"I knew you'd bring it up." Andrew stared down into his coffee cup. "It never fails. For the last forty years, every time I see you, we talk about that night."

Mick shrugged and sipped his Scotch. "It made a lasting impression, I guess."

"Well, my father was right. There was nothing to it."

"Maybe." Mick frowned. "Actually, I have another reason for mentioning it this time."

"Oh?" Andrew laid his fork and knife across

his plate and looked around for the waitress. She was nowhere to be seen.

"I've got a new boss," Mick said. "Well, not new, exactly. He's been here two or three years now, but he's new enough not to have heard the old stories, or the local legends."

"What's that got to do with anything?"

"He's put me onto doing a story about Tom Jacobs. That's right. And while I was doing some research, I learned some very interesting things."

"Such as?"

"Well, for one thing, Borden—my editor—lives in the house down the road from the senator's old digs."

"Really?" He definitely had Andrew's attention now. "Wait a minute. Borden? There's a neighbor woman by that name. Kindhearted, a bit smothery with baked goods."

"That's the boss's wife."

Andrew nodded. "Seems like a decent sort. She was the one who found my father the day he had the stroke."

"Hadn't heard that." Mick swirled the ice in his glass. "A bit dumpy for my taste."

"Say, that's not kind, especially when we both know your taste is rather eclectic."

Mick shook his head in dismissal of Janet. "Well, anyway, you remember that night."

"Of course I remember. What's your point?"

"That night." Mick set his glass down on the

table with a thud. The waitress approached, pulling a sales pad from her apron pocket.

"Refill?" she asked Mick, and he nodded. She picked up his glass and looked at Andrew. "Anything else for you, sir?"

"Just more coffee."

When she had left them, Andrew focused on Mick and decided he was still marginally sober. "I don't see what that night has to do with your boss."

"Think, Andrew. We were so stupid, so ignorant back then."

"We were kids."

"Yes, I know. We never put it together."

"Put what together?"

"Think," Mick insisted. "Make your brain work. What day was it?"

Andrew shrugged, feeling just a little cross. "How should I know? Early summer. Had school ended? It was a warm night."

"School was still in session."

"You're right. It seems like we couldn't wait for the freedom of summer."

"But it was hot that day. We'd been out fishing after supper." Mick watched him expectantly.

"Early June, I suppose," Andrew said, a bit pleased that he could pull that out. "School got out later then, didn't it?"

"Seems like it. Do you know what day Senator Jacobs disappeared?"

Andrew stared at him, feeling a bit stupid. "Surely not that day."

"He went missing in May, Andy."

"You don't say. That same year?"

"Yes."

"But . . . he wasn't in Belgrade when he vanished. Everyone knows he was in Washington. He left his office in the Capitol for lunch, and no one ever saw him again. You're telling me it was that day? The day we . . . No, come on. Dad told us what we saw was nothing."

"And when did you ever listen to your father?" Mick leaned forward and dropped his voice. "I looked it up this afternoon, Andy. He vanished May sixteenth. I'm thinking that was two or three weeks earlier than what we saw."

The waitress brought their drinks, and Mick grinned at her. "Thanks, sweetheart." He took a gulp from his glass and frowned at Andrew. "I wish I'd kept a journal then."

"We were kids," Andrew said again, feeling the futility of it.

"Yes, we were kids."

"My father was right. It was nothing. You've said so yourself."

"Was it?"

Mick's attitude was beginning to make Andrew uneasy. "If it were something to do with the senator, surely my father would have realized it."

"One would think so."

“It couldn’t be.”

Mick just looked at him.

Andrew decided Mick was more drunk than he’d realized. The poor fellow had been hitting the bottle too much lately, and now he was imagining things. He glanced at his watch and stood up. “I’d better get going. Family stuff, you know.”

Mick nodded. “I’m sorry about your father.” He picked up his empty glass and peered into it. “Guess I’d better call it a night.”

“Let me drive you home,” Andrew said.

Mick stood and held on to the edge of the table. “Nah, I walked. I’m staying just around the corner with a buddy of mine. That apartment house—”

“Come on, I’ll drop you off.” Andrew placed a ten-dollar bill on the table for a tip. He let Mick out at a rather rundown brick building and watched him weave to the door.

All the way back to the house by the lake, he turned over in his mind what Mick had said. It was ridiculous, to think that night had anything to do with the most famous missing persons case of the century. Andrew wasn’t even sure Mick was right that the two events had occurred the same year. Maybe he wanted it that way, to make his news story more exciting. That was it—Mick would embellish what had happened, turn it into a first-person, coming-of-age piece for the

New Yorker or some such highbrow periodical. Fiction, under the guise of a childhood memory.

Andrew vaguely remembered when Jacobs had vanished. It had been in the news for weeks, but it hadn't worried him. He'd been eleven years old. Politics didn't interest him then. Maybe that was Mick's point. They'd been so innocent. It was nothing, really, a misinterpreted moment. But Mick was a good writer. He would turn it into something spectacular and make a lot of money.

Chapter 4

Janet swallowed hard and tried to decide how to approach the topic. Sharon and her sister sat opposite her on the threadbare sofa in Elwood's parlor, and their brothers sprawled in armchairs. Janet sat on the edge of Mrs. Fairmont's old Boston rocker.

She was relieved when Sharon took control of the gathering.

"Thanks for coming, Janet. I asked you to do this now because Paul is planning to leave soon. I don't know if what Dad said to you is important, but it seemed to me we should all hear it. There's a chance—" Her voice caught, and she paused then took a deep breath and went on. "There's a chance Dad won't ever be able to speak again, and I wanted the others to know what he said to you when you found him on Wednesday."

Janet nodded and looked around at the Fairmonts. They all seemed to have done well for themselves, if their clothing was any indication. Geneva was obviously successful. Her well-cut, navy blue pants and silk blouse didn't come from a discount store. She'd made a point of saying that she'd recently sold a seaside mansion in Camden to a movie star. Sharon had hopped into the conversation and changed the subject, and Janet suspected she did it to keep Geneva from revealing how large a commission she'd received.

Andrew's hair showed a little gray. His height and classic features gave him a distinguished air. Paul, the younger brother, was less impressive, slightly pudgy, but still a handsome man. He fidgeted and shifted his position often. He was dressed casually, while Andrew wore a jacket and tie. Both men nursed mugs of coffee.

Janet could see a family resemblance; all of them had slightly pointed chins and those soft, liquid brown eyes. The Fairmont kids were popular when they attended high school, she concluded. They were outgoing, good-looking, and opinionated.

Sharon had attended church that morning with Kurt and Janet, which had pleased Janet immensely. Geneva had turned down the invitation to join them and gone to the hospital instead. Both the Fairmont brothers had opted to sleep in. Janet tried not to draw conclusions from that, since all were probably weary from travel and anxiety over their father, but she couldn't help liking Sharon and being a bit wary of her siblings. Janet didn't know any of them well, but Sharon seemed the friendliest and the most concerned about their father. Geneva exhibited more of a dutiful, let's-get-this-done attitude. The brothers were still unknown quantities, but Janet thought she saw a bit of arrogance in Andrew, and an attention deficit in Paul.

Janet cleared her throat. "Well, it wasn't much. Your father was completely disabled when I arrived. He was lying on the floor." She looked toward the braided rug. "Over there, just between the piano and Paul's chair. He spoke to me, and I assured him help was on the way." She looked up and met Andrew's eyes, feeling that he was the one who held her most responsible. "I called 911 immediately, of course."

She looked toward Sharon for support, and Sharon nodded.

"He did speak to me. He mentioned you all." Janet smiled. "He called you his 'kids.' At first I thought he wanted me to call you right away. He made it clear he wanted me to relay a message to you. But he had trouble getting it out. The only parts I understood clearly were, *I'm sorry,* and then, *I shouldn't have kept it,* and *I should have done what he told me.*"

"What?" Andrew's face was wrinkled in question.

"What on earth does that mean?" Paul asked.

Janet raised her hands in helplessness. "I have no idea."

Geneva crossed her legs and looked toward the ceiling. "Kept it?"

"Yes."

"Kept what?" Paul leaned toward Janet eagerly.

"I don't know."

"An appointment?" Andrew hazarded.

"Janet suggested he meant a promise," Sharon said.

"It was just a thought, but now I'm guessing he may have meant something tangible." Janet shook her head. "I'm at a loss. I'd seen your father a couple of days earlier, and he seemed fine at the time. In fact, he was quite cheerful. But that day . . . Wednesday . . . I'd say something was definitely worrying him."

"What do you suppose it means?" Sharon asked them all, looking around as though expecting one of them to reveal the answer to the riddle.

"This isn't a party game," Paul said. He jumped up and walked to the window overlooking the front yard then turned to face them. "Mrs. Borden, did you think he was desperate? I mean, if he thought he was dying . . ."

Janet felt tears spring into her eyes. "He seemed agitated, upset. I'm sorry, very sorry, that he had to go through that time of agony." She wondered if she was wise in telling them of Elwood's words to her, but she had promised, after all. He had wanted his children to know he was remorseful about something, some past action he had taken. If he died, she would at least know she had carried out his wishes. She sent up a silent prayer for his recovery.

"I think we should go through his papers," Andrew said suddenly, and they all stared at him.

"But . . ." Sharon looked from one sibling to the next. "It's only been a few days, and the doctor said this morning that Dad might improve. His facial muscles looked more natural, didn't you think so?"

"No," said Paul.

"I saw a small change," Geneva said. "But I think Andrew's right. Most of us have to go home soon. If you can stay and look after the house and keep us up to date on Dad's condition, Sharon, why we'd all appreciate it. But I think we should go through his desk and file cabinet while we're all here together. Locate his important papers, that sort of thing."

"It's just common sense," Andrew agreed. "And maybe we'll find something that clues us in on what he wanted so badly for Mrs. Borden to tell us."

"I wonder if he has life insurance," Paul mused. "I asked him once, and he hung up on me."

"He must have some." Geneva turned and stared pointedly at her sister. "Sharon, do you know?"

Sharon shook her head. "All I've dealt with

so far is health insurance and Medicare, for the hospital."

Janet stood up. "I'll be going, but please call or stop at the house if you need anything. Anything at all. And it's Janet." She smiled at the room in general. Sharon followed her to the porch and saw her out.

Sharon rose early the next morning, scrawled a note to Geneva, and drove to the hospital.

She could never sleep late here. The loons calling on the flat lake at dawn woke her without fail. She didn't mind. She liked to make a cup of tea and sit out on the porch, where she could sip it and enjoy the silence of the morning.

It was so good to be out in the country again. She hadn't realized how stressed she was until she got away from the pressure of the business. Her husband, Vic Schlesser, owned a construction company outside Boston, and Sharon kept the books for him. Business was brisk, and for the last six months neither of them had taken a day off. Her father's illness was an excuse to get away, and she saw now how much she'd needed this break. She missed Vic, but she'd hardly seen him while she was home, either. They'd talked more the last few evenings, when she'd called him, than they had in the previous months.

She felt an urgency this morning and headed straight for the hospital in Waterville. Visiting hours didn't start until eight o'clock, but since her father was in the intensive care unit, the nurses let Sharon and her siblings visit at any time. It was just after six when she greeted the young woman at the nurses' station.

"Any change in my father's condition?"

"No, Mrs. Schlesser. He's resting comfortably."

Sharon entered Elwood's glassed-in cubicle. His eyes were closed and his breathing shallow and soft. She sat down and watched him.

"Good morning, Dad," she said.

The monitor hummed and flashed numbers at her. Being here so early made no difference. She ought to have grabbed something to eat. She closed her eyes for a moment. She would go down to the cafeteria as soon as one of the others got here.

She had never been a religious person—none of their family was deeply spiritual. Yet she found herself wondering about prayer these days, and God and faith and all sorts of abstract things. Janet Borden's pastor had made it sound like anyone could just talk to God and expect an answer.

She had found the church service yesterday refreshing. Not only had the serenity she felt in the meeting lifted her spirits, but the relief of getting out of the hospital room and away from her siblings for a couple of hours had buoyed her. Now she felt she could face whatever came.

"Please, God," she whispered, "I don't know You, but I'm beginning to wish I did. If You truly care about every person on this earth, the way Janet said You do, could You please give my dad a little attention? I don't feel as though I should ask anything of You, and yet . . . Well, You know how it is, I guess. We kids all left home more or less angry with Dad. Since Mom died, Dad and I have made up and become friends, and I'm thankful for that. I guess what I'm asking for is a chance for Geneva and the boys to do the same."

She opened her eyes and froze. Her father's eyes glittered behind half-closed eyelids.

"Sharon."

She caught her breath. "Yes! Yes! Oh, Dad!" She seized his hand and leaned toward him, careful not to jostle the tubes and wires that ran to his IV pole and the monitor. "Dad, can you hear me? Talk to me!"

"I'm . . . sorry. Tell the boys."

"Yes, I will." Sharon fumbled for the call button and pushed it with trembling fingers. "Dad, you're going to get better. I'm calling the nurse."

Elwood closed his eyes and muttered a few more words. Sharon leaned close to listen.

Kurt sat at his desk, reading Dave Carpenter's latest article on the mayor's plan to cut property taxes in the city. Normally Mick would have handled that story, but Mick was off on his odyssey in Belgrade.

Dave had done an adequate job on the piece, but it lacked the zing Mick's years of experience on the city hall beat gave his stories. Kurt was almost at the end of the file when Wally Reed breezed in from the hallway.

"Hey, Kurt."

Kurt looked up. "Yeah?"

"What's the deal with Mick?" Wally asked around a wad of chewing gum.

"What do you mean?"

"I waited forty-five minutes for him out at the lake. He never showed."

Kurt frowned. "Seriously?"

"Do I look like I'm kidding?" Wally shook his head in disgust.

"Did you get any pictures?"

"I snapped a few, but Mick told me Friday he'd be there and show me some particular things he wanted shots of."

Kurt remembered Mick's enthusiasm when he'd asked for a photographer. "I'm sure there's an explanation."

"Oh, so am I." Wally tipped up an imaginary bottle as though drinking from it.

"No, he was here this morning. I only saw him for a minute, but he looked all right."

"If you say so."

Kurt watched in fascination as Wally unwrapped

a new piece of gum, folded it in half, and tucked it into his cheek with the wad.

Wally caught his stare and said apologetically, "I quit smoking."

"I see. How long now?"

Wally glanced at his watch. "Eleven hours and twenty-seven minutes."

"If you make it 'til noon tomorrow, I'll buy you lunch."

"Cool." Wally grinned and headed down the hallway, swinging his camera bag.

Kurt picked up his telephone receiver and punched in Mick's cell phone number. After four rings, the recording for voice mail greeted him.

"Mick, check in with me ASAP." Kurt sat for a moment, tapping his fingers on the desktop, then shook his head and went back to work.

Paul pulled out one of the drawers from his father's oak dresser and upended it on the bed-spread. He quickly spread out the contents.

"Nothing here. Just underwear and socks." He reached for the next drawer.

"Paul, stop," Sharon cried.

He hesitated, and Andrew agreed, "You can't just tear the house apart."

"Why not? I've already stayed here too long. If there's something to be found, let's find it."

"Not this way." Geneva came to his side and began packing the clothing neatly back into the drawer. "If there's something worth finding, we'll find it, but let's not make a shambles of the house doing it."

Sharon sighed in relief. "Yes. We can go through all Dad's things systematically. If there's something significant, it will turn up."

Paul shook his head. "I've already wasted enough time here. I'm not going to spend weeks looking for this mysterious treasure."

"Who said anything about treasure?" Andrew shouted.

"Well, there's got to be something here!"

Sharon tried to hold back her tears. Paul's impatience had worn her out. "Why don't you just go?" She sat down on the bed and buried her face in her hands.

Andrew stepped over to her side and placed his hand on her shoulder. "Hey, buck up, Sharon. You're tired, and you've been through a lot this week. Just relax while we go through Dad's things."

"There was nothing significant in his desk. I suppose it wouldn't hurt to look through the dresser and closet in here," Geneva said, looking toward the unopened drawers.

"What if it's not papers or valuables?" Paul asked. "What if it's something . . . I don't know, something bigger."

"Tell us again what he said, Sharon," Paul coaxed.

She sighed. "I don't know, I don't know. I've told you what it sounded like. It could be nothing. You're making too much of this!"

"Take it easy." Geneva pulled the rocker over close to her and laid a hand on Sharon's wrist. "Relax, honey. Just think back and tell us what happened this morning."

Sharon took a deep breath. She was beginning to wish she'd said nothing to her siblings. "Well, I got to his room early. I was just sitting there thinking that you all would be coming in soon, and I would go down to the cafeteria for something to eat when you did."

Geneva and Andrew nodded in synchronization. Paul beckoned with impatient fingers. "And then?"

"And then Dad said my name." Sharon closed her eyes, and two tears slid down her cheeks. "I couldn't believe it. I leaned down close to him and said, *Dad? Dad, can you hear me?*"

"Were his eyes open?" Geneva asked.

"Not completely. Maybe part way, I don't know." Sharon looked around at all of them, wishing she could give a more coherent account of that morning's incident.

"And what did he say then?" Paul asked, taking the tone a kindergarten teacher would use with a five-year-old.

Sharon scowled at him. "He said, *I'm sorry. Tell the boys*. And then . . . then it sounded like . . .” Again she paused. She didn’t want to misrepresent their father’s words or intent, but she was almost certain. “It sounded like, *I hid it.*”

“See?” Paul almost shouted. “He hid something. It could be anything. Money, jewelry, anything.”

Andrew looked skeptical. “Come on, Paul. Anything? You might as well say Dad hid some stolen property, or a cache of drugs, or a body.”

Geneva’s brow furrowed as she thought it out. “It could be something fairly simple. Something like a letter. Or maybe he’s slipped into dementia and is remembering something that happened years ago.”

“Yes,” said Andrew. “He might have hidden something when he was a child, even.”

“But he said he was sorry. I’m sure of that.” Sharon looked around at all of them, daring them to deny it.

“Maybe he hid something from Mother,” said Paul.

Geneva rose slowly, staring out the window toward the lake without seeing it. “Put this together with what he said to Janet Borden—”

“I shouldn’t have kept it,” Paul said triumphantly. “You are so right, Gen!”

“Well, whatever it was that he hid or kept, it probably isn’t here now.” Sharon stood up. “I don’t think we should rummage through his things. I'd rather wait until Dad can tell us himself what this is all about."

"Not me." Paul pulled out the second drawer and flipped his father's sweaters onto the bed.

Sharon winced. "Tory is coming up Thursday. If Dad still can't communicate by then, we can start sorting through things methodically. Maybe we'll find something."

"I don't think there is anything," Andrew said. "His mind is confused. There's no treasure."

"We don't know that." Paul's taut facial muscles revealed the stubbornness he always felt when he was angry with his older brother, and Sharon felt a headache beginning. She rubbed her forehead at the hairline. Why couldn't Paul and Andrew ever get together without bickering?

"Sharon's plan sounds sensible," said Geneva. "Now I'm going back to the hospital. Who knows? Dad may be talking again."

Paul turned back to the dresser and pulled out another drawer. "They'd have called us."

"Well, I'm going anyway."

"I'll go with you," said Andrew. "Let's stop for a bite to eat on the way."

Geneva nodded. "Thanks. Dr. Ridge said Dad was about the same when he examined him, and things can go either way, but he also said he'll have the neurologist in to take another look at Dad later today."

“We might have some news when we get there,” Andrew agreed.

“Wait for me.” Sharon grabbed her sweater from the bed. “And Paul, don’t you dare trash this place while we’re gone.”

Paul sighed and slid the drawer back into its niche. “Quit crabbing at me. I’ll come along. I’m serious about leaving tonight, though, so I guess I’d better put in one more appearance.”

“Maybe Dad will know us this time,” Geneva said as they headed for the door.

“I think he knows us now.” Sharon patted her pocket to be sure she had the house key. “I know he was back in his trance when you got there, but he really did say my name.”

Geneva squeezed her hand before going down the porch steps. “Of course he did, and I’m glad you were there when he had that one lucid moment.”

“Trance,” Paul muttered scornfully, and Andrew jabbed him with his elbow.

Chapter 5

Janet was tired, but she was glad for the chance to get to know the Fairmont siblings a little better. She had invited them all over for dessert and coffee after supper, and they sat around the Bordens' pine dining table, eating one of Janet's delectable cheesecakes. Kurt's eyelids drooped a bit, and she knew he was tired, but he had assured her before the guests arrived that he was anxious to meet the rest of the Fairmonts and would enjoy the evening.

"Did he speak any more after that?" Janet asked Sharon as she refilled her mug with decaffeinated coffee.

"No, but he seemed quite alert when we all went in this afternoon. One of the nurses thought so, too. I can't wait to hear what the neurologist thinks. Maybe Dad's going to recover!"

"Did you give them our phone number, in case there's a change in your father's condition while you're here this evening?" Kurt asked.

"Yes, and my cell phone number," Geneva said.

"We probably won't get the neurologist's report until tomorrow." Sharon sipped her coffee. The dark crescents under her eyes told Janet that she no longer cared enough to try to hide her fatigue with makeup.

"Maybe he didn't say *I hid it,*" Andrew said suddenly. They all stared at him, and he flashed an apologetic glance at Sharon. "I mean, he wasn't speaking distinctly; Sharon told us that. Maybe he said . . . oh, I don't know . . . *I did it.* Just for example."

"Oh, right." Geneva was clearly angry at the suggestion. "You just don't like Dad. Next you're going to say he was confessing to a crime."

"No, nothing like that." Andrew chuckled. "Maybe he was trying to remember if he shut the stove burner off, and he suddenly remembered and said, *I did it.*"

"Oh, that is so logical." Paul's sarcasm made Janet uneasy, and she looked toward Kurt for assurance. Kurt smiled, but he seemed a bit unsettled, too.

Paul went on, "Maybe he was saying *I bit it,* and there was a half-eaten cookie on the floor. Or better yet, *I hit it,* and—"

"Enough," Sharon cried. "Just cut it out!" A strained silence followed, and then she sobbed. "I'm sorry. I'm just so strung out by all this. Can't you guys get along for five minutes?"

Janet went to Sharon's chair and patted her shoulder. "You're exhausted. This has been a terrible strain on you, worrying about your father and being away from your family for so long."

Paul stirred his coffee in silence, but Andrew said, "I'm really sorry, Sharon. And to you, too, Kurt and Janet." He nodded at them deferentially. "I didn't intend to bring our family squabbling over here with us. It's just that we were all excited that Dad spoke to Sharon this morning, and for the last twelve hours I've been trying to figure out what Dad meant."

"We all have," Paul said, "but the truth is, we don't know for sure what he said, let alone what he meant."

"I want to go back to the hospital." Sharon pushed her plate away.

"No, you can't," Geneva said. "Janet's right. You need some sleep. If anything happens, the nurses will call us. Let's go over to the house and get to bed. We'll both go in early tomorrow." She stood up and waited for Sharon's response.

"You're right." Sharon got up slowly. "Janet, Kurt, thank you. That was delicious."

"We've enjoyed the visit, but I suppose you do need rest," Janet said. "Will you let me know tomorrow how your father is?"

"Of course." Sharon gave her a weary smile.

"Paul, you said you're heading back to Missouri tonight?" Kurt asked, walking with them all to the front door.

"Yes, I'm flying out of Bangor at 11:30." Paul

looked at his watch. "Guess I'd better head up there right now. My business is suffering without me, and I've got my youngest son's college tuition payments to think of."

Kurt nodded and extended his hand. "I'm glad to have met you. If you come back again, stop by."

When the door was closed behind the Fairmonts, Janet slid into his arms.

"Whew!" she whispered. "That family's hard to take all at once."

Kurt chuckled. "You were marvelous, but I agree. Small doses, sweetheart."

"Yes. I really like Sharon, and we had quite a discussion after church yesterday." Janet turned back toward the dining room. "I should have sent the cheesecake home with them."

"You didn't eat any," Kurt noted. "I was very proud of you."

"That's because I knew there would be leftovers and I'd have another chance."

"Why don't you take a piece over to Mrs. Vaughn tomorrow?"

"Good idea." She sighed. "I've got to do something. Seems like I walked every inch of Belgrade this summer, and I didn't lose a pound."

"Well, you didn't gain any, either, did you?"

Janet shrugged and began picking up the dessert plates. "Maybe a little."

"Oh, come on. Really?"

She stacked the plates together. “Three and a quarter pounds since my checkup in May.”

Kurt’s eyes widened in surprise. “A quarter?”

“That’s just this week. From that rhubarb pie.”

He smiled. “Maybe you’d better let me take the cheesecake to the office and let the sports writers and photographers finish it off.” He gathered up the coffee mugs.

“You think that’s funny,” Janet said, “but I think it’s a good idea. Let the reporters have it. Maybe it will inspire them.” Her weight was becoming a constant source of frustration. Although she wanted to think it was under control, the way the scale’s indicator slowly moved upward told her otherwise. Maybe she should just stop cooking.

Kurt followed her into the kitchen. “That reminds me, I’d better give Mick Tyler a call.”

“Something newsworthy happening tonight?”

“No, but he missed an appointment today, and I’m a little concerned about him.”

“Is he sick?”

“I don’t know.” Kurt pulled out his pocket calendar, flipped through the pages, then lifted the wall phone’s receiver to make the call.

Sharon went to wipe off the dining table, and when she returned to the kitchen Kurt met her look with troubled eyes.

“Did you get him?” she asked.

“No. I just hope he shows up at the office in the morning.”

• • •

Tuesday morning Kurt paced the newsroom restlessly for an hour, then went to his office cubicle and flipped his address file open to the T's. He hesitated with his hand over the telephone buttons, then sat down abruptly and closed his eyes in prayer. Twenty minutes later he was ringing the doorbell at Mick's home address.

The lawn needed one last mowing for fall, he noted, but overall the brick ranch house was in good repair. The garage doors were closed, and he decided no one was home, but just as he turned away the front door opened.

"Mr. Borden?"

"Hello, Callie."

"Is something wrong?" She wore a housecoat, and her hair was in disarray. It appeared that he had interrupted the process of blow drying it. She didn't have her makeup on yet, and her leathery, tanned face was a grim contrast to Janet's smooth, creamy skin. He guessed they were about the same age, but Callie Tyler looked at least ten years older than Janet.

"I was wondering if Mick was here," he said.

"No."

Kurt nodded. "Thank you. I'm sorry I bothered you. I should have called first."

She frowned. "He didn't come in to work?"

"No. And he missed an appointment yesterday."

"Are we surprised?" Callie asked with a

tinge of bitterness. "He's missed a lot of family appointments, too, this past year."

Kurt grimaced. "I'm getting a little concerned about him. Do you know where I can find him?"

"Last I knew, he was staying with his friend Lionel."

"Do you have a phone number?"

"I don't think Lionel has a landline, but I may have his cell."

Kurt waited, trying to calm the uneasiness that prodded him. Mick had missed a day or two of work before, but he always called in sick. This time he'd been eager to do his assignment. Kurt had hoped the new drive he'd exhibited would keep him on track.

In the car, he used his cell phone to try Lionel's phone number, but no one answered. Kurt turned in to the newspaper's parking lot with a sigh. It was a good thing he hadn't counted on Mick doing any hard news stories today.

He parked in his reserved spot and got out of his car, then stood looking around the lot. Dave Carpenter's car; Molly, the receptionist's; sports reporter Alan Houghton's SUV; the company car the photographers used during the day shift. There were several more he couldn't place, but Mick's car wasn't there.

Wally was climbing the steps that led up from the larger parking lot below, down at the river's edge where the staffers were encouraged to park, leaving the upper lot free for customers. Kurt ambled toward him. The uneasiness was growing. They met at the top of the stairs, and Kurt caught a whiff of cigarette smoke.

"Hey, boss," Wally said. "What are you doing out here?"

"Just came in from an errand. Say, you didn't see Mick's car down there, did you?"

Wally's eyes narrowed, and he shook his head. "I just took a look around. You think he's okay?"

Kurt frowned. "I don't know. I stopped by Callie's, but she hadn't seen him."

Wally turned and they stood side by side, looking over the cars in the riverside lot below them. Mick's was not among them, but they'd already known that. Kurt pulled in a breath, and the tobacco smell was strong now. He could imagine Wally strolling around the overflow parking lot, eyeing all the cars carefully, shifting the strap of his camera bag on his shoulder, and puffing away on a cigarette. He probably stayed down there checking out the cars as an excuse to have a smoke where the boss wouldn't see him.

"So, are we going to lunch?" Kurt asked.

Wally winced. "Not today, boss."

Kurt nodded. "Another time."

Just before five o'clock, he reached Lionel Gibson by phone.

"Well, let's see," Lionel said slowly, after Kurt

had identified himself as a friend of Mick's at the paper. "I saw him yesterday."

"What time?"

There was a pause. "Well, I guess in the morning. He was chewing me out for not having any more coffee, and I said, *Hey, if you don't like it here, go crash someplace else, man.*"

"So you think that's what he did? Found another place to stay?" Kurt asked.

"Hey, Mick comes and goes, you know? I let him sleep here, but it's getting to be a pain. He's a lousy roommate, you know what I mean?"

"Does he kick in on the rent?"

"He gave me fifty bucks a couple of weeks ago. That didn't go far."

Kurt hesitated. "Lionel, have you known Mick a long time?"

"Sure. Twenty years, at least."

"Well, nobody here at the paper has seen him since about 8:30 yesterday morning. I'm thinking of calling the police." There was a prolonged silence, and Kurt said, "You there?"

"Yeah, yeah, I'm here. But, man, I wouldn't do that."

"You wouldn't?"

"No." Lionel's tone was decisive. "Mick can take care of himself. He'll show up. He always does."

Kurt thought about that, trying to see things from Lionel's perspective. It wasn't good enough. He wondered if revealing more would be a mistake, but decided Lionel was a necessary link. If Mick turned up at his friend's apartment, he would need Lionel's cooperation. "He's never missed work before without calling in."

"Yeah?"

"Yeah. Listen, if Mick shows up, or even if he calls you, would you give me a call? Let me give you my phone number at the office, and my cell phone, too."

"Okay. Just a sec."

Kurt waited, assuming Lionel was searching for a pen.

"Okay," came the gravelly voice.

"Right. My name is Kurt Borden."

"Huh. The boss, right?"

"Well, yes, I'm Mick's editor. I'm not the *big* boss." Kurt felt suddenly juvenile, trying to explain his relationship to Mick. He gave the phone numbers and resisted the urge to have Lionel read them back so he'd know the man had actually written them down. "Be sure and call me."

"Okay, man."

Kurt hung up and scowled at the phone.

"I suppose it's all I can do for now," he told Janet over supper an hour later.

Janet watched him. She didn't like the way

Kurt's brow furrowed. "I don't know, honey. What if he's had an accident?"

"Lionel seemed to think calling the police at this point would be a mistake. And he knows Mick pretty well."

"But not in a work setting."

Kurt drew in a deep breath, and she could see he was dissatisfied with the situation. "Have you talked to anyone else about this?"

"Wally Reed's worried, too, but he won't admit it. He keeps implying that Mick is off in some dive drinking himself into a stupor, but I don't buy it. I saw Mick just briefly yesterday morning. He stopped at the office for a few minutes, and he was whistling. He was primed for the new assignment I gave him, Janet. He wasn't despondent or angry."

"And his ex-wife wasn't worried, you said."

"I think they're still married, but, no, she seemed to think this was status quo."

"Maybe he's dropped in and out on her a lot," Janet suggested.

"But not his job."

He looked across at her, and her heart ached for him. She wished she could give him some advice that would put him at peace, or even go out and help him search for the reporter. She had loved Kurt since their senior year of high school, and over the years they had faced a lot of tough times together. Financial crises, Anne's bike accident when she was eleven, the death of Kurt's parents and her own mother, the kids getting married and moving away, and the upheaval of Kurt's changing jobs and moving to a new location. This seemed comparatively minor, but she could see that he was deeply concerned.

"I think you'd feel better if you called the police," she said.

Kurt bit his lip. "Maybe I should have called the publisher today and told him."

"Why didn't you?"

He sighed and rubbed the back of his neck. Janet realized he was exhausted. She got up and went around behind his chair. "Relax." She started rubbing the tense muscles in his neck and shoulders, and Kurt slumped a little under her firm touch.

"Thanks. That feels good. Mick's been on the hot seat with Grant for a while. I was taking a chance, giving him a new assignment when Grant wanted me to make him take a leave. I get the feeling that Grant's looking for a loophole in Mick's contract, so he can fire him, and I don't want to get him in worse trouble than he's already in."

"Call the police in the morning."

Kurt seized her hands and pulled them around in front of him, dropping a kiss on each one. "I'll do that. If he's not at his desk by eight, I'll go to the police station and talk to them. And we'll pray about all this tonight."

Janet bent and rested her cheek against his head. Kurt being Kurt, he had certainly been praying about this all day. She closed her eyes, savoring his warmth and steadiness. His golden brown hair was still thick and soft against her cheek, in spite of the hint of gray.

He tightened his hold on her hands, and she leaned to kiss his temple. "You want dessert?"

"No, do you?"

"No." It wasn't a lie. Of course, she always wanted dessert, but pleasing Kurt was better than leftover cheesecake. If she kept the comparison in mind, the choice was simple.

"Want to walk along the shore path?" he asked.

"Yes."

Kurt stood and helped her clear the table. "All quiet at the Fairmonts' tonight?"

"Geneva left today. She's got a big sale pending, I gather. Sharon and Andrew went back to the hospital tonight. No change in Elwood today. So far as I know, he hasn't spoken again since that one time on Monday when he talked to Sharon." She stacked their plates on the counter. "I'll start the dishwasher later."

As she slipped on her zippered L.L. Bean sweatshirt, she remembered another concern of Kurt's. "How's Wally doing? Did you have lunch together?"

"No. He relapsed again."

"Maybe he needs a bigger bribe."

They went out through the deck door and walked slowly toward the lake. The water was calm, and ten yards out a trout broke the surface. A chilly offshore breeze promised a frost soon.

"You should have worn your jacket." Janet's voice was loud in the stillness.

"Keep me warm." Kurt slid his arm around her waist. "Are you keeping next Friday night free?"

"What for?" she asked, but she knew. She wanted to hear him say it.

"Thirty years together is something to celebrate, don't you think?"

She smiled up at him. "What are we doing?"

"It's a surprise. But it involves reservations, which I made this afternoon." He stopped on the path and kissed her.

"Why are people so scared of getting older?" she murmured, snuggling closer in the curve of his arm as they walked on. Kurt gave her a squeeze.

Thank you, Lord, Janet prayed in silence. *I'm fifty, and my life is perfect.*

Chapter 6

Kurt couldn't stand to put it off any longer. After the morning news meeting with his staff, he lost no time getting to the police station.

He stopped at the window and gave the dispatcher a brief version of his mission, and she immediately called the patrol sergeant. The uniformed sergeant opened a door farther down the hall and guided Kurt into a tiny office that was more a niche than a room.

"I know Mick Tyler. How long has he been missing?" Sergeant Bedard opened a small notebook and sat with his pen ready. He was young, in his early thirties, clean cut, and exhibited the right amount of concern and efficiency.

"Since Monday morning." As Bedard wrote, Kurt felt as if something was finally being done, and things would turn out all right. He had come prepared with all the contact information he had for Mick—Callie's phone number and address, Mick's cell phone, Lionel's phone and address, a description of Mick's car.

"Do you have the license plate number?"

Bedard scrutinized the memo sheet Kurt had given him.

Competent and thorough, Kurt thought with relief. “No, sorry. Callie might have some records at the house.”

“I can check it.” Bedard wrote something else in his notebook, then looked up at Kurt. “Pardon my asking, but is there a chance Tyler is hiding from you?”

“Oh, I don’t think so. He never has before.”

“But isn’t he a hard drinker on the weekends?”

“I guess he can be, but I saw him for a minute Monday morning, and he was sober.” Kurt watched the sergeant, waiting for an expert opinion on Mick’s erratic behavior. “He was upbeat that day,” he added. “I had put him on a new assignment last Thursday.”

“What was it?”

“A nostalgic piece about an old family that used to live in Belgrade. He went out there Friday and scoped the house involved. One of our photographers, Wally Reed—”

“I know him.”

Kurt nodded. Sgt. Bedard apparently knew everyone at the paper. “Wally was going to meet him there at ten Monday morning and take some photos for the story. But when he got to Belgrade, Mick wasn’t there. Wally waited a while and then came back. But Mick hasn’t checked in since, and as I told you, his wife and the friend he was staying with haven't heard from him either."

Bedard frowned and studied his notes. "You say he and Mrs. Tyler were having some problems."

"Well, I don't know any details." Kurt shifted in his chair, uncomfortable to be revealing another's private affairs. "All he told me was that he wasn't currently living at home. And when I stopped by the house yesterday, Callie seemed . . ."

The sergeant zeroed in on his hesitation. "How did she seem?"

Kurt groped for the right word.

"Mr. Borden, if Tyler's in trouble, any little thing could be important."

"Well, to be honest, she was pretty bitter. Sort of a *good riddance* attitude. She said . . . she said he'd been a no-show for lots of family events."

"So she considered this part of a pattern."

"I don't know. I only know that at work he either shows up or he calls in. But not this time."

Bedard nodded. "I'll have one of our officers do some checking. Could be he decided to get away for a few days and forgot to let you know."

Kurt doubted that. "If he was involved in an accident, wouldn't his car show up in your reports?"

"Depends on where it happened. Sometimes it takes a while for our system to get updates from other agencies. But I'll put someone on it right away. Meanwhile, if there's any word from him, you let us know."

"Of course." Kurt stood, wishing he'd come in sooner to file the report. Now to tell Grant. He wished he didn't have to, but they needed to inform the newspaper staff right away. Terry Fallon, the reporter covering Mick's former police beat, would find out soon anyhow, when he went to collect the daily reports from the police log. Kurt didn't want the employees to find out that way.

On Thursday morning Janet went next door to help Sharon prepare for her daughter's arrival.

"Tory ought to be here by suppertime," Sharon said with a smile.

"I'm glad she's coming." Janet stood on the opposite side of an old, oak-framed double bed from Sharon, tucking in the sheets.

"So am I. I'd rattle around in this big old house all by my lonesome, now that Andrew is gone."

"Oh, he left this morning?" Janet asked.

"Yes. He was the last. I was surprised he stayed this long, but I'm glad he did."

"What does he do? He lives in Knoxville, right?

"Yes, Tennessee." Sharon reached for a pillowcase. "He's a city planner. They've had a lot of growth in that area. I think he's good at it. At least, he's always busy. He doesn't call me very often, and I have to admit I don't know that much about his work."

Janet nodded, thankful again for her close, loving family. Although her only brother lived in Idaho, they kept in touch, and she and Kurt received phone calls from their three married children often.

"He was a bit put out that he couldn't get hold of his school friend again before he left." Sharon smiled ruefully. "At least he got to see Dad conscious."

"I'm so glad your father's improving," Janet said.

Sharon's smile widened. "Me, too. He's not saying much yet, just a few words here and there, and I can tell by the look in his eyes sometimes that he's terribly frustrated."

Janet nodded and picked up a pillow. "Can't communicate the way he wants to."

"Right. But the doctors are optimistic. They say that with time and therapy, he may regain a lot of his speech and mobility."

"That's wonderful." Sharon didn't say anything about Elwood's previous attempts to convey messages to his children, and Janet didn't bring it up. It would only add to Sharon's stress. They were both aware of it, and if Elwood was able to shed any light on the mysterious events he had mentioned earlier, Sharon would tell her.

"Today I started looking into options for long-term care," Sharon said. "The doctors aren't sure if he'll be able to come home, and he certainly can't live alone anymore."

"I'm sorry."

Sharon shrugged. "Part of life. But I can't stay forever. Vic says he needs me. He's getting way behind on the financials for the company. So I figured I'd better start making arrangements. You know, tie up loose ends as soon as I can. I told him it may take me another week, and he wasn't happy, but he said to do what I have to for Dad."

"That's nice of him," Janet said.

"Yes, he's pretty good about things like that. But I could tell he wished I was home. I suggested he might have our accountant help out a little extra, but that would be expensive." She laughed. "I work cheap."

"Is Tory flying up?" Janet asked.

"No, she's driving. She lives in Providence now, and she got the rest of the week off, and all of next week."

"Why don't the two of you have supper with us?"

"Oh, thank you, but Tory asked me especially if we could eat at the seafood restaurant in Waterville after she sees her grandfather tonight. Dad took her there the last time she was in Maine, and she hasn't forgotten the scallops. Maybe another time?"

“Sure. Have you got another blanket for this bed? The nights are getting colder.”

Kurt and Janet sat in the family room watching the tail end of Jeopardy. The final category was “U.S. Presidents.” Janet thought she might have a chance of guessing the answer if the relevant president lived before 1920. She enjoyed reading historical novels and dabbled in genealogy, which had taken her on some lively forays into colonial and early American history. But if the question involved a more recent President, Kurt surely had the advantage with his exhaustive news background.

“He was the youngest man ever to be President of the United States,” Alex Trebek said.

Kurt smiled at her. “You know this.”

“Hmm. Kennedy?” She squinted at the screen. “Does it say *elected?*”

“I don’t think so, but I don’t have my glasses on.”

“Then it must be Theodore Roosevelt,” Janet said with certainty. “He was younger, but he wasn’t elected to his first term. He inherited the job from McKinley.”

“In a manner of speaking,” Kurt agreed.

The music ended, and they listened carefully to the responses. Kennedy . . . wrong . . . Kennedy . . . wrong . . . Roosevelt . . . correct!

“There you go,” said Kurt, pushing the off

button on the remote. "You win tonight. If you'd been on the show, you'd have almost forty thousand dollars."

Janet laughed. "If I'd been on there, I wouldn't have made it to Final Jeopardy. All those questions about business moguls and rock music! Besides, you knew it before I did."

"Speaking of the Kennedys," Kurt said, rising and picking up his empty coffee mug, "do you remember the summer of '68? Bobby Kennedy's assassination?"

"Well, sure. I was in school when we heard the news. Why?"

He frowned. "Nothing. Just something Mick Tyler said to me a few days before he went missing."

"About Robert Kennedy?"

"Well, about Senator Jacobs."

Janet eyed him in confusion. "The man who used to own the house down the road."

"Right. He said Jacobs disappeared the same year Robert Kennedy was shot, so no one thinks of it anymore. All they remember is Kennedy's assassination."

She nodded slowly. "I sure don't remember much about the Senator's disappearance. Just Kennedy and Martin Luther King, Jr. But I was pretty young. Kurt, don't you think it's strange that Jacobs disappeared, and when Mick started digging into the story, he disappeared, too?"

The doorbell rang, and they looked at each other in surprise.

"Must be Sharon." Janet hurried to the entry and flipped the switch for the outside light. She could see Sharon through the glass in the door. A young woman was with her.

"Well, hi!" Janet swung the door wide. "Been to the hospital? You must be Tory. Come on in."

The two women spilled into the hallway, and Sharon clutched Janet's arm.

"Thank heaven you're home! Call the police!" Sharon's eyes were wide with fear.

"What's wrong?" Janet asked.

Tory smiled at her in wan apology. "We just got back from dinner, and someone has broken into Grandpa's house."

Chapter 7

"Do you think it's safe for them to stay in the house tonight?" Kurt asked the state police detective who had come to investigate the break-in. The idea of sending the two women home alone to the rambling farmhouse didn't sit right with him.

"Oh, I think so. Just give us another half hour or so to finish up. I doubt we'll get any fingerprints, but you never know. Sometimes they get sloppy."

Kurt shook his head. The burglar had broken the glass in one of the ground floor windows and unlocked the sash. They were old, twelve-paned window casements. Kurt hadn't been over to put the storm windows on yet this fall. He usually did that for Elwood in late October.

"Professional or amateur?"

"Hard to say." The detective smiled as though he were humoring a mystery buff. They were lucky to have him here—normally a county sheriff's deputy would have handled the break-in, but the detective lived nearby, and Kurt had called him at home. "They didn't use a glass cutter or pick the lock. On the other hand, they could have just kicked the back door in."

"They?" Sharon's voice quavered. "You think there was more than one?"

"We're not sure," Detective Robbins said. Kurt figured he wouldn't tell them everything he knew, anyway. Robbins seemed to know what he was doing, and he definitely had experience on the job. He had to be near retirement age. The old-timer would play his cards close to the bullet-proof vest. "Now, Mrs. Schlesser, according to what you told us, you're not sure whether anything was stolen."

Sharon was sitting at the Bordens' kitchen table, where Janet had settled her and Tory with a pot of tea after Sharon had gone through her father's house with the detective. "That's right. I haven't lived here for twenty-five years, so I can't be certain. But isn't that odd? I mean, Dad has a few nice antiques and a nearly new TV set and DVD player. They weren't touched. But his desk and bedroom were torn apart."

Robbins pressed his lips together. "Yes, they seem to have concentrated on your father's papers and personal items."

"My own things don't seem to be disturbed," Sharon noted.

"They didn't even open my luggage." Tory's tone hovered between outrage and insult. "I left it on the bed, and we rushed off to see Grandpa.

You'd think they would have opened it to see if there was anything valuable in my bags. I've got a laptop in there!"

"Be thankful they didn't steal it." Sharon reached over and squeezed her hand.

"Oh, Mom, I'm so ripped that they did this to you!" Tory's chestnut curls were pulled back in a ponytail, and her makeup consisted of mascara and lip gloss. She stood behind Sharon's chair, facing the detective and massaging Sharon's shoulders.

"Maybe they were interrupted," Janet offered.

"Oh, please." Sharon's face paled. "Don't even suggest that they were in the house when we came home. I won't sleep at all tonight."

Kurt listened to the fragments of memory and speculation, trying to fit it all together.

"You folks were home all evening?" Robbins asked him.

"Yes."

"See or hear anything unusual?"

Janet shook her head.

Kurt said, "I did hear a car drive past during dinner, but I didn't think anything of it. With all the Fairmont family coming and going this week, there's been more traffic on the road than usual."

Robbins's eyebrows drew together. "What time was that?"

Kurt focused on the recollection. Janet stared at him, her eyes round and wary. He smiled at her, and at once her expression softened. "I'd say around six-fifteen. Certainly between six and six-thirty. Right, Jan?"

She nodded. "You got home about quarter to six, and we sat right down to eat."

"Yes, but we were down to coffee when the car went by, I think."

"It was a car, not a truck or an SUV?" the detective asked.

Kurt smiled with regret. "Sorry. I didn't look. I guess I assumed it was one of the Fairmonts."

"But it wasn't," Sharon insisted. "Tory got here just after five, and we left almost immediately for the hospital. We sat with Dad for about an hour, then went over to the restaurant. We didn't get home until almost eight."

"That's right," Janet said. "Jeopardy had just ended when you rang our doorbell." The detective threw her an inquisitive glance, and Janet flushed.

"It's our favorite program," Kurt said with a smile, and Robbins nodded and wrote something in his notebook.

"All right, folks, we'll let you know when we're finished over there."

Robbins walked diagonally across the dirt road toward the Fairmonts' house, and Kurt shut the door.

Janet turned to smile at Sharon. "Listen, you

two can stay here tonight." She looked expectantly from Sharon's face to Tory's.

"Sure," Kurt agreed. "Janet keeps the guest room made up all the time."

"Oh, no," Sharon said.

"No trouble," Janet told her. "I'll probably sleep better if you do."

"Tory?" Sharon looked a little lost as she moved toward her daughter.

"We'll be okay, Mom." Tory put her arm around Sharon. "The police are going to patrol off and on all night. Those burglars won't come back now that we've got the big, bad cops out here."

Kurt called Sergeant Bedard of the Waterville Police Department as soon as he got to the office the next morning.

"I don't suppose you have any news on Mick Tyler?"

"No, sorry," Bedard said. "We've checked all the leads you gave us—even talked to the town office in Belgrade to see if he'd been out there Monday morning. They said he was there last Friday, but he didn't come back Monday."

"What about Callie?"

"We talked to Mrs. Tyler, and she gave us the names of some friends and relatives. No luck. I'm sorry, Mr. Borden. Maybe he'll turn up Monday as if nothing happened. Have you checked your vacation schedule?"

Kurt fought to keep the irritation out of his voice. "Mick was not due for vacation this week."
"Well, there's not a lot more we can do, sir."
"All right, thank you. Oh, Sergeant?"
"Yes?"
"My neighbor's house was broken into last night."
"Where do you live?"
"Belgrade."
"Ah. Who's handling it?"
"The state police. Detective Robbins. Do you know him?"
"Sure, I've met him several times. You're not suggesting a link between Tyler's disappearance and this break-in, are you?"
"Oh, no. But here's the thing of it: the house that was burglarized is right across the road from the house Mick Tyler was going to write the big article about."
"Odd," said Bedard, "but these things happen. And they've had some break-ins at summer homes out there within the last month."
"Yes." Kurt remembered the article Dave Carpenter had written a couple of days ago. Those thieves were targeting antiques, but Elwood Fairmont's collectibles were undisturbed.
He had just hung up from talking with Bedard when his phone rang.
"Borden, is Tyler still AWOL?"
"Yes, Grant." Kurt leaned back in his chair and

held the receiver six inches from his ear. When the publisher quit raging at him, he cautiously brought it closer.

"I've had six calls about it already this morning," Grant was saying.

"Readers?"

"Readers, advertisers, and the owner. I'm telling you, Borden—"

"I'll update you as soon as I hear anything, Grant." Kurt hung up and pulled in a deep breath. "Okay, Lord, I need Your strength more than usual today."

Tory stood on a stepstool, handing things down to Janet and Sharon. They were in Elwood's pantry, which was a tight fit for three adults and a stepstool. But Sharon had decided to start her cleaning there, and Janet thought it was a good idea. If Elwood needed to go into a nursing facility, the house would have to be closed up. Sharon might as well begin now. It would keep her busy, and there would be less work for the family to do later. Even better, it would keep Sharon's mind off the break-in.

"Okay, this shelf is all pots and pans." Tory lifted a stack of pie plates and lowered them carefully to Janet's waiting hands. They were followed by bread tins, cookie sheets, a quiche pan, and a spaghetti pot.

"I didn't realize Mother had so many pans."

Sharon laughed as she set a stack on the kitchen table. "Dad probably hasn't used that quiche pan since she died."

"Yard sale," Tory called. Her voice was muffled as she reached back into the corners of the high shelves. "What's this?"

Janet smiled. "A potato ricer."

"A which?"

Sharon chuckled. "A gadget we'll never use."

"Yard sale," Janet and Tory said in unison. They all laughed.

"Okay, that's it for that shelf." Tory extended her hand toward Janet. "Give me the dish cloth."

Janet wrung out the cloth and handed it up to her, and Tory began scrubbing the shelf down.

"I should hold a sale," Sharon mused. "It's kind of late in the season, but still . . ."

"Wait until next summer," Janet said.

Sharon frowned in indecision. "It's just that there won't be a better time than now for nine months or so, but if Dad should . . ." She swallowed hard. "If Dad should die . . ."

"Oh, come on, Mom." Tory straightened and stared down at Sharon. "The doctor said this morning that he's doing great."

"Yes, he did look better to me," Sharon agreed. "But even so, if he's not going to live here, we might as well sell the house, don't you think?"

"I don't know." Tory looked at Janet.

Sharon's bleak expression prompted Janet to say, "Surely there's time. You can talk it over with Geneva and your brothers and see what they want."

"And Grandpa," Tory added. "You should ask him if he wants to sell the house."

Sharon nodded. "I guess you're right. No sense being too hasty. We don't have a power of attorney or anything, and there's a chance that in a week or two Dad will be able to make some decisions."

"Yes," said Janet. "Let's just scrub this pantry down and find out what's here."

"I'll make a list if you want," Tory offered.

"All right," her mother said. "That might be useful later."

Tory descended one step on the stool. "This shelf seems to be mostly canned goods, and some baking supplies." She handed Janet two cans of spaghetti sauce.

Janet and Sharon filled the counter on one side of the sink with containers of food.

"Dad probably didn't realize how much stuff he had up there," Sharon said.

"He shouldn't have to go shopping for a year," Tory called. "Hey, Mom, lookee here."

Sharon went to the pantry and took the square tin Tory held out.

"That looks old," Janet said.

"I'll say. Whitman's chocolates." On the hinged

cover of the rusty tin, a woman's profile was still visible on a blue and yellow mosaic background. Sharon lifted the lid. "Well."

"What is it?" Tory stepped down from the stool and came to look over her shoulder.

"It's a pen and . . . Hmm, what is this?" Sharon held up a small, rectangular silver object.

Janet glimpsed a hinge on one side of the tarnished item. "May I?"

Sharon surrendered it to her readily, and Janet held it up in the light that streamed through the window. "I think it's a card case."

"Are those initials?" Tory leaned close.

"A monogram," Sharon said.

"It's a J." Janet frowned. "Or is it an I?"

Tory giggled. "I thought it was an S."

"Open it," Sharon prompted, and Janet released the catch.

"Empty."

"Too bad." Tory smiled at her mother. "You should keep it. If it's not an S, you can pretend it is."

"Funny." Sharon frowned down at the trinket. "No one in the family has a name starting with I or J."

"It's real silver," Janet said.

"Oh, I think I saw a can of silver polish up on the shelf," Tory cried.

"Don't polish it," Janet advised. "At least, not if you think you want to sell it."

Sharon nodded, turning the case over. “That’s right. I’ve heard that people do a lot of damage to antiques trying to clean them up. Maybe I’ll take these things to a dealer just the way they are and get an appraisal.”

“Couldn’t hurt. Maybe we can go tomorrow.” Tory reached into the tin and took out the silver pen. “Look, this has the monogram, too. They’re a set.”

“I almost think I’ve seen that thing before.” Sharon scowled at the small case then shook her head. “Oh, well. Let’s get back to work. I want to go back to the hospital after lunch.”

Chapter 8

Kurt scrolled down the article about Senator Thomas Jacobs. He'd spent most of the morning researching the man's disappearance, and the more he read the less he liked it. A large sum of money, earmarked to fund a study on pesticides, had disappeared at the same time Jacobs did. Kurt clicked on the Print button, then went to the printer for the sheets that came out, adding the article to the thick file he was building on Jacobs.

He stood for a long moment with the file in his hand. It was Friday. The *Sentinel*'s weekend pages were being laid out, except for those reserved for breaking news. Most of the reporters would have the next two days off, and the paper would be filled with features and wire service stories. One local reporter worked each weekend day to catch the events that had to be covered: accidents, fires, community happenings.

Right now all of the reporters were eager to get out of the office for the weekend. They wouldn't want to think about a new assignment, but Kurt felt he couldn't wait until Monday to start moving on this.

The question was, who?

It was the type of story he would have put Mick on. In fact, he *had* put Mick on it. Which of his four remaining reporters could do it justice? They were already stretched to the max, covering for Mick. Terry Fallon had rescheduled his vacation because they were shorthanded. Kurt had even written up an accident report himself near deadline yesterday.

Terry could do this job, but Kurt immediately rejected that idea. Terry was a good writer, but he was slow. He wanted everything in his articles to be perfect. As a result, the night editor often waited for Terry to submit his stories at the last minute. He needed someone quick-witted for this.

Joy Liston? No way. Her style ran to purple paragraphs of description, which was fine for parades and graduations, but would be out of place on this story.

Kurt didn't even consider handing it to Roger Clifford. Why the paper had kept Roger for ten years, Kurt had no clue, except that the reporter had a contract that was next to unbreakable. He couldn't spell, and his stories often needed reorganizing that amounted to virtual rewriting. What was more, he resisted all Kurt's efforts to teach him to do better. Kurt had spoken to Grant Engstrom and managing editor Steve Basner about Roger more than once, but Grant was afraid to mess with contracted employees. His predecessor had been the cause of the newspaper's paying out a large wrongful termination settlement, and Grant didn't want that to happen on his watch.

That left Dave Carpenter.

Kurt watched Dave from across the room. He was on the phone, listening more than he talked, and scrawling in a notebook throughout the conversation. He was probably getting quotes for the article he was doing on the new municipal playground. Dave had only been with the paper a few months. He was young and inexperienced, but he had excellent writing mechanics and an innate sense of what was newsworthy. His style was in its infancy, but Kurt had great hopes for the rookie. Confidence—that was what Dave needed most.

Still Kurt held back. With Grant's reluctant permission, he had written a press release that announced Mick's disappearance in yesterday's paper. It was time for a follow-up giving the police's official word that there were no clues, a little background data on Mick, and an appeal to the public to come forth with any information on Mick's whereabouts since Monday morning.

Beyond that, he wanted the reporter assigned to the story to start working on the Jacobs angle. They wouldn't print that yet. They would only tell the readers Mick had been detailed to work on an article in Belgrade the day he vanished. But if Mick wasn't located soon, someone would have to dig into the same research Mick had been doing.

The story of Mick's disappearance was already large, and it could become huge if he didn't turn up soon. On Wednesday, Kurt had reasoned with Grant to convince him to print the one-paragraph press release. It was a judgment call, but Kurt felt the paper was in a stronger position to announce it early. If Mick was found safe and it was all a misunderstanding, fine. But if not, they were better off having acted. No one could accuse them of ignoring Mick's plight or trying to cover it up.

Kurt sat down at Mick's desk to think for a minute. What if Mick was off on a drinking binge, as Wally seemed to think? What if he'd given in to depression and committed suicide? Or what if Mick's abrasive personality had gotten him into hot water? He had made plenty of enemies over the years, with his blunt reports and caustic comments about local officials.

Even so, Kurt decided, it was to the newspaper's advantage as a business to make the announcement early and follow the unfolding events in print. If necessary, management could distance itself from Mick when an explanation was found. If he had met with an accident, the paper would be praised for quick action.

Still, he might take a lot of heat if the story turned sordid. So could the reporter writing the daily articles. Did he really want to put Dave in line for that? Maybe he should just hand it to Joy. She was tough enough to take it.

Kurt took a deep breath, imagining Joy's lead paragraph. No, Dave was the one for the job. He closed his eyes to offer a brief prayer before approaching Dave.

When he opened them, Wally was breezing down the aisle between the work stations.

"Hey, Wally, how's it going?"

Wally stopped and grinned at him. "Terrible. And you, boss?"

"I'm fair to middling." Kurt leaned toward him and gave an exaggerated sniff.

"Uh . . ." Wally wrinkled up his face in a sheepish grimace. "Sorry. I had a rough time this afternoon. Pics for the story on after-school programs. Kids screaming and carrying on. You wouldn't believe it."

Kurt nodded. "Sure, I would. It's too bad, though."

"What?"

Kurt reached into his shirt pocket and withdrew two slips of card stock. "These tickets."

"Wow, you got Red Sox tickets?" Wally's eyes gleamed with appreciation.

"Third game of their series with the Cards next month."

“Oh, boss.”

Kurt pulled the tickets away. “Don’t drool on them, Wally.”

“Is it on a weekend?”

“A Saturday. I figured we’d drive down together, catch the game . . .”

“You mean it?”

“Only if you can make it ’til game day without a cigarette.”

Wally stood silent for a moment, then drew a deep breath. “That’s awfully ambitious, but I’ll take a shot at it.”

Kurt nodded. “All right then. But if you blow it, I’ll take Janet. I’m serious about that.”

Wally eyed him with suspicion. “I didn’t know she liked sports.”

“She doesn’t. But she likes the Sox.”

Wally nodded in perfect understanding.

“Besides,” Kurt added with a grin, “she’d go anywhere with me.”

Dave Carpenter hung up his telephone receiver, and Kurt stood up. “See you later, Wally.” He walked over to Dave’s desk. “Sorry to interrupt you, Dave, but could you join me in my office? I’ve got a new project I’d like to discuss with you.”

Dave sized up the papers covering his desktop on both sides of the keyboard. “Sure . . . uh . . .”

“Take a minute to organize your notes if you

need to," Kurt told him, "and I'll get us some coffee. This is important."

Twenty minutes later, Dave was sitting across from him in Kurt's private office, engrossed in the Jacobs file.

"Why have I never heard about this?" he asked, turning a page on one of the printouts.

"It was before you were born," Kurt said.

"But you say Mick remembered it?"

"Yes. He was just a boy, but his best friend lived near the senator, and I guess when Jacobs vanished, it made a big impression on him."

"This is a great story." Dave's brown eyes took on a faraway look. "I'd love to do something like this. Talk to a lot of the senior citizens and find out what they remember. Maybe I could even locate one of his old Senate colleagues. But I don't know, Mr. Borden. I've got the school board tonight, and that big charity auction is Tuesday. Plus there's that historical society thing in Fairfield—some big-time author is speaking. I have to cover that. And the—"

Kurt held up one hand to stop the verbal traffic. "Take the file home, Dave. Read it over the weekend. Do some more research online if you want. Then call me at home and tell me what you think."

Dave nodded. "We may hear something before Monday. Something about Mick, I mean."

"I hope we do." Kurt folded his hands on the

desk top. "Dave, if Mick hasn't turned up by then, or if he's found, but he's not in the best of health . . ." Kurt looked down at his hands, then back at Dave. "I need to have a reporter primed and ready to do this story, no matter which way it goes."

"The story about Mick."

"Yes."

"What about this Jacobs thing?"

Kurt sighed. "I've been thinking about it for days. It boils down to this: if we find that Mick's disappearance had anything to do with his assignment, then you'll need to jump into it."

Dave nodded. "I'll be ready."

"Good. And if that happens, I'll reassign your other stories to give you the extra time."

"But what if it doesn't have anything to do with this?" Dave tapped the folder. "What if he just decided to cut loose and is backpacking through Slovakia?"

Kurt smiled. "Then the Jacobs story would make a nice nostalgia piece for the Sunday paper."

"The way Mick planned it."

"Right. Meanwhile, take the information I gave you and start on the follow-up about Mick for tomorrow's paper. Touch base with Sergeant Bedard at the P.D. Your playground piece can wait if it needs to."

"Got it." Dave stood up and tucked the folder

under his arm. “Remember you mentioned the other day having a Bible study at noon? I was wondering if you were serious about that.”

“Yes, absolutely.”

“Great. Tim Savage from advertising and I were talking this morning, and we thought maybe Tuesdays would work. Are you free for lunch Tuesdays?”

“Sure.” Kurt reached for his day planner. “Dave, there’s one other thing about this Jacobs project.”

“What?”

Kurt looked up at him and wondered again if he was doing the right thing. He liked Dave, and they’d had a couple of deep conversations about spiritual things. Kurt was delighted to discover that they were brothers in Christ, though Dave had some questions about his faith. Kurt was sure Dave could handle the complicated assignment he was giving him, but there were still things that made him uneasy about putting the cub reporter on it. “If researching the senator’s disappearance got Mick into trouble . . .”

Dave blinked. “You think it’s dangerous?”

“No. But . . . maybe you shouldn’t tell anyone else just yet that you’re looking into this aspect of Mick’s work. And be careful.”

Chapter 9

"This was always one of my favorites walks," Sharon said. "It's so beautiful this time of year."

She and Janet strolled down Pine Lane, away from the paved road. The dirt lane extended for about half a mile beyond the Fairmont house, giving access to several more summer cottages on the lake shore. Janet loved the fall, too, when all the seasonal occupants had departed, leaving the only year-round residents, the Bordens and Elwood Fairmont, in peace.

"The privacy means a lot to me," she admitted. "In summer, there's a lot of noise on the lake, and traffic in and out on the road, but between Labor Day and Memorial Day, the tranquility is astounding."

"It was a great place to grow up," Sharon said. "We always wished our house had shore frontage, though. Being on the side of the road away from the lake, Dad's house has a fabulous view, and we always had swimming access, thanks to kind neighbors, but it would have been nice to have our own little beach."

"I'm sure your father's taxes are a lot lower

since he doesn't have it." The annual property tax bill always made Janet wince, but Kurt rightly noted that it was part of owning shore property. She hadn't considered how the young Fairmonts had reached the water for recreational purposes.

"The maples are turning." Sharon walked along with her face turned upward, and Janet followed her gaze. The pines for which the lane was named had given way to hardwoods, and their leaves showed splashes of red, maroon, orange, peach, gold and yellow.

"I love the birches," Janet murmured. They were not as showy as the maples, but the yellowing leaves waving against the slender white trunks gave her a glad feeling of rightness. The colors, lines and proportions God placed here in the woods had become part of her soul, and she couldn't imagine living anywhere else. She often wished her three children could have grown up here.

"Tory should be up when we get back to the house," Sharon said. "She was so tired last night, I told her to sleep in. We'll have some tea with her if she's awake, then get started on Dad's den."

"Do you think the burglar took anything from your father's desk?" Janet asked.

"I don't know. Andrew and Geneva gave it a quick once-over when they were here. Yesterday

I started sorting through the papers that were dumped out, but it was such a mess! I didn't really know what was there to begin with, so how can I tell what's missing, if anything?"

Her voice cracked, and Janet knew the strain was taking a toll on her. She reached out and patted Sharon's arm. "I'm sorry you had to go through that, on top of your dad's illness. Maybe Andrew and Geneva can remember what papers in the desk seemed important."

Sharon sniffed. "It's been rough. When I called Andrew and told him about the break-in, he was upset. He'd just left that morning. He said maybe they'd been watching the house and thought we were all gone, so it was safe to ransack the place."

Janet shook her head. "That doesn't make sense to me, since they didn't grab any of the obviously valuable things."

"I know. But Andrew said maybe they were looking for the same thing we were."

"You mean . . ."

Sharon laughed. "The mythical treasure. Or maybe there was something in Dad's papers. I should have listened to Paul when he wanted to tear into things and do a thorough search. Now we'll never know if there was something there worth stealing."

"Is there a will?" Janet asked.

"Yes, and Andrew and I have copies. I don't

think it's that, but I don't have any idea what they wanted."

"What did Paul say about the burglary?"

"I didn't tell him." Sharon made a face. "I'm chicken, but I knew he'd be furious. Andrew said to wait, and if nothing else strange happens we don't have to tell Paul and Geneva. If we feel they need to know later on, he'll do the telling."

Janet nodded. It wasn't the way her family would do things, but she understood by now that the Fairmont family was not like other families. At least Andrew was offering to take a small part of the burden off Sharon's shoulders. That was an improvement.

"In a way, I'm glad the others weren't here," Sharon reflected, "although it would have been easier for me to let Andrew and Paul deal with the police."

"Well, things were quiet last night," Janet said.

"Yes. I'm not going to think about it anymore." They reached the turnaround at the end of the road. Through the trees they could see the placid lake. Far out on the water, a red kayak glided over the surface.

"Ready to head back?" Janet asked.

"Sure." As they ambled along, Sharon told her of the attempts she had made to find long-term care for her father. "Dr. Ridge says he'll need nursing care, so there's no question of him coming home now."

"That's too bad."

"Yes, but at least we'll all know he's in a safe place this winter. Vic told me to go ahead and close the house up."

Janet had never met Vic. Sharon said Tory looked like him, and if their daughter's thick, curly chestnut hair, sparkling hazel eyes, and sweet face were any indication, Vic was a handsome man. Sharon's wistful tone also dropped a hint of how much she missed him, and Janet was glad Sharon had a solid marriage. The other Fairmont siblings had all been through at least one divorce, it seemed.

"Would you like Kurt to put the storm windows up next month, like he usually does?" Janet asked.

"We're going to have the power shut off and drain the pipes. I don't think the storm windows will be needed."

Janet nodded. "Maybe you ought to remove some of your father's nicer pieces of furniture."

"I'm going to. Andrew told me to take Mother's best dishes home with me for safekeeping and have the antiques put in storage."

"Probably wise, but it's a big job."

Sharon shoved her hands into the pockets of her light jacket. "Yes, but Tory will be here all next week to help me. And I've already found a storage company that will come for the things."

"Great."

"Oh, say." Sharon turned toward her with a new eagerness. "I don't know if you've seen my mother's paintings before . . ."

"Yes, your father showed me a couple. There's the view of the lake in the living room, and isn't there a still life she painted over the dining table?"

"That's right. There's one of a loon family in Dad's den, and several more upstairs. Mother wasn't very good, but she enjoyed painting. I thought I'd take them down and wrap them for shipping, and each of us kids could have one. I'll save the loons for Dad to have in his room wherever he goes for care. That was his favorite."

"What a wonderful idea."

"Well, I don't know. Tory says they're all rather bad, and the still lifes are depressing. And Paul always ridiculed Mother's painting. He probably won't want one."

"Not even as a keepsake?"

"It wouldn't surprise me." They had reached the Fairmont driveway, and Sharon turned in, producing the house key from her pocket. "We never used to lock the doors when I was a kid, but after living in suburban Boston for so long, I hardly dare walk to the mailbox without locking up."

Janet understood. She felt secure leaving the doors unlocked, especially after the summer people had left, but since Thursday evening's break-in at the Fairmonts', she'd been extra careful, too.

"Hey," Sharon said as she mounted the porch steps, "would you like one of the paintings? I mean, I know they're not great art, but since you've been so good to Dad and all . . . and there are seven of them."

"How thoughtful. Are you sure your father wouldn't mind?"

Sharon turned the key and they went into the entry. "Well, I'm facing reality, Janet. It's been ten days since his stroke. He seems to know me, and I think he knows Tory. He answers yes and no questions, but I'm not always sure he knows what he's agreeing to. Most of the time he just sits and stares. He can't move his left arm. He can't walk. I doubt he'll ever live outside a nursing home again."

Tears filled Sharon's eyes, and Janet drew her into a warm embrace.

"There now," she whispered. "It's hard to see him like this, isn't it?"

Sharon nodded with a little sob.

"When he's up to it, I'd like to go in and visit him."

"He'd like that." Sharon wiped a tear from her cheek with the back of her hand.

"Why don't you show me the loon painting?" Janet asked softly. "I don't think I've ever seen that one."

They went through the living room and into the smaller den. Sharon led her to the roll-top desk. It was still in disarray from when the intruder had rifled it, but at least all the papers and office supplies had been picked up off the floor.

Janet gazed at the oil painting above the desk. The colors and long, pointed beaks of the loons were recognizable, but the attempted feathering effect was amateurish and inadequate, and the unnaturally green water looked as solid as a linoleum floor.

"Maybe I could sell them as primitives," Sharon said with a chuckle.

"Hey, any coffee?"

Tory stood in the doorway. Without her customary makeup, she looked like a teenager, not the sophisticated city girl who had arrived from Providence Thursday evening.

"Janet and I were just about to get a cup of tea," her mother said. "I was showing her the loon painting."

"It's better than the one in the dining room," Tory said.

They all headed for the kitchen, but with unspoken consent paused to study the framed painting over the dining table.

"Sharon," Janet said. She squinted and peered closer at the dark still life. Her excitement grew, and she inhaled sharply. "Sharon?"

"Hmm?"

"It's the card case."

Tory gasped. "You're right, Mrs. Borden! Mom, look! Right there. It's the silver card case we found in the chocolate tin."

"Do you think so?" Sharon eyed the rectangular blob in the picture critically. "I thought it was a bar of soap."

"No, no! It's the card case all right! Look, Mom. There's the monogram."

"I suppose you're right." Sharon's voice still held a strong hint of doubt.

"Of course we're right. Consider it from Grandma's perspective. All of her paintings are a bit unfocused and vague. Look at that apple. It could be a pot holder, but, no. In Grandma's point of view, that's an apple, and we all accept that it's an apple."

"Well, yes . . ."

"Now think about the card case. If Grandma was going to paint that, what would it look like?"

Sharon smiled. "You're right. It's the card case."

Janet laughed. "You'd better put that and the pen in a safe place."

"I had them appraised yesterday," Sharon said. "They're not worth much. Maybe fifty dollars or so. But I thought I'd put them away until the others have a chance to see them. Maybe Geneva can tell us where they came from."

"When did Grandma paint this?" Tory asked,

and Janet thought that was a very good question.

But Sharon only shrugged. “It used to be in the upstairs hall when I was a teenager, but then she put the sunset up there and moved this one in here. I don’t remember her painting it. It’s got to be at least thirty-five years old. Maybe older.”

“Hey, I’m starving here,” Tory said. “Are we going to the hospital this morning?”

“I’d like to see that card case. The real thing, I mean.” Kurt studied the framed painting Janet had brought home from the Fairmonts’ house. It was an amateurish depiction of a few pieces of fruit in a blue bowl, with a silver blob Janet insisted was a card case lying in front of it.

“The case is quite elegant, and the pen has the same design.”

Kurt pointed to a hazy swirl on the object in the painting. “You’re sure it’s a monogram?”

“Uh-huh. It’s old-fashioned script. A capital J, I think, but it could be an I. Tory says it’s an S, though.”

Kurt frowned. “And none of them have those initials.”

“Well, Sharon’s is an S, but those things are older than Sharon, I’m sure, and I’m ninety-nine percent certain it’s not an S.”

“Ask her what her grandparents’ names were.”

“Good idea. They could have belonged to someone in another generation.” Janet eyed the painting, then looked speculatively at Kurt. "Where should we hang it?" He stared at her in mock horror, and she began to chortle. "I guess you weren't in the market for new art for your office, huh?"

"I'd be the laughingstock of all the snooty liberals I work with if I took that thing to the office. It's awful. And besides, who wants a picture of a pumpkin hanging over his desk?"

"That's an apple."

"Oh? Then I really hate it."

"Are you sure you want to pass on it?" Janet asked with a grin. "What if twenty years from now Olivia Fairmont paintings are all the rage? There's a limited supply."

"Are you sure she painted it?"

"Positive. It's her style, and this is her signature." Janet touched the lower left-hand corner of the canvas. "O.B.F."

"Hm. So her maiden name wasn't a J, either."

"Nope. Now, if those things had been found across the lane in—"

"In Senator Jacobs's house." Kurt almost felt things click in his brain. He snatched the painting from her hands. "Janet, you're a genius. He was rich enough to own something like this."

"Like that painting?"

"No, no, the silver accessories. I want to see them."

Janet stared at her husband, feeling out of

breath and lightheaded. “You think the pen and card case belonged to the vanishing senator?”

“Why not? Anything is possible.”

“But . . .” They looked at each other. “But if none of the Fairmont children knows where they came from, and if Elwood can’t tell us . . .”

“Maybe there’s another way to check out your theory.” Kurt thrust the frame back into her hands and marched across the room to the telephone stand.

“*My* theory?” Janet shrugged. “Okay, my theory. Are you saying that so you won’t have to claim it if you’re wrong?”

Kurt thumbed through the phone book and punched in Dave Carpenter’s home number.

“Dave! Glad I caught you. Listen, I know it’s Saturday and all that, but could you come out to my house and bring the file I gave you yesterday? Great. I have to leave at four o’clock. I’m speaking at the Lions’ Club in town tonight, but there’s something I want to check on first, and it may be helpful on the Jacobs story.”

“What’s in the mysterious file?” Janet asked as soon as he had hung up. She gave him back the painting and turned toward the kitchen. Kurt set the frame down, leaning it against the wall so that the picture was hidden, and followed her.

“Articles about Senator Jacobs. I printed several pictures off the Web yesterday.”

“So? Was the card case in one of the pictures?”

"You're quick, babe." He pulled her toward him and kissed her. "Not the card case. The pen. I distinctly remember a very clear photo of him signing a document. He was chairman of the Appropriations Committee for a while, you know."

"Regular big shot."

"Yes, he was."

"Couldn't you have just pulled that picture up again on your computer, instead of making Dave come all the way out here?"

"Probably, but I don't just want the picture. I want Dave."

"Go get a shower." Janet stretched on tiptoes to kiss him again. "If you're going to be the main speaker to all those hungry Lions tonight, you can't be all sweaty and covered with garden dirt."

Kurt smiled. "All right. Those are the last of the tomatoes, I'm afraid." He nodded toward the windowsill.

"Yum. I'll make myself a fabulous salad for supper. Too bad you have to eat rubber chicken."

Kurt headed for a soak in the shower. He'd worked all day in the yard, getting things ready for winter. It was too early to put away the patio furniture and the canoe, but there always seemed to be a million jobs that needed his attention on weekends. He was hoping for a long Indian summer, so that he and Janet could enjoy a few more leisurely paddles up the lake to view the foliage as the color peaked.

When he came out into the living room dressed for his presentation to the Lions, Dave was sitting on the sofa with the fat file folder open on the coffee table before him, and Janet sat beside him, her face earnest as she pored over a sheet of paper in her hand.

"Hi, Mr. Borden." Dave stood up, and Kurt gave him mental brownie points.

"Dave, thanks for coming." They shook hands, and Kurt looked expectantly at Janet.

"It's the pen, all right," she said.

"You're sure?"

"Pretty sure. I could ask Sharon to show it to you."

"Do you think she's home?" Kurt asked.

Janet shook her head. "She and Tory were going to get groceries and go to the hospital. I doubt they're back yet."

"I don't know if we should tell her," Kurt mused. "There's no way to be sure, really, and you said she has no idea where the things came from."

"But they were neighbors. There could be a reasonable explanation." Janet handed the picture back to Dave, and he laid it on top of the file folder. "You saw how Sharon gave me the painting today, as a memento. Maybe Mrs. Jacobs did the same thing when she closed up the cottage here. She was leaving for good, and

Olivia had been her summer neighbor for years. She might have given her the silver pen and case as a reminder of the good years."

"No way it could happen," Dave said.

"Oh?" Janet arched her eyebrows.

"You're right, Dave," Kurt said. "The early reports after Senator Jacobs disappeared said that, when last seen at his office, he was wearing a gray suit, red, silver, and black striped tie, white shirt, black belt and shoes, Waltham wristwatch, and he had his reading glasses and a monogrammed silver pen in his pocket."

"I don't think they ever found those things," Dave said. "All the descriptions published for weeks afterward included them."

Janet frowned. "Then how did the pen get to be up here in Maine? He disappeared in Washington."

"That's the two-hundred-fifty-thousand-dollar question," Kurt said.

"I thought it was the Sixty-four Thousand Dollar Question."

Kurt smiled at her. "You get an A in trivia today, Mrs. Borden, but your Final Jeopardy answer is wrong. Did I neglect to tell you that when Jacobs pulled his vanishing act, two hundred fifty thousand dollars also went missing?"

"Money that wasn't his, I suppose."

"You suppose correctly. It belonged to Uncle Sam."

Dave looked up from examining the photo. “So, maybe it’s not the same pen after all. There could be lots of similar pens.”

“With a J monogram?” Kurt asked, but he knew Dave was right. His theory would never stand up in court.

“Or maybe he had more than one,” Janet suggested. “It could be a set.”

Kurt frowned at her.

“Sorry,” she said, “but I don’t think we can assume the artifacts in Sharon’s pantry belonged to the senator. We don’t have anything solid.”

“Not yet.” Kurt glanced at his watch. “I’ll have to get going soon.” He picked up the file folder, wishing he could stay and go through it all with Dave again. There had to be a connection between the former senator and Mick’s disappearance, if he could only find it.

“I stayed up late last night reading the articles,” Dave said with an air of confession. “I couldn’t quit once I started.”

“What about the card case?” Kurt asked, shuffling the stack of papers. “Did you come across anything about that?”

“No, I don’t remember anything like that.”

“I wonder if it was a gift.” Kurt sighed. He couldn’t think of a way to find out when so many years had intervened.

“If we told Sharon and the rest of the family,” Janet said slowly, “maybe one of them could shed some light on it. Obviously their mother knew about those things. She put the card case in one of her paintings."

"Why did she do that?" Kurt asked. The whole problem bothered him.

"Because it was pretty?" Janet suggested.

"But if the card case was important to her, why did she hide it behind the soup and anchovies, and why don't the kids know about it?" Kurt shook his head. "I'm thinking that if any of the surviving Fairmonts could shed some light on it, other than Elwood, of course, it would be Geneva."

"The oldest girl." Janet's brow furrowed. "You may be right. She has the longest memory, and she might have been closer to their mother than the others."

"Or we could ask the senator's family," Dave said.

Kurt smiled. "That's a thought." He stood up. "Time for me to go, but let's think about that, Dave. We ought to be able to find out if Mrs. Jacobs is still alive, or if there are any living children."

"Sure, they're public figures. I'll bet we can." Dave's smile lit up his eyes. "If nothing else, a phone interview would be a great addition to my story."

"I wish you didn't have to speak at that club tonight. The three of us could dig up a lot." Janet sounded eager and childlike, and Kurt wished he could stay home.

He smiled apologetically at Dave. “Not the way you wanted to spend your Saturday evening, I guess.”

“No, actually, I was going to ask you if I could see the house. Since I’m so close, I’d like to take a look at it. Maybe Mick came out here to meet Wally, and there’s some evidence of that.”

“Great idea,” Janet said.

Kurt reached for her hand. “Well, it will have to be the two of you, or I’ll be late for the meeting.”

“I’d be happy to walk over there with you, Dave,” said Janet. “The people who own it now live in New Jersey. It’s all locked up, but you could see the outside.”

“That’s all Mick saw, right?” Dave asked.

“Right.”

He nodded. “That would be great. Wally Reed showed me the pictures he took Monday while he was waiting for Mick, but I’d like to see it in person, and how it sits in relation to the road and the lake.”

The three of them walked toward the door, and Kurt said, “Do you really think we should ask Sharon about the pen? She’s had so much stress lately.”

“I know.” Janet pressed her lips together for a moment. “But it would be a distraction from her father's situation, and if there really is a connection to the Jacobs family . . ."

"Hold on," Kurt said. "So far the only link between Elwood and the senator is that they used to be neighbors. I wouldn't want to upset Sharon by implying we think there was something sinister there."

"I can be discreet." Janet almost pouted, and Kurt smiled. He leaned over and kissed her cheek.

"Yes, you can, sweetheart. Go for it, then, but take Dave with you so he can get it all firsthand."

Chapter 10

Janet and Dave walked across the grass and down the slope toward the Hillmans' cottage.

"Wow, that's the house?" Dave asked. "It's small."

"It's just a summer cottage."

"Their camp," Dave said with a smile. Locals heading for their lakeside cottages always said they were "going to camp."

The two-story cottage was sided with weathered shingles. A glassed-in porch faced the driveway. On the side toward the Bordens' property sat a small, detached garage with a padlock securing the old-style rolling door.

"You can't really see much," Janet said.

"It's all right." Dave watched the ground as he walked toward the garage. He stopped and prodded something with the toe of his sneaker. A cigarette butt.

"Does Mick smoke?" she asked.

"No, but Wally does."

They looked around and found several more butts, all the same brand. "Gotta be Wally's," Dave said. "Your husband's trying to get him to quit, but it's a losing battle."

"I heard."

They strolled to the back of the house, climbed the steps to the deck facing the lake, and stood looking out over the rippling waves. They could just see the marina, across half a mile of water.

"Nice," Dave said.

"This deck is new. It was added a couple of years ago. I think there was another porch before that. As you can see, there's no foundation. The Hillmans have had quite a bit of work done. Town ordinances won't let them add on to make it bigger, but they can renovate what's here."

"I'm surprised the senator didn't have a bigger place." Dave turned around and scrutinized the little cottage. "He bought it in 1941. That was long before he was elected to the Senate."

"What did he do before that?" Janet asked.

"He was a teacher. Got married in 1940."

"The year before they bought the cottage," Janet noted. "Prices were lower then."

Dave nodded. "He served in the army in World War II. Didn't go in until 1942. After the war, he went back to teaching. Then he ran for the state legislature. It kind of snowballed after that. State Senate, campaign for governor—he lost that one—a couple of years of lobbying for the paper industry, then he ran for the U.S. House. Two terms there, then the Senate."

"This was their summer cottage," Janet said. "Where was their permanent home?"

"Portland."

A faint sound reached her ears, and she looked toward the lane.

"Sharon Schlesser and her daughter are back from their grocery shopping trip. Would you like to meet them?"

"Her mother was the artist, right?" Dave asked.

Janet smiled. Some artist. It was all she could do not to laugh. "That's right."

"Should we get the file folder?"

"Let's stop in and chat first," Janet decided. "It might scare her to see how much material you and Kurt have amassed on Senator Jacobs. But we can run over to our house for the picture if it seems appropriate."

"The lady's been traumatized enough, from what you've told me."

"Right. Her father's stroke, and the house being burglarized. I wouldn't want her to think we're trying to blame Mick Tyler's disappearance on her family. That would be irrational, but when you're already tired and under stress, things don't always make sense."

Tory opened the door to Janet's knock.

"Hi!" Her gaze flicked past Janet to land on Dave. She looked back at Janet with obvious expectation.

"Tory Schlesser, I'd like you to meet Dave Carpenter. He's a coworker of Kurt's, and he's fast becoming a friend of the family."

Dave smiled and extended his hand. Janet watched in fascination as Tory took it. She could have sworn a spark jumped between them when their hands clasped. Dave's intent concentration on Tory's face was endearing. The boy was smitten, no question. A motherly glow warmed Janet's heart. Dave reminded her a little of Eric, her and Kurt's only son. Not his looks, but his manners and mannerisms.

She shifted her attention back to Tory. A slow flush crept up from the scoop neck of Tory's lavender top, and her eyelashes swept down to hide her hazel eyes, but Janet had seen them glitter.

"How's your grandfather today?" Janet asked.

"I thought he was doing pretty well, but Mom's discouraged. She was hoping to see a bigger change, I think."

Janet nodded. "Is he talking?"

"Just a little. A word at a time, mostly. He said *juice* when he wanted a drink. The therapist was there when we went in, and she seems to think Dad will keep improving."

"That's great."

Tory looked past her, at Dave. Janet turned to include him. He was watching Tory avidly.

"We were wondering if your mother could take a look at a photo Dave brought to the house." Janet hated to break the mood, but she feared they would all be embarrassed if she didn't.

"Oh, sure. Come on in." Tory stepped back. "She's putting away groceries. I'll tell her you're here."

A few minutes later they were all in the Fairmonts' kitchen helping put away the food. Tory gave Dave the job of stuffing the empty plastic sacks into a long sleeve her grandmother had made for the purpose, and Janet added to Elwood's array of canned goods.

"You want me to look at a picture of Senator Jacobs?" Sharon asked in confusion.

"That's right," Janet said.

"I don't understand. I mean, I'd like to see it. I barely remember him, from when I was little. But why?"

"I have another reason for showing it to you." Janet looked over toward Dave and Tory. They were laughing together, and Tory pulled a grocery sack out the bottom of the fabric sleeve and held it out for him to put in again at the top.

"Hey, you're making more work for me," Dave said in mock offense.

Tory laughed and tossed it at him.

"I'll ask Dave to run over and get it," Janet said.

Sharon shook her head. "We're done here. Why don't we walk over with you?"

Janet hesitated. "There's something else . . . oh, dear, I'm not doing a very good job of this."

"What is it?"

Janet pulled in a big breath. "Can you bring the chocolate tin over with you?"

Sharon's eyes grew wide. "What in the world . . . ?"

Janet wished she'd led up to it more smoothly. And she'd promised Kurt discretion! "I don't want to say any more yet. Just play along with me and bring it, all right?"

Sharon shrugged and reached up to the third shelf. "Fine. Be that way." She laughed and pushed the canned vegetables aside.

Janet was glad Sharon hadn't lost her sense of humor. "You and Tory might as well stay and have a sandwich and salad with me. Kurt's away for the evening, and I'll be lonesome."

"Tory," Sharon called.

Tory whirled around, and Sharon seemed to notice for the first time the interplay between her daughter and Dave. "Sorry, sweetie, but I need your help. Can you bring the stool? I can't reach the tin."

"May I help you, Mrs. Schlesser?" Dave stepped forward, his brown eyes shining.

He is just too cute, Janet thought. She hoped Sharon was bright enough to recognize prime son-in-law material when she saw it.

"Yeah, Dave's tall enough." Tory pushed him forward. "It's right behind the spaghetti sauce."

Sharon stepped aside. "An old tin box. That's

it. Thank you so much." Dave passed it down, and she took it from his hands.

"What do you want it for?" Tory asked.

"Janet wants it for some reason. She's being very mysterious." Sharon tucked the tin under her arm, and Dave rearranged the canned goods he had disturbed.

"I've invited you and your mother over for a light supper," Janet added. "Are you game?"

"Sure, but let us bring the doughnuts." Tory skipped across the kitchen to the old walnut sideboard.

"Of course." Sharon chuckled. "We bought the yummiest looking crumb doughnuts. It's a good thing you two dropped in, or Tory and I would have had to eat them all ourselves."

"You're invited, too, Dave," Janet added, and he grinned.

"Sounds good. Thanks."

Sharon and Tory got their jackets, and they all walked over to the Bordens' house. Tory and Dave chattered all the while, and Janet was amazed to hear Dave laughing and bantering so freely. She didn't know him well, but she'd pigeonholed him as reserved. Tory was certainly drawing him out.

She led them all into the living room and settled Sharon in a comfortable armchair. Tory drifted to the sofa, and Dave followed. Janet pulled her rocker a bit closer to Sharon.

"I know all of this seems odd, but Dave and Kurt are working on a project for the paper, and Kurt located a photograph of Senator Jacobs." She nodded at Dave, and he opened his folder and passed the black and white printout to Sharon. She took it and held it in front of her for a couple of seconds.

"Yes, that's Senator Jacobs."

"Let me see," Tory said eagerly. "I've never seen him."

"Before you pass it to Tory," Janet said, "is there anything else you recognize in the photo?"

Sharon frowned and again studied the picture. "I don't see . . ."

Tory stirred, but Janet didn't take her eyes off Sharon's face. In her peripheral vision, she saw Dave reach out toward Tory to keep her in her seat.

Sharon's eyes widened. "It looks like . . ." She lowered the paper and stared at Janet. "It can't be."

"Let me see," Tory cried. She jumped up and bounded to her mother's side.

Sharon gave her the picture, still looking at Janet. "I don't understand."

Tory gave a little yip. "Mom! They're identical. Get the pen out."

Sharon looked down at the tin in her lap. "They can't be the same. Can they?"

Janet shrugged. "I don't know. When I saw the photo, I thought they looked the same. Comparing it to the real thing may prove me wrong."

Sharon opened the lid and took out the silver pen.

Tory held the picture up next to it. Her gaze skipped from the paper to the pen and back. Sharon stared at the two items, frowning.

"What do you think?" Janet asked.

"They look the same."

"They sure do." Tory took the pen from her mother's hand and went to the sofa, holding it and the picture out to Dave. He took them, and Tory sat down beside him. They bent over the pen and the picture. Janet smiled. They didn't mind getting close in the investigation.

"Awfully alike," Dave said. "I wish the picture was clearer."

"And closer." Tory looked up and seemed startled by his nearness. She sat up. "What happens now?"

Janet cleared her throat. "Well, we thought perhaps your mother would ask her sister and brothers, but especially Geneva, if she knew anything about the things in the tin. For instance, does she know where they came from, and does she remember when Olivia painted the still life with the card case?"

Sharon nodded. "I can do that."

"We're also considering trying to contact any remaining members of the Jacobs family," Dave said.

Tory brightened. "Sure. If those things were the senator's, they might recognize them."

"Right." Dave gazed at Tory. Janet wondered if he knew he was staring. Tory was worth staring at. She was a beautiful young woman, animated and smart.

"You got this online?" Tory reached for the paper once more and read the slug at the bottom. "Why didn't I think of that?"

"We didn't connect the silver things to the senator when we found them," Janet said.

"No, but all my life I've heard about this man, and I never once thought of googling him." Dave laughed, and Tory eyed him coyly. "What do you do for the paper, anyway?"

"I'm a reporter." Janet thought he sat a little straighter as he said it.

"So, you're reporting on this, or what? I don't get it. You're not putting the burglary in the paper, are you?" Tory darted a glance at Janet.

"No, dear." Janet looked at Sharon to see if the suggestion upset her, but Sharon listened with rapt attention. "It's just that Kurt had already found this picture while he and Dave were working on something else. When I brought the painting home and told him about the card case and pen, he . . . well, we're from away, you know?"

Tory blinked at her.

"The Jacobs story was a novelty to us," Janet hurried on. "We didn't know anything about the senator living here until last week, and Kurt was going to have Dave do a story on it."

Tory nodded. "I see. But what made you put that together with . . . Oh, the monogram, of course."

"That's right." Janet was relieved that Mick Tyler's name hadn't come up. Tory probably hadn't heard about Mick's disappearance. "We were trying to think whose initial it could be . . . your grandparents' for instance. Then Kurt suddenly thought of the nearest neighbor, Thomas Jacobs."

"Right across the street." Tory looked at the photograph again, and Dave sat watching Tory, his lips parted in a contented smile.

Sharon caught Janet's eye. She raised her eyebrows and nodded slightly toward Dave and Tory.

Janet smiled and gave a tiny shrug. "Well, anyone for grilled cheese?" she asked, perhaps a bit louder than was necessary.

"And doughnuts," Tory said.

Janet laughed. "Sandwiches and salad first."

"Let me help you." Sharon followed her hostess to the kitchen, leaving the two young people behind. As soon as they were out of Tory's earshot, Sharon whispered, "Janet! That is a gorgeous young man, and so polite!"

"You noticed." Janet grinned and plugged in her electric skillet. Already her mind was out of control, trying to come up with an excuse to bring Dave and Tory together again soon.

"I've been worried about Tory," Sharon said. "We thought she was about to get a diamond when she graduated from college two years ago, but it ended in a messy breakup."

"She's a beautiful girl."

"Yes, and she deserves a rock solid man. Her old boyfriend treated her badly toward the end, and Vic was furious. She was so hurt. Can you vouch for this fellow?"

"Kurt likes him. I haven't known him long, but he's bright, courteous, and has a decent job."

Sharon nodded. "Well, there's definitely an attraction there. Probably nothing will come of it, though."

"All in God's time." Janet threw her a smile and rummaged in the refrigerator for the cheese.

"Speaking of God," Sharon began, and Janet noticed a serious inflection. She straightened and looked at her friend. "I mentioned church to Tory this afternoon, and she said she'd like to go with us tomorrow. Do you mind?"

"I'd love it."

Sharon gave her a tremulous smile. "I've been thinking about your pastor's message all week. I even bought myself a Bible."

"That's wonderful! In fact, I considered asking if you wanted to get together to study the Bible, but you've been so busy, I hated to put another thing in your schedule."

"I think I'd like that," Sharon said. "Things are slower, now that it's just Tory and me at the house. And I have a lot of questions."

Janet nodded. "What time is good for you?"

"How about right after Kurt leaves for work in the morning?"

"Terrific. Why don't you come over Monday around eight, and I'll have tea ready. If the weather's nice, we can sit out on the deck." Janet got out the lettuce and chose a plump tomato from the windowsill.

"Let me do that. I'll make the salad while you cook the sandwiches."

"Thanks." Janet handed her a paring knife.

Sharon's face went sober again. "Do you really think that pen belonged to the senator? It just doesn't make sense to me. Wouldn't his wife have kept it for one of the family members? It's a pretty expensive trinket to just give to a neighbor, and I don't think my folks were ever that close to Senator and Mrs. Jacobs. Mom always felt a little lower-class around them."

"I don't know," Janet said. "The pen looks like the one in the picture, but it's only a computer printout, and we can't be certain. Maybe Dave or Kurt can find the photo online again and enlarge it. But just in case it's the same pen, you might want to put that tin in a more secure place."

"Yes. I can put the things in Dad's safe deposit

box. Do you think I should? My name is on his bank card."

"It might be a good idea, at least until your siblings get to see them."

Sharon nodded. "I'll do it Monday. I wouldn't want them to be stolen." Her eyes flared, and she whirled toward Janet. "You don't think that's what the burglar was after, do you? I mean, if someone else knew they were in the house . . ."

Janet caught her breath. "I hadn't thought of that."

"Perhaps we should tell the police." Sharon's lower lip trembled. "I don't like this, Janet."

"I'm sorry." Janet put her hand on Sharon's shoulder. "We didn't want to upset you. In fact, we almost didn't show you that picture. I don't want you to worry about this."

Sharon took a shaky breath. "I'm glad you did show me."

At the supper table, Janet noted how readily Dave bowed his head when she announced that she would say the blessing. She liked him more and more. How could this handsome young man with the impeccable manners still be single? She'd have to ask Kurt to probe a little about his situation. It would be awful if Tory lost her heart to Dave and then found out he had a girlfriend.

When they had eaten, Sharon and Tory put on their jackets and prepared to walk back to Elwood's house. "We're just going to make a quick run to the hospital this evening," Sharon said. She carried the chocolate tin in her arms, and Tory took the bag of leftover doughnuts.

"Why don't you call instead?" Janet suggested. "You're so tired."

"Let's do that, Mom," Tory agreed. "If the nurse says he's sleeping, we won't go."

"Well . . ."

"Let me walk you home," Dave offered.

"Oh, we'll be fine," Sharon assured him. "It's just a few yards down the road."

Dave seemed a little mournful, and the romantic in Janet made her wish Sharon hadn't turned him away so blithely.

Janet suddenly realized she was daydreaming, not acting the gracious hostess. "Here, take my flashlight. It gets dark so early." She opened the drawer in the hall table and put her small rechargeable light in Tory's hand.

"Thanks, Mrs. Borden. Supper was fabulous."

"Oh, you're welcome, dear. I hope to see more of you soon." Janet leaned close to Tory and whispered, "Put your mother into a bubble bath and then get her to go to bed early."

Tory smiled and nodded.

They all stepped out the front door.

"Goodnight," Dave said, grasping Tory's hand for an instant. "I'm glad we met."

"Me, too."

Janet and Sharon called a last goodnight to

each other, and Janet stood by Dave, watching them out the driveway.

"Well, I'd better start the dishwasher." Janet turned back toward the house.

"I should hit the road," Dave said.

Janet was sure his mind was still on Tory. "Kurt ought to be home soon. You're welcome to stay."

"No, but thank you. If I'm here when he gets back, I'll be tempted to stay up late again talking about this story, and I have to be at Sunday school with my brain functioning in the morning."

"I know what you mean. Where's your church?"

They walked through to the living room, and Dave gathered up the papers and the thick file folder.

"It's out in Fairfield. Just a small, country church, but I love it. I'm helping with a skit in the opening tomorrow."

She nodded, even more pleased with her emerging view of his character. "That should be fun. Sharon and Tory are going to church with us. We go to the Community Church in—"

There was a frantic pounding on the front door, and Janet stared at him for a fraction of a second, then ran back into the entry. Without bothering to look through the peephole, she threw the door open.

Tory came in first, pulling Sharon by the hand. Both their faces were pale.

"Police," Tory gasped.

Chapter 11

"Oh, no." Janet hurried to the phone. "Another burglary?"

Tory caught her breath. "There's a strange car under the pine trees at the end of the driveway. We almost fell over it."

"And there's someone in the house," Sharon added.

Tory nodded in confirmation. "We saw a light moving around in the dining room."

"A flashlight?" Dave asked, and Sharon nodded.

"Looked like it. We didn't stick around."

"It couldn't be one of your brothers, come back again?" Janet asked.

"If it's someone with any business being there, they'd have turned the lights on," Tory said.

"Are you all right?" Dave asked.

"We're fine," Tory replied, but she was shaking all over.

Janet spoke with the 911 operator, requesting a patrol car immediately. When she hung up, she looked at Dave. "The nearest trooper lives in Oakland. Well, there's one in Augusta. Either way, I'm afraid whoever's in the house will be gone before the police arrive."

"There's no police in Belgrade?" Tory asked.

"We're too small," Janet said.

"Did you get the license number of the car?" Dave asked.

Tory shook her head. "I didn't even think of it. That was brilliant, wasn't it?"

"I was petrified," Sharon said. "I just wanted to get to where there were lights and people and telephones."

"Come sit down." Janet took them into the living room. Sharon complied, and Janet took the afghan off the back of the sofa and spread it over her friend's knees. Sharon still clutched the chocolate tin to her chest, and Janet gently pried her fingers away. "Let me put this somewhere safe."

Tory gaped at her. "You think that's what they're after?"

"I don't know," Janet said, "but let's just get it out of sight."

"Do you have a safe?" Dave asked.

"No. But the deep freezer locks." Janet hurried to the laundry room, shoved the tin into the freezer, and took the key they seldom used from its hook.

When she returned to the living room, Dave was sitting next to Tory, with his arm protectively across the back of the sofa behind her.

"I'll make some hot tea," Janet offered.

"No, I'm fine," Sharon insisted.

"We ought to go over there and wait for him to come out," Tory said. "I am so mad! They can't do this to us."

"Tory, dear, calm down," Sharon said.

"I want to go wait by his car." Tory jumped up.

"What if he has a gun?" Dave stood, too, and Tory stared up at him, then scowled in defeat.

"Come on, sit down," Dave said, and Tory obeyed him.

Janet's brain whirled. "Dave, could you help me for a minute? I think hot chocolate is in order." She all but pulled him into the kitchen.

"What's up?" he asked.

"If that car is gone when the police arrive, what do we have to show for it?"

He frowned. "I wouldn't mind doing a little investigating. You want me to sneak out the back so Sharon and Tory won't know?"

"No, I think we'd better go together. Safety in numbers. But I don't want to drag Sharon over there."

Dave nodded. Janet pulled a box of cocoa packets and four mugs from a cupboard, then filled the teakettle and set it on the stove.

"All right, then," she said. "Tory brought my flashlight back. It's on the hall table."

"I'll get it."

Janet went back to the living room doorway. "Listen, Dave and I are going to go out to the end of our driveway and see if we can tell whether that car is still there or not."

"I'm coming." Tory jumped up.

Janet said gently, "No, dear, you ought to stay here."

Dave spoke from behind her. "Don't leave your mom alone, Tory."

Tory stared at him, then nodded. "All right, but if you're gone long, we'll worry."

"We just want to see if it's still there and maybe get the plate number," Janet said. "If the police car arrives we'll come right in, and if the mystery car is gone we'll come tell you."

Tory pursed her lips, but she nodded.

"Meanwhile, the kettle is heating, and I put out the hot chocolate things. Can you take care of it, Tory?"

"Sure."

Janet took Dave back through the kitchen and out onto the back deck, seizing her jacket and a tablet and pen in passing.

The night was still. They walked down the steps and across the lawn, avoiding the crunchy gravel of the driveway. At the edge of the road, they both halted. Janet looked toward the main road and listened. Nothing. She looked down Pine Lane toward Elwood's house, but could see nothing amiss.

"You hold the light, and I'll write the number down if he's still there," she whispered.

Dave nodded. "Do you need the light now?"

"Not on the roadway. If a car comes, duck into the trees on the other side."

They crossed the road swiftly. Dave led the way, and Janet jogged to keep up. The big pines at the end of Elwood's driveway loomed dark and foreboding. Dave slowed, and they advanced cautiously, peering into the shadows beneath the trees.

"There it is," Dave whispered.

"I see it."

They crept closer to the dark bulk of the car, and Janet looked toward the house. "I don't see any lights inside."

"Me either."

Dave bent low and dashed to the front of the sedan. He turned on the flashlight and shone the beam on the license plate.

"Three-one-five-three-BK," Janet breathed. "Three-one-five-three-BK."

"Got it?" Dave asked.

"Yes, but I'd better write it down."

She held the tablet low, and he shone the light on it. Janet scribbled *3153BK.*

Footsteps sounded nearby—too close. Janet gasped and looked toward the sound, and Dave snapped the light off. A startled exclamation reached them.

Suddenly a bright light blinded her, and Dave grabbed her hand, pulling her aside. Janet realized someone had opened the car door, and the inside light had shone brilliant in the night.

The motor started, practically under her nose, and she stumbled. Dave jerked her to her feet and behind a large pine tree. He held her tight against the tree trunk while the motor roared and the car bumped out into the lane and tore off toward the main road.

Dave released her, and she grabbed a deep breath.

"Sorry," he said.

"It's all right, but I lost my tablet."

"We'll find it."

"I remember the number. Three-one-five-three-BK."

He exhaled with a relieved laugh. "You're good, Mrs. B. Let's go back. Tory's probably hopping with frustration."

"Listen." Janet caught the faint wail of a siren.

"The cavalry, I presume. There's your notepad." Dave stooped and retrieved her tablet from where the car's nose had been.

"I didn't even notice what kind of car it was," Janet groaned.

"Mitsubishi Eclipse."

"Was it black?"

"Some dark color."

The siren was loud now, and they looked up the lane to see the flashing blue light approaching.

"Go brief the ladies," Dave said. "I'll tell the trooper what happened."

Janet ran across the road to the end of her driveway and looked back. Dave wagged the flashlight back and forth, shining it low, and the cruiser slowed down. She stood watching, knowing she should go inside, but hating to miss the action.

The front door of the house opened, and Tory came out onto the steps. "Is he gone?"

"Yes, but we got the plate number." Janet looked down at the tablet in her hand. She'd better take it over to the trooper. Looking back toward Tory, she called, "Tell your mom everything's all right. I'll be right there."

She walked across to where Dave stood by the police car talking to the officer.

"Here's Mrs. Borden," Dave said as she came even with them. "Was that 3-1-5-3-BK?"

"You got it."

The officer was writing in a notebook. "All right, good. Do you know which way he went when he hit the paved road?"

Dave and Janet looked at each other and both shook their heads. "You can't see all the way to the corner from here," Janet said.

The trooper nodded. "I came from Belgrade Village. Think about how long he'd been gone when I came down the road. Do you think I passed him if he was going that way?"

"Could be," Dave said. "It wasn't long."

"He didn't turn the lights on at first," Janet recalled. "The dome light came on when he opened the door, but no headlights when he pulled out."

"Did you get a look at his face?"

"No, I was too busy jumping out of the way. He almost ran over me, but Dave pulled me out of his path."

"It was definitely a man," Dave said. "He was alone, and he had a light-colored shirt or jacket."

"Glasses?" the officer asked.

Dave gritted his teeth. "Maybe."

"Beard?"

"I don't think so. It was pitch dark, until he opened the door. I only got a glimpse, because I saw that he didn't care if he mowed us down. I was thinking more about our safety."

"All right, I'll call this in, then we'll see what the house looks like."

Another car rolled down Pine Lane. Janet looked toward her house and saw Tory and Sharon standing together at the end of the driveway. The car pulled in at the Bordens' and stopped.

"It's Kurt." She left Dave and ran up the road, into her husband's arms.

"What happened?" Kurt demanded, staring at the police cruiser.

"The burglar came back."

"Is everybody okay?"

"Yes."

Kurt held her close and peered toward the police car. "Is that Dave?"

"Yes."

"He's still here?"

"He stayed for supper. Tory and Sharon did, too. I've got so much to tell you!"

Kurt squeezed her. "Let's go inside, and you can tell me everything. The officer can come find you if he needs you."

Janet clung to his hand as they walked back toward Kurt's car.

"We think he was after the chocolate tin," Janet said. She handed Kurt a mug of hot chocolate. The police had left, and Sharon and Tory had insisted on going back to the Fairmont house.

"Chocolate tin?" Kurt looked down at the cocoa in his cup. He was tired, and Janet's disjointed narrative had ceased to make sense.

"You know. The one Sharon found the pen and card case in. That's right—you haven't seen it yet."

"Did he find it?" Kurt asked.

"Not unless he robbed our freezer while I wasn't looking."

She burst into laughter, and Kurt realized his expression must be a comical sight.

"I'm sorry," Janet gasped. "This has been awful for Sharon."

Dave met her gaze with troubled brown eyes. "Do you think she's really all right?"

Kurt had asked him to stick around, but now he felt guilty about making the request. He was keeping Dave out when he ought to be enjoying his free time, not to mention sleep, and his ulterior motive was to ask Dave to do some extra work.

"She still seemed shaken," Janet said, "but she was wonderful when Detective Robbins had her go over and do another walk-through."

"And nothing was stolen this time, either." Kurt stirred his mug and reached for the bag of marshmallows. "So you think the burglar was after the silver pen and card case."

"I don't know," Janet admitted, "but if not that, then what? Sharon can't imagine what else he might be looking for. She says her father was living on his Social Security. He didn't have any big investments."

"Where are those things now?" Kurt asked.

"Locked in our freezer until she can get them to the bank. Want to see them?"

Kurt cracked a smile. "That would be *cool.*"

"Ha, ha."

Janet brought the old tin, and Kurt opened it. "Interesting." He fingered the icy card case. "Fit for a senator?"

"Sharon and Tory think so."

"Those things were sort of hidden in the pantry," Dave said thoughtfully.

"Yes. And maybe they were hidden for a reason," Janet said. "It was a fluke that I asked Sharon to bring the box over here. We could just as easily have taken the picture of Jacobs over there to her. But, anyway, it wasn't in the house when the thief came back, for which we're thankful."

"Technically, he's not a thief." Dave blew on the surface of the liquid in his mug. "He didn't steal anything."

"We think," Janet added. "But only because we had it over here."

Kurt nodded, processing that. "Whether this is what he wants or not, it appears he didn't find what he was after."

"I didn't see him carrying anything but a flashlight," Dave said.

"It happened so fast, I'm not sure." Janet dipped a spoonful of hot cocoa from her mug and sipped it, then asked, "Are you still mad at me?"

Kurt scowled at her, feeling once more the dismay that waylaid him when he first heard about Janet's escapade. "Yes, I'm livid. Can't you tell? But I'm relieved, too. You know that was a stupid thing to do." He glared at her and Dave, and they both murmured sheepish assents.

"Dave, I expect you to use your brain on this job, not get my wife killed."

"Yes, sir. I'm sorry, Mr. Borden."

"All right, then, I've been thinking this over. Can you have your first story about Senator Jacobs ready by tomorrow night?"

"Sir?" Dave's big brown eyes widened.

"I was thinking we should run a story on the front page Monday, giving all the background on Jacobs's disappearance and telling the readers that this is the story Mick was working on when he vanished Monday."

Dave took a deep breath. "I guess I can do that tomorrow afternoon."

Janet's eyes widened. "Do you think that's wise, publicly linking Mick Tyler's disappearance to Senator Jacobs? And what about the burglary?"

"It's all one story," Kurt said with certainty.

"Even the burglary?" Dave asked.

"It's got to be." Kurt thought about it some more and sipped his cocoa. "But you've got a point. There's no proof. The police wouldn't like it if we hinted that the burglaries are connected to Mick and Jacobs. And Grant Engstrom would hit the roof."

Dave flinched at the mention of the publisher's name. "So, do you want a report on the burglary?"

"A one-paragraph brief. We can't ignore it this time. If anyone found out, they'd accuse me of a self-serving cover-up. After all, it's my close neighbor, and a friend of mine." He looked Dave in the eye. "Type it up and send it to Kate, will you? She can bury it in the local news. But I want this Jacobs thing on page one."

Janet put her mug down with a little thump. "You want the burglar to see it."

"I do. He's had things his way too long."

"You want to flush him out?" Dave guessed.

"Maybe. Put him on edge, anyway."

"Did the detective say whether they'd traced the plate number?" Janet asked.

"They must have," Dave said.

They all sat looking at each other, and Kurt wondered if he was doing the wrong thing. Janet had almost been injured tonight. Was he inviting further risk? The last thing he wanted to do was put his wife in danger.

Thirty years of marriage, he thought. *Thank you, Lord. I love her so much.*

Dave drained his mug and stood. "I'd better get going. Got a lot to do tomorrow. Thanks for everything, Mrs. Borden. Today was great. Supper, tour of the neighborhood, sleuthing, everything."

Janet smiled at him with the same sweet affection she usually reserved for their offspring. "You're welcome, Dave. Come back anytime."

Kurt walked him to the door. "You didn't have to enjoy almost getting your clock cleaned quite so much," he said, shaking his head.

Dave smiled. "I'm just glad I was there to get Mrs. B. out of the way of that car."

"Yes, well, you know my feelings on that. Next time, play it safe."

"Yes, sir." Dave hesitated with his hand on the doorknob. "Mr. Borden, how well do you know Tory Schlesser?"

That was easy. "I just met her Thursday, when she came up from Providence to help her mother. Why?"

"Oh. Just asking."

"She seems like a nice girl."

"Yeah."

He still didn't leave.

Kurt said, with some amusement, "She's going to be here all week."

Dave nodded, leaning on the door knob so heavily that Kurt was afraid he would break it.

"Why don't you just call her tomorrow and tell her how much fun you had chasing burglars? Her grandfather's number is in the book."

Dave chuckled and looked down at the rug. "Yeah, maybe. Thanks, boss."

He was out the door at last. Kurt tested the lock set, and it seemed to have withstood the strain. He turned the deadbolt and switched off the outside light. In the kitchen, Janet was rinsing out the mugs. Seeing her performing the mundane task reminded him again of how much he loved everything about her. Her silky brown hair; her soft, rounded form; her compassion; her fierce loyalty.

"You tired, babe?" he asked, reaching up and stretching against the lintel. He used to do pull-ups in the doorways of their old house, but the woodwork there was thicker. He ought to join a gym and add weightlifting to his running routine, but who had time?

Janet hung up her dish towel. "I should be, but my mind is racing. I've never had a chance to be involved in a real mystery before."

Kurt laughed. "I was hoping for some TLC, not more investigating."

She came to him smiling and stroked his cheek. "You got it, Mr. Editor."

Kurt slipped his arms around her and bent to kiss her.

She pulled away suddenly.

"Where do you think Mick is now?"

She had to think of Mick Tyler at this moment? Kurt shrugged. "I don't know."

She frowned. "I hope he's safe. I pray for him constantly, Kurt. Him and Elwood."

He leaned his forehead against hers. "I do, too. Well, at least I do when I'm not worrying about you or the paper."

"Well, quit that worrying." She kissed his chin.

"Should we add Dave and Tory to the prayer list?" he asked.

She smiled up at him. "Isn't that something?

I've never seen so intense a blaze of instant attraction."

"Never?" He stooped lower and kissed the side of her neck.

"Well, hardly ever." Janet was a little breathless. He pulled her closer.

Chapter 12

Sharon and Tory waited while the physical therapist helped Elwood stretch and flex his arms and legs.

"Can you wiggle your fingers for me? Can you feel that? Can you lift your foot?" The questions and manipulations went on for twenty minutes, and Sharon was encouraged by what she saw. She looked at Tory, and Tory smiled and nodded. She could see her grandfather's progress, too.

Sharon blinked back tears. He was getting better. His recovery was slow, but she could see definite improvement. *Thank you, God,* she whispered silently. A new peace enveloped her. After yesterday's church service, her heart had yearned for a deeper understanding of God and the right to call Him *Father.* At this morning's study time with Janet, she had surrendered to the longing and gained a faith she knew was real but couldn't comprehend.

"You need to trust Him," Janet had told her, smiling tenderly over a steaming cup of green tea.

They sat on the Bordens' back deck, overlooking the misty, flat lake. A loon called to its mate, and as they swam into view, Sharon felt the glory and wonder of the creation. She'd grown up in this majestic setting. Why had she never seen God's hand in it before?

She had shivered at first in the thin early morning sunshine and zipped her fleece jacket tight. But gradually the tea and the sun's rays had warmed her, as the truth warmed her heart.

"That's all?" she'd asked.

"That's all. Just believe."

It seemed too easy, but Janet showed her scriptures that bore out her words. The tranquility stayed with Sharon, and now, looking into her father's wrinkled face, she let go of worry and fear.

The physical therapy session ended at last, and the therapist helped Elwood lie back on his bed.

"Better rest a little now," she told him.

Elwood smiled, although his mouth didn't want to cooperate completely on his left side. "Thank . . . you."

The therapist put her hand on his shoulder. "You're welcome. You're doing great! I'll see you tomorrow." She smiled at Sharon and Tory and left the room.

Sharon pulled her chair close to the bed.

"Dad, that was wonderful. You did so much better today!"

He pulled in a shaky breath and let out a groan

that was speech. Sharon leaned close to catch his words.

"I . . . make . . . trouble . . . for you."

She smiled and shook her head. "No, you don't. Don't think that. I'm glad I got to come visit you this week, but I'm sorry you're not feeling well."

He struggled to speak again. "Tory?"

Sharon looked around quickly, and Tory moved closer to the bed. "She's right here, Dad. She's been here with me while you had your therapy."

Tory smiled and took his hand. "Hi, Grandpa. I think you're doing fantastic."

He gazed up at her. His faded brown eyes were watering, and Sharon grabbed a tissue to wipe his cheeks.

"You . . . help . . . mother," Elwood said.

"She is helping me," Sharon assured him. "We cleaned the oven yesterday."

He sighed and closed his eyes.

"Is he sleeping?" Tory whispered.

Elwood's eyes fluttered open. "Vic . . ."

"Vic's not here," Sharon said. "He couldn't come this time." She wouldn't disturb him by saying that Vic was getting anxious for her to return home and had asked several times how long she was planning to stay in Maine.

Elwood looked around, peering toward the corners of the room, as though searching for someone else.

"Andrew and Paul and Geneva were all here last weekend," Sharon said. "Do you remember them being here, Dad?"

Slowly he nodded.

"They'll all come back and see you soon, I'm sure. I'm going to call everybody this afternoon and tell them how well you're doing."

"We're proud of you, Grandpa," Tory agreed. "Before you know it, you'll be walking again."

Sharon didn't contradict her, although the doctor was noncommittal as to how much mobility Elwood would regain. Today anything seemed possible.

Once more he opened his mouth, and Sharon leaned forward, watching his lips.

"Jan . . . et."

"Janet?"

He nodded.

"You want to see Janet Borden?" Sharon asked.

Again he nodded.

Tory looked at her in confusion, but Sharon smiled. "He and Janet are good friends, isn't that right, Dad?"

"She's . . . nice . . . to . . . me."

Sharon patted his hand. "Yes, I heard about all those pies and cookies she brought you."

He smiled wearily.

"I think you should rest, Dad. I'll tell Janet you'd like to see her. Maybe she can come in tomorrow. Would that be all right?"

Elwood's eyelids drifted down.

"We'd better let him sleep," Tory said. "He's exhausted after all that hard work."

Andrew Fairmont drove his rental car down Pine Lane faster than he ought to on the narrow dirt road. Why hadn't someone told him the news earlier? He wouldn't have gone back to Tennessee on Thursday if he'd known about Mick. And his plane had hardly left the ground when Dad's house was ransacked!

He turned in at the driveway to the farmhouse. There was no car in the yard. *Great. Sharon's not here.* Just to be sure, he parked and got out. He pounded on the door, and when there was no answer, turned the knob and rattled the door in its frame.

He sighed. Any chance she'd left a key somewhere around the porch? He doubted it. Sharon was always cautious, but in the four days since the break-in she'd probably become obsessive. He felt under the porch steps, risking spider bites, and lifted a plant pot on the railing. Nothing. He moseyed to the shed door that opened into the ell connecting the house and the old barn, but it was locked.

He stood in the driveway for a moment, considering his options. It was warm for mid-September in Maine, and he took off his jacket and tossed it into the car, then walked out the driveway and the few yards up the road to the next house.

Nice place the Bordens had. It hadn't been there when Andrew was a kid. The lot had been vacant, and the little natural beach was used by the Fairmont children without anyone raising objections. They'd even kept a rowboat there in summer, pulled up on the shore.

After he'd been away to college—Brown University—and gotten married—the first time—he hadn't been home to see the folks for more than five years. He and his father had always been like sandpaper and chrome, two substances that should stay away from each other.

Then, after Beth left him, before the divorce was final, he'd made a trip home. Mom had begged him to come, and he had, but he could only stand to be around Dad for about three days, max. As always, his father was critical and demeaning. Andrew had left in a rage, as usual. He'd mellowed some now, but he'd noticed last week that Paul was still in the angry stage. Andrew was glad he'd outgrown that.

But anyway, that was when he'd first seen this house. It was built sometime in there, while he was away.

He'd resented it at first. It took away the Fairmonts' private piece of the lake shore. Which was a silly attitude, since they'd never owned it in the first place. He'd always thought they had, but when he asked about the new house, his father told him the property was part of what the Jacobs family had owned. Mrs. Jacobs had sold the cottage and the acreage back in the late ’60s, and one of the later owners had subdivided. That was before the town’s zoning regulations were so strict. And so his parents had new neighbors.

Andrew had been home several times since then, but he’d chosen to ignore the new house and its occupants, viewing the lake from his parents’ front porch and staying on the farmhouse side of the road.

So it had surprised him on this latest visit to learn that his father had made friends with the current owners. In fact, to hear Sharon tell it, Dad adored Janet Borden and treated Kurt like a son. *Like he should be treating me,* Andrew thought. The old bitterness resurfaced. Dad had always been more affectionate to outsiders than to his own children.

But it was a nice house.

Mrs. Borden apparently liked to garden. Most of her perennials had bloomed and gone to seed, but chrysanthemums and foxglove still splashed color against the lawn and the house’s natural redwood siding. If he remembered correctly, she was also a good cook. Of course, she could have bought that cheesecake, couldn’t she?

He rang the doorbell and squinted toward the

garage, trying to see through the dusty windows in the overhead door so he could tell if there was a car inside.

The door opened. Janet Borden was the classic homemaker. She actually held a dust cloth in her hand. Her light brown hair spilled over her forehead in disarray. It was probably blond when she was a child, Andrew decided. She ought to lighten it and lose about fifteen pounds. She would be quite attractive.

She smiled, and he revised his critique. She was attractive now, just not his type. He preferred willowy women with a sense of fashion. Janet's jeans and fuchsia polo shirt didn't cut it.

"Andrew! What a surprise. Sharon didn't tell me you were coming back so soon."

"She doesn't know. It was sort of a spur of the moment decision. But she's not at the house, and I couldn't get in. I was hoping she might be over here visiting you."

"Oh, I'm sure she and Tory are at the hospital. Come on in." Janet stepped back and gestured to the interior of the house with her yellow dust cloth. "I'll get you our key."

"Thank you, that would be very helpful."

Janet led him to the kitchen, talking all the way. "We've had a key since the summer after we moved in. Your father locked himself out once. Kurt found a window in the woodshed unlocked and got in that way to open the front door for him, and after that Elwood insisted we keep a key here."

She plucked the key from a rack near the back door and put it in his hand. "Would you like something to eat? You must be hungry."

"No, thanks, I got a bite to eat when I left the airport in Portland. I'm fine."

She nodded doubtfully. "Long drive up here. I've got baked beans and half a blueberry pie left from yesterday's church potluck."

He opened his mouth to refuse, but the sudden sharp craving for homemade blueberry pie ambushed him.

"Uh . . ."

Her smile broadened. "I sense wavering. Sit down. I'll put on fresh coffee."

Andrew sat on a bar stool on the opposite side of her work island, his anticipation outweighing his pride. "It's been years since I've had homemade blueberry pie."

"Then you came to the right place." She worked quickly, measuring out the coffee and water, starting the machine, then bringing the pie plate from the refrigerator and cutting a generous slice. "Shall I microwave it for a few seconds?" Before he could answer, she looked up and winked. "I'll bet there's vanilla ice cream in the freezer."

Andrew couldn't help smiling. "Do you spoil your husband this badly?"

"I try, but Kurt's a hard case. He's the one who does most of the spoiling around here."

She popped his plate into the microwave and pulled a carton from the freezer compartment. "I admit this is one of Kurt's favorites."

"Be sure and save him plenty."

She laughed. "I will, but he'll probably tell me he's had too many sweets this week." She turned sincere and sober then. "I'm sure your father will be delighted to see you again. Sharon tells me he's progressing every day."

"Thank you." Andrew hesitated. "Of course I want to see Dad, but that's not the thing that made me hop the plane this morning."

"Oh?"

"I went online to read the local paper—" He hesitated, very aware that Janet's husband was the city editor at the paper in question. "The lead story this morning was about Mick Tyler."

She nodded, frowning a bit. "Yes. Do you know him?"

"We were friends all through school. I had dinner with him last week. I was shocked to read that he's been missing so long."

"Yes, it's been a week since anyone's seen him." The microwave timer pinged, and she took the plate out and fussed over it, making sure the scoop of ice cream stayed on the center of the crust until she placed it in front of him.

"But it was just reported now?"

"No, my husband contacted the police last Wednesday." Janet's sad, pensive expression didn't make Andrew feel much optimism for the outcome of the story. "The paper ran a couple of small stories last week, saying he was missing and asking for information. But today's story was the first time they told what Mick was working on when he disappeared. Kurt and the others at the paper are hoping someone who saw Mick last week will come forward with information."

"I must have missed the earlier reports. Today was the first time I looked at the *Sentinel* since I left here." Andrew took the first bite of pie and melting, creamy ice cream. He closed his eyes. "Oh, Mrs. Borden."

"Janet."

"Janet. I can see why my father esteems you so highly."

She laughed. "Thank you. But tell me about you and Mick Tyler. Were you close?"

"Yes, at least while we were in school. Of course, we don't see each other much anymore, but I always make it a point to contact him when I'm in Maine."

"And you saw him last week?"

Andrew nodded and swallowed. "Saturday night. A week ago Saturday, that is. Before he . . ." He paused, looking to her for denial. "I can't believe he just vanished like that. And the police have no leads?"

She shook her head. “No one knows what to think. His car is missing, too, you see, so the police say he could have disappeared on purpose. Or . . .” She hesitated. “He did have some issues at home and work.”

Andrew considered that. “I know he and Callie were on the outs. I dropped him off at a seedy apartment building Saturday. He said he was staying with a friend. But I didn’t think he was depressed enough to consider suicide. Mick always lands on his feet. And I doubt he’d run away from a fight.”

Janet poured his coffee and brought it to the work island. “My husband and Dave Carpenter, the reporter who wrote today’s story, have been trying to retrace Mick’s path on the day he disappeared, but they haven’t had much luck so far.”

Andrew glanced up at her. “Wasn’t Mick coming out here? That’s what the article said.”

“Yes, I’m afraid it’s true. He was supposed to meet a photographer just down the road, at the Hillmans’ cottage. That is, at Senator Jacobs’s old cottage.”

“So something happened to him between the newspaper office in Waterville and the cottage here in Belgrade.”

“That’s all they know for sure.” They were both silent for a long moment, and then Janet said, “I keep wondering if I should have noticed something that day. I went into town to shop that morning, and when I came home I didn't see his car in the neighborhood or anything. I guess the photographer had come and gone by then."

Andrew came to a decision. "Janet, do you suppose your husband would have time to see me this afternoon? There's something I think I should tell him."

"Oh?"

Andrew sipped his coffee. Good coffee. In his book, Janet Borden was due for a homemaker award. "Yes. You see, when Mick and I had dinner on Saturday, we talked about Senator Jacobs."

She blinked at him, her lips pursing. "Is that a coincidence? Or was it because he was getting ready to do a story about Jacobs?"

"Maybe it was partly that. But every time I've seen Mick since high school graduation, he's brought up the subject of a certain night in 1968. But this time was different. This time he told me he thought the events that happened that night had something to do with Jacobs's disappearance."

Janet's gray-blue eyes flared. "Let me call Kurt. I'm sure he'll see you."

Chapter 13

Kurt and Dave waited in the conference room. Every time the elevator doors opened in the hallway outside, Kurt looked to see who got off. Dave sat fiddling with the tape recorder.

Kurt got up and went out into the newsroom and stopped at the receptionist's desk. Molly was chewing gum while she typed, and she blew a large, pink bubble, popped it, and scooped the gum back into her mouth with her tongue.

"Molly, could you please do me a favor? I have an important meeting coming up, and I was wondering if you'd bring coffee for four to the conference room."

"Sure." The phone on her desk rang, and she shifted the wad of gum into her cheek as she picked up the receiver.

Dave stood by the window when Kurt rejoined him, looking down at the park across the street. He turned as Kurt entered. "So, I heard you and Wally have a bet going."

"A bet? First I've heard of it."

"Yeah, he said you bet he can't quit smoking, and the stakes are Red Sox tickets."

Kurt shook his head vigorously. "It's not a bet. I look on it more as a behavior modification reward. I just want him to quit smoking."

"Oh. Well, Wally thinks it's a bet."

Kurt sighed. "Next we'll have to cure him of gambling."

"Right. Say, are we on for Bible study tomorrow? Tim was asking me."

"You bet." Kurt reached for his pocket calendar, and Dave pointed an accusing finger at him.

"Watch it, boss."

"Oh, right. It's not a bet, really."

Dave laughed. "I just hope it works."

"At least they don't let him smoke in the building." Kurt looked at the page for the week. He'd already written the time of the Bible study in his calendar. He noticed the note on Friday: *Anniv. Dinner 7 p.m.* The big day was creeping up on him. At least he'd remembered to make dinner reservations at the best restaurant in Waterville. *Yikes. I'd better call the florist.*

The elevator doors opened, and he raised his head. Andrew Fairmont and Janet stepped off the elevator. Janet turned toward the conference room, saw Kurt through the doorway, and came toward him with a somewhat self-conscious smile. Kurt could almost read her mind. *She never comes to the office in her grubbies,* he thought. *She's convinced this is urgent.*

He met her in the doorway and kissed her cheek. "You look great, babe."

She scowled, telling him she knew better. "I'm just glad you weren't busy."

Kurt didn't tell her how much pressure he was under from Grant Engstrom and Steve Basner. Not only was he expected to put out a decent paper without his best reporter; he was also on notice to keep the lid from blowing off the Tyler-Jacobs story and landing them in a lawsuit. At least the publisher and managing editor had their offices in Augusta and weren't looking over his shoulder all the time.

"Kurt, thanks for seeing me." Andrew stepped forward, and they shook hands.

"I'm glad you came." Kurt introduced Dave and asked Andrew if he minded the use of the tape recorder.

Andrew hesitated then shrugged. "Why not?"

"It will ensure that I don't misquote you if any of this material makes it into an article, Mr. Fairmont," Dave said.

"You're the one who wrote the story in today's paper?"

"Yes."

Andrew nodded and sat down in one of the padded chairs. "You were fair to Mick. Made him look good, but not too good. Mick's no saint. And all that background material about Jacobs . . . I'd say you did a lot of homework."

Dave smiled. "Thank you, sir. It was a challenge."

He turned on the tape recorder. Kurt was about to shut the door, but Molly was coming down the hall with a coffee pot and four mugs on a tray.

"There you go, Kurt." She popped her gum for emphasis and handed him the tray.

Kurt cringed inwardly. "Molly, one more favor."

"Yeah, boss?" She blew a bubble and stared cross-eyed at it.

"That. Lose the gum."

She stared at him over the collapsing bubble.

"Now," Kurt said.

She slurped the pink mass into her mouth. "Gotcha. Professional demeanor and all that."

Kurt nodded and closed the door. He set the tray down and took his seat at the end of the long table, where he had left several file folders and a notebook. Janet had settled in the chair next to his, on the back side of the table. Andrew was at his right, and Dave sat beyond him.

"Coffee, gentlemen?"

"Thanks," Andrew said, "but your wife just gave me a cup of such good coffee I'd hate to spoil the memory."

Kurt smiled and looked questioningly at Janet and Dave.

Janet shook her head, but Dave said, "Yes, please."

Kurt poured him a cup and then one for himself.

"So, Andrew, Janet says you and Mick Tyler are old friends?"

"Yes, we go way back."

Kurt nodded. "What can you tell us about Mick? You saw him recently?"

"Saturday, the ninth of September." Andrew ran a hand over his face. "Nine days ago. We ate dinner together and caught up a little on the news. You know, family stuff."

Dave began writing in his reporter's notebook, but Kurt sat relaxed, trying to make it seem like a normal conversation.

Andrew's eyes met his. "Every time I visit my father, which isn't often, I call Mick. If we can schedule it, we get together."

"How did he seem last Saturday?" Kurt asked.

"The same, or maybe worse. Cynical, critical, self-centered."

Dave stared at him, and Kurt found himself a bit surprised by Andrew's frankness.

Andrew smiled. "He wasn't always that way, at least not so bad. As a kid, he was kind of a smart mouth, but he was intelligent, sort of a loner, and I liked him. We understood each other. And old friends put up with a lot." Kurt nodded, and Andrew went on. "Last week he told me about his problems at home. He wasn't happy, but I wouldn't have said he was suicidal."

Dave gulped audibly, and Andrew turned toward him. "Well, that's what they think, isn't it? He's holed up somewhere and shot himself? Or overdosed on alcohol and pills, maybe."

"I'm not convinced of that," Kurt said.

"Neither am I." Andrew met Kurt's gaze. "He talked about you."

"Me?" Kurt wondered if this interview was such a good idea after all. If Mick had used a three-martini dinner to trash his boss's reputation, how could it profit him to know that?

"Yes," Andrew said with a trace of a smile. "It was in passing. He said you lived out near my father, and I told him I'd met Mrs. Borden. That was before my family had all been over to your house for dessert."

Kurt nodded, and Janet smiled as though it was wonderful to be included in the story. Kurt was glad she had come with Andrew. It would make things so much easier later, when they were alone. He wouldn't have to relay everything to her, and he knew that tonight they would discuss the interview in detail. Janet would zero in on the salient facts, just as she had with the silver card case. Her mind worked that way. Kurt stifled the impulse to reach for her hand, but threw her a smile. *Do you know how much I appreciate you?* Her eyes were intent on Andrew's face, but he thought she knew.

"Well, Mick started telling me about how he

was going to do a story on Tom Jacobs," Andrew said.

Kurt picked up his pen, then laid it down. Nothing new here. What was the point?

Andrew stood up and walked past Dave to the window. "I see they're renovating at City Hall."

"Yes," Kurt said. "They've worked on it all summer." He and Dave looked at each other. Dave's brown eyes were full of questions. Would Andrew Fairmont reveal something useful about Mick, or was he just fretting over his boyhood chum? Kurt shrugged.

Andrew turned around to face them. "That's when he brought up the subject he brings up every time I see him."

"And what was that?" Kurt leaned back in his chair.

"The night he and I were convinced we'd witnessed a crime."

Kurt waited. No one spoke until Andrew continued.

"Mick and I were at the end of fifth grade. We were about to start the summer. Late May or early June, I think. He came over one evening after supper, and we took the rowboat out and did a little fishing. Didn't catch anything." He smiled at Kurt. "Mick's family didn't live near the water, so he liked to come over and swim and fish with me and Paul. We used to keep a rowboat over where your beach is. There wasn't any house there at the time. It was getting dark, so we came in and tied the boat up, then we headed up the path, carrying our fishing poles. The path went along toward the Jacobs place, then up toward the road, where we always crossed. That's when we heard it."

The tension was back. Kurt leaned forward, ready to play along. "Heard what?"

"A popping sound."

Kurt eyed him in speculation. "And?"

"Well, like I said, it was nearly dark, and it scared us a little. Mick said, 'What was that?' I didn't know, but we were excitable kids. We both thought it was a gun, although it wasn't terribly loud. It sounded like it came from over by the next house."

"Jacobs's cottage," Kurt said, and Andrew nodded.

"We dropped our fishing rods and headed over that way, along the shore. It's rocky in there, so we had to hop from rock to rock for a ways, but when we got over close to the Jacobses' dock, we heard voices, and we stopped." Andrew sat down. "Maybe I'd take some coffee after all."

Janet reached for the coffee pot.

Kurt smiled at him. "It won't be as good as what you had at my house."

Andrew took the mug and sipped the dark liquid. "Right."

They all chuckled.

"So, anyway, there were a couple of men over there in the driveway, and the garage door was open. It was pretty dark by then, and Mick and I were trying to stay out of sight, so we didn't get a good look at them, but there were also two cars in the driveway. I'm sure about that. After a couple of minutes they drove out."

"Both cars left?" Kurt asked.

"Yes. It was nothing, really, but Mick and I saw that they didn't turn their headlights on until after they passed my folks' driveway. That clinched it. We were sure something sinister had happened, and we were scared silly. We ran home to my house and forgot all about the fishing poles. I had to go out and find them the next morning."

"So, what happened after that?" Dave asked.

Andrew shook his head. "My father was in the kitchen when we got to the house, and we told him this incoherent tale about shadowy men and gunfire and mysterious cars pulling out in the night. My dad just laughed."

Kurt raised his eyebrows. "He didn't take you seriously?"

"He said we had big imaginations. The noise was probably a backfire." Andrew frowned. "But those cars weren't running when we got over there. I tried to argue with Dad, make him see that something really had happened. He said something like, 'You know the Jacobs family hasn't been up here in weeks. Probably Mrs.

Jacobs sent someone to close the cottage for the season.' " He paused, then took a long swallow from his mug.

"And you connected that with Jacobs's disappearance?"

"Not at the time," Andrew said. "See, I was only eleven, and I wasn't paying much attention to the news. I'm not even sure I realized the senator was the cause of such an uproar. Anyhow, I didn't put it together. In fact, until now I'd pretty much forgotten that it was about the same time he disappeared. But Mick didn't forget. I think over the years he's brooded about it. And last Saturday he told me that incident took place within two or three weeks after Jacobs vanished in Washington."

"That long after?" Dave's startled question hung in the air.

Andrew nodded slowly. "If what Mick said is true, we heard the noise at the cottage a few weeks after the senator went missing. But I hardly ever saw the senator, you know? The family came up summers, but they didn't really mix with us, and Senator Jacobs himself was only there once in a while, for a few days. So it hadn't really affected me, and when Dad said to forget it, I pretty much did."

"But Mick didn't," Kurt said.

"Apparently not. He didn't mention it for a long time. Dad was pretty stern with us that night. He told us not to go poking around over at Jacobs's place. I think he intimidated Mick a bit, because Mick didn't come over for a while, and then school let out. I don't think Mick and I talked about it again for years."

"When did he bring it up next?" Kurt asked.

"I'm not sure. We both went off to college. I'm thinking it was when we came home on Christmas break that first year. We got together and talked about what we'd been doing at school, you know? Mick was packing the beer away pretty fast, and I started being concerned about him, even then."

Kurt sat back and stared at the coffee pot, letting his mind run.

"That night you heard the noise," Dave said, "did you recognize the voices of the men?"

"No."

"So you don't think one of them was Thomas Jacobs?"

"I'm not sure I'd have recognized his voice, but, no, at the time I didn't think so."

"Did you hear what they said?" Kurt asked.

"Not really. Just mundane things. 'You ready? I'll follow you.' Things like that."

Dave asked, "Could they have been fishing and taken their boat out at the Jacobses' landing?"

Andrew shook his head. "I didn't see any boats or trailers, and it didn't seem like that. People who've been out on the lake are usually pretty loud and jolly. These guys were quiet. Very quiet and businesslike."

Janet stirred. "Didn't Mrs. Jacobs sell the cottage soon after that?"

"I guess so."

"The next year," Kurt said. The dates were ingrained in his brain, after all the research he'd done.

"So possibly it was a real estate agent and a prospective buyer who came to look the place over," Janet suggested.

Andrew shook his head. "Anything's possible, I guess, but . . ."

Dave looked across the table at Janet. "I don't know, Mrs. Borden. The Senator had only been gone a few weeks. I doubt his wife was thinking of selling the cottage yet."

"And it was dark," Andrew added. "If they were viewing the place, they'd do it in daylight."

Janet nodded, and Kurt gave her an empathetic smile. There went her analytical mind. She would consider every angle, every option. So would he, and then they'd hash it out over ice cream and think of some new possibilities.

Andrew clasped his hands around his coffee mug. "That's about it, I guess. You see, there was nothing, really. And yet . . ."

"And yet?" Kurt prompted.

Andrew inhaled deeply. "Saturday night, Mick was hinting that it *was* something. That it had to do with Jacobs, and we were just too naïve to realize it."

"You never told anyone else? I mean about what happened in '68."

"I don't think so. My family, maybe. But my dad made me feel . . . kind of stupid. So I didn't say anything to my other friends. I don't think Mick brought it up, like I said, but if he tried, I probably would have shut him down. Dad had a way of . . ." He shook his head and let the thought die.

"You didn't want to make your father angry," Janet said softly, and Andrew nodded, pressing his lips tightly together.

Kurt watched Andrew's face for a moment and then turned the tape recorder off.

"Andrew." He used the quiet but firm voice he'd always used with the children when having a parental talk with them. "Andrew, you don't have to answer this question, and you won't be quoted if you do, but it could be important. At that time, was your father . . . difficult to please?"

Andrew let out a short bark of a laugh. "At that time and every time." He ran a hand through his thick brown hair. The gray was more noticeable in the harsh light, and his weary disillusionment showed in the fine lines around his eyes. "I gave up trying to please Dad a long time ago. But back then, I certainly didn't want to set him off."

Kurt pondered his choice of words and

wondered if he should pursue the line of questioning. Janet saved him the trouble.

"Did your father mistreat you, Andrew?"

The slash of Andrew's mouth wrinkled into a bitter smile. "I know you like him, and you think he's a sweet old guy, but there were times . . . There were times when I hated him."

Kurt could see that Janet was disturbed by his answer. He said, "I'm sorry to hear that, Andrew. You know, people do change over time."

Andrew sighed and rubbed his eyes. "I expect you're right. In fact, Sharon told us a week ago that one of the first things he said after his stroke was, 'I'm sorry. Tell the boys.' I didn't say so at the time, but I wondered if he meant he was sorry for the things he did to Paul and me."

Janet cleared her throat. "Andrew, this is a very difficult time for you. Just let me tell you that your father and I had several conversations this summer that lead me to believe he had a genuine change of heart. Oh, he never told me just how bad things were with you and your brother when you were young, but several times he expressed remorse, and I could tell he regretted the way he'd behaved as a father. I thought he meant he hadn't spent enough time with the family or some such thing, but now I see that it went deeper."

Andrew nodded. "Do you think that's what he meant when he first had the stroke, and he told you he was sorry?"

"I don't know." Janet leaned toward him and spoke earnestly. "He seemed to have a particular action in mind then, when he said what he did to me."

"I shouldn't have kept it," Kurt quoted.

"Yes. To me, that doesn't fit with his feeling regret about the poor relationship he had with his children." Janet looked to Kurt for support, and he nodded.

"I agree. It seems he also regretted a particular thing that he did or didn't do. Didn't he say something to you about how he'd ought to have done what someone told him to do?"

"Yes." Janet was sure about that. Kurt remembered her writing it all in her journal that night. She wouldn't forget Elwood's panicky words to her.

Andrew pushed back his chair. "Well, maybe he'll be able to talk more soon, and I can ask him some of these questions. But for now, I've taken up enough of your time. I hope this was helpful in some way. I'd better get home and see if Sharon's there."

Chapter 14

Andrew dropped Janet off at her house, and it wasn't five minutes later that Sharon appeared on the Bordens' doorstep.

"Janet, thank you for taking care of my brother. If Andrew had told me he was coming, I'd have left a key for him."

"It's all right," Janet assured her. "Would you like to come in?"

"Oh, no, I need to get back to the house and get supper. But I also wanted to tell you, Dad asked for you today."

"For me?" Janet was surprised and pleased. Andrew's unsettling words about Elwood niggled in the back of her mind, but she refused to think about them right now. When she had time to sit down with her Bible and a cup of tea, she would thrash it all out with the Lord.

"Yes," Sharon said. "He'd like to see you. I can tell you've become very special to him. Thank you for that."

Janet smiled. "He's been a dear. We talked about spiritual things, you know."

Sharon nodded. "You told me. It was a great

comfort to me, especially when we were afraid Dad was going to die."

"Well, I don't know his heart, but he has certainly been considering things. Kurt and I both told him quite plainly that he needed to get things right with God."

"Goodness, I hope he didn't get angry with you."

Janet shook her head. "I've never seen him angry. Well, except when he got his property tax bill last spring and saw how much the rates had jumped."

They both laughed.

"Maybe you can go in to the hospital tomorrow," Sharon said.

"I'll try to do that."

"He was tired this afternoon, but his therapy went well." Sharon grimaced. "Andrew wants to see him, too, but I'm not so sure that's a good idea."

"Oh?"

"He and Dad can't be in the same room for more than a few minutes without fireworks going off."

"Maybe that will change now."

"Tell you what," Sharon said. "We'll both pray really hard, and if you can drop by the hospital at 8 a.m., when visitors are allowed in, we'll let you go in first and see what Dad wants to talk to you about. Then, if he's up to it, Andrew and I will go in."

• • •

Detective Robbins came to the Bordens' house between Double Jeopardy and Final Jeopardy. Janet was mildly put out, because the category was "Royalty," and she was sure she would know the answer, but the detective took precedence.

Kurt ushered him into the family room, and Janet clicked the television set off.

"Well, Mrs. Borden," Robbins said with more heartiness then she felt the occasion warranted, "we've found the owner of the car that nearly plowed you over Saturday night."

"Oh?" Inside, Janet thought, *It's about time! After all, we did give you the license plate number.* But she would never be that discourteous. Instead, she offered the detective coffee and some of the oatmeal cookies she had baked to take to the neighbors tomorrow.

She could see that he was about to decline. *Fine! The more for Marguerite Vaughn and the Fairmonts.*

But Kurt smiled at Robbins and said, "Oh, yes, join me, won't you? Janet makes the best oatmeal-raisin cookies in New England. I'm encouraging her to enter them in the Skowhegan Fair next year."

Robbins wavered, and Kurt soon had him seated at the kitchen table with a tall glass of low-fat milk (Robbins, it seemed, had to watch the caffeine these days) and a plate of delectable cookies.

Kurt somehow got it out of the detective that he collected old ink bottles and launched an animated discussion of the antiques market. Janet nibbled on a cookie, determined not to eat more than one, sipped her tea, and waited. Her husband was very good at putting people at ease and getting information out of them, sometimes more than they intended to give. She was fascinated to see him at work. Twice in one day she'd watched him interview a cagey subject.

Robbins was actually smiling. Janet felt herself relax a notch, too.

"So," Kurt said pleasantly after ten minutes of small talk, "you found out who the driver of the mystery car was."

"William Dunning," Robbins said readily.

"Dunning," Kurt said. "Is he local?"

"Yes, lives in North Belgrade. We questioned him yesterday."

"Does he have a criminal record?"

"No." The detective reached for another cookie, and Kurt refilled his milk glass. "He admits being out here Saturday evening, but said he was just driving down to take a look at one of the camps farther down this road. He claims he knows the owner and was asked to see if the electric company had shut the power off like they said they would."

"Have you checked that out?" Kurt asked.

"Not yet. The cottage owner lives in Pennsylvania. Haven't got ahold of him."

Kurt nodded.

Janet could keep still no longer. "But that car was parked at the end of the Fairmonts' driveway, under the pines. And he was in the house. Sharon and Tory Schlesser saw a light moving around in there."

Robbins winced at that and rubbed the back of his neck. "Well, he says he wasn't in the house."

"Oh, really?" Janet glared at him, and Kurt stepped in hastily.

"What does Mr. Dunning say exactly?" Kurt picked up the cookie plate and offered it to Robbins.

"Just what I said." Robbins selected another cookie. "He came out here and checked his friend's camp. Everything was okay, so he drove out. He says he saw a couple of people walking beside the road, but he denied parking the car at the Fairmonts' or being in their house."

"He almost killed me," Janet insisted.

Robbins shrugged and slurped his milk. "Your word against his."

"Mine and Dave's."

"Well, yes, there is that." Robbins looked a bit uncomfortable for the first time.

"We could probably show you tracks where

he parked," Janet said, although she wasn't sure about that. The bed of spent pine needles was pretty thick under those trees, and it had rained some last night, after midnight.

"Could be he parked there and walked on down the road."

"That doesn't make sense," Janet said.

Kurt reached over and took her hand. "Maybe he was disoriented in the dark, sweetheart."

Robbins nodded as if that satisfied him and stood up. "Well, I need to get going. Thanks for the refreshments, Mrs. Borden. You folks take care."

Janet fumed until Kurt had shown him out and come back to the kitchen. In that short amount of time, she devoured two more cookies and put the rest away.

"Some investigator," she cried.

"Oh, babe, come here." Kurt took her in his arms and rubbed her back. "Let it go."

"But that Dunning character may be dangerous. You know as well as I do that he was in Elwood's house, and he wasn't there to check the electric meter."

Kurt laughed. "Oh, come on. You and Dave didn't see the light in the house, did you?"

"No, but Sharon—"

"Sharon and Tory may have been mistaken."

"You don't believe that."

"Well . . ." Kurt nestled his cheek against the top

of her head. "What if this Dunning was walking down the lane with his flashlight and they saw the reflection of the light in the windows?"

"No! I'm not that stupid, and neither is Sharon. It just doesn't make sense for him to park at the Fairmonts' and walk down to check on another house. Not one bit of sense."

"Hey, hey. Let's just forget it. Why don't you call Sharon and see if she watched Jeopardy? Maybe she can tell us what the final answer was."

"You're trying to sidetrack me, Kurt Wayland Borden, and I want to know why."

He was quiet for a moment. She expected him to parry with a retort, addressing her by her full name, but he didn't, and that worried her. She pulled away from him and looked into his clear blue eyes. Her husband was tired and vulnerable.

"Jan, I want this to go away."

"You mean . . . ?"

"All of it. I want Mick to show up at the office tomorrow and laugh at us for all the fuss. I want Elwood to get better and come home, and most of all, I want you to be safe. I don't want there to be cars almost driving over you and Dave, and I don't want people threatening me."

Her heart lurched, and she stared at him. "Someone's threatened you?"

He closed his eyes and sighed. "I wasn't going to tell you."

"You can't do that."

"I know. I can't keep anything from you, and I don't want to, really. But I don't want you to worry, and mostly I want you to be safe."

"Come here." She pulled him by the hand, through the hall and up the stairs. He hung back and flipped off light switches as they went. When they got to the bedroom, she pushed him down gently on the bed. "Sit." She kicked her shoes off and settled beside him, sitting cross-legged. "Now tell me."

"After you and Andrew left the office, I was doing some work in my cubbyhole, and I got this call. I couldn't tell who it was. A man, but I didn't recognize the voice." Kurt squeezed her hand. She reached over and stroked his fingers until he eased his grip a bit.

"What did he say?"

"Not much. 'Take your reporter off the Jacobs story.' That's it. Then he hung up."

"Did you call the police?"

"No, I . . . I didn't know whether or not to take it seriously."

"I think we have to take everything seriously where Senator Jacobs is concerned." Janet thought about the phone system at the newspaper office. "Was it an outside call?"

Kurt gritted his teeth. "Yes. Someone dialed my extension direct."

"How could you tell?"

"There are different rings for inside and outside calls. Even for outside calls that have been transferred in the building."

"No one at the paper would threaten you."

Kurt chuckled. "Grant Engstrom threatens me every day."

"Well, sure." She knew about the clashes Kurt had with the publisher over management style and company policies. "But he wouldn't say it that way. If he wanted you to take Dave off the assignment, he'd call you and say, *Borden, I want you to kill this Jacobs story. It's too creepy, and we're losing advertisers.*"

He nodded. "Something like that. Besides, Grant actually likes this story now."

"Really?"

"Yeah, he wants Dave to do a new installment every day until Mick is found. We're selling lots of papers this week because of it, and some of the business owners in Belgrade are calling and asking if they can run ads on the same page as Dave's next article."

"So it couldn't have been Grant who threatened you."

"No."

There was pain in his voice. Kurt was the one who made her feel secure, and he didn't like losing control of that, she knew.

"Does Dave know about the call?" she asked.

"I told him. I figured it was a crank, but he ought to be careful just the same."

"Well, sure."

"And he's taking Tory out tonight."

"What?" She jumped a little, making the bed bounce. "How can I not know this?"

Kurt laughed. "There's a new exhibit opening at the Colby College Art Gallery. They're going to the reception tonight, and Dave's doing a write-up."

"That is so . . ." She broke off and glared at him.

"Romantic?"

"No! A working date? I expected better things of Dave."

"Well, I guess it's my fault. He asked her to go to the exhibit just as a date, and when he told me about it, I remembered the college asked for a story, and I got so hung up in this other business that I forgot to assign it."

"So you're making Dave work tonight when he should be romancing Tory?"

"Eh." His smile was artificial. Guilty, guilty, guilty.

Janet reached for a pillow.

"Don't do that," Kurt said.

"You gonna stop me?"

"Yeah."

"You talk big," she said.

"You've never won a pillow fight with me

in thirty years, and you're not going to start tonight."

She swung the pillow back, holding tight to the ruffle on the sham. Kurt dodged and dove for his pillow.

Chapter 15

"Elwood, how are you?"

The old man's brown eyes focused on her face, and he smiled. Janet was glad she had come, although knowing that Andrew was pacing impatiently in the waiting room made her nervous.

She took a chair at the bedside and reached for Elwood's hand. "You're looking chipper today."

He opened his mouth, but no sound came out.

Janet turned and looked at her husband. Kurt was leaning in the doorway, but he stepped forward now, and she said to Elwood, "I brought Kurt to see you, too. We've been thinking of you and praying that you would get better."

Elwood's lips parted, and she listened closely.

"Than . . . nk . . . you."

Kurt grinned. "Sharon says they're getting you up every day now."

"They . . . won't . . . leave me . . . alone."

Janet smiled and patted his hand. "No, and they won't, until you're ready to walk out of here."

They sat with him for a few more minutes, and

Kurt and Janet made small talk. The leaves were changing; a squirrel kept raiding Janet's bird feeder; Kurt was going to take the dock out of the water soon.

The nurse came in and called loudly, "Good morning, Mr. Fairmont! How we doing today?" She checked his plastic identification bracelet against his chart, then studied the monitor. "Did you get breakfast yet?"

Elwood's eyebrows went slowly up. "What . . . did . . . she . . . say?"

"Did you have breakfast?" Janet repeated.

"Nooo . . ."

"I'll make sure you get it soon," the nurse promised, straightening his blanket. "How do you feel?"

"Tired." He dragged the word out as though it was all he could do to produce it.

"You'd better rest," the nurse said, shooting a meaningful glance at the Bordens.

"Yep, we'd better leave," Kurt said.

Janet frowned at him. Kurt never said *yep.* Either the nurse made him antsy, or he was thinking of a million things he needed to do at the office, probably the latter.

"How about if I come back again in a day or two, Elwood?" Janet asked, bending close and holding his hand.

"You . . . come."

"I will." On impulse, she kissed his wrinkled

cheek, then straightened and followed Kurt to the waiting room.

Sharon and Tory stood up, and Andrew came from the coffee machine with a steaming paper cup in his hand.

"How is he?" Sharon asked.

"Not too talkative," Kurt admitted.

Janet tried to hide her disappointment. "He seems wrung out."

Sharon nodded. "He's been that way since the stroke, but at least he can talk a little bit." A worried frown crossed her face. "Did he say anything to you?"

"Yes, a few things," Janet said. "The nurse seemed to think he needed his breakfast and a rest."

Andrew sighed. "Why did I even bother to come?"

"Don't be that way." Sharon's eyes pleaded as she scolded him. "It will mean something to Dad just to know you're here again, even if you can't carry on a real conversation."

"There are things I want to ask him," Andrew insisted, catching Kurt's eye.

"Maybe it would be best to wait," Kurt said. "He's not very strong yet."

Sharon nodded emphatically. "Andrew, you will not bother him about what happened over forty years ago." He scowled, and she said, sharper, "I mean it."

"Mom." Tory laid a gentle hand on Sharon's sleeve. "Mom, just go in and say hi and see how he is. If you think he's up to it, Uncle Andrew can step in for a minute. I'll wait here."

"Oh, no, you should go in, dear," Sharon said with a wobbly smile. "Grandpa would love to hear about the artist's reception you went to with David last night."

"You can tell him," Tory said. Sharon's eyes widened in question, and Tory nodded. "Go ahead. Uncle Andrew can wait outside the door until you tell him to come in. I'll just wait for you here."

Janet said, "I'll wait, too, if you don't mind giving me a ride home after. Kurt needs to take the car and get to the office."

She went out into the hallway with Kurt, and as they waited for the elevator to reach their floor, they watched Sharon and Andrew walk toward Intensive Care.

"What do you think?" Kurt asked.

"I'm not sure. When Sharon told me he asked for me, I thought maybe he wanted to tell me something, but it didn't seem that way this morning."

"Maybe he just wanted to visit with you," Kurt said.

She sighed. "I wish I knew. He does seem exhausted, poor man. Kurt, do you think I was right to tell his children what he said to me the day he had the stroke?"

"How could you not tell them? He begged you." The elevator doors opened, and Kurt got in.

"That's what I keep telling myself." She blew him a kiss as the doors closed.

When Kurt got to the office, he had twenty minutes to prepare for the morning staff meeting. He looked over the list of local stories they knew would be going into Wednesday's paper. Nothing major, but there was the charity auction, and a city council meeting tonight. Sometimes that led to fireworks. You never knew until the last minute if it would need space on the front page or in the local section.

He decided to put Dave's story about the art exhibit on the top of the split page, unless something more urgent came up. Simon, the new photographer, had taken a nice photo of a couple of students admiring the artworks. Not dramatic, but a well balanced, upbeat shot. Kurt always told Kate, the local section editor, to put an interesting picture above the fold on the split page, which was the first page of her section. It caught people's attention and kept them from skipping from the national news to sports.

When Kurt walked into the newsroom, Joy and Roger looked up from their monitors. Kurt headed toward the conference room, knowing the reporters and editors would follow him. Terry fell into step with him.

"How are you, Terry?" Kurt asked.

"Fine. I've got that story about the Fairfield Fire Department today, and an advance on History Days."

"Good. We'll find spots for both of those. Do we have art?"

"Simon is supposed to go to Fairfield with me this morning and swing by the History House for a photo op there after we do the fire department."

"Good."

Kurt sat down in his customary chair at the end of the table, and Terry took the chair next to him.

He leaned toward Kurt and said in a confidential tone, "I was wondering . . ." Terry glanced toward the door and continued, "If Mick never comes back, can I have his desk?"

Kurt's mouth went dry, and he stared at Terry. Dave, Joy, and Roger, along with the local and special sections editors, came through the door laughing and chatting. Kurt decided he could put off answering the question.

"All right, here's the lineup for today," he began as soon as everyone was seated. He avoided looking at Terry, but asked each staff member to quickly give him an update on planned stories.

Wally, as head photographer, also sat in the

meeting, and when he came around to him, Kurt asked, "Wally, what's your department up to today?"

"The usual. A couple of school sports shots this afternoon. Simon and Joe are following reporters around most of the day. I've got a 100th birthday girl, a restaurant opening, and a shot at the paint store on Elm Street."

Kurt glanced at his list, but it was no help. "What's going on at the paint store?"

"They're naming a new color after the mayor's first grandchild."

Everyone laughed, and Kurt said, "Are you serious?"

"I'm so serious I'm almost critical."

Kurt laughed, too. "A new color? Is that possible?"

Wally shrugged. "It's one they've never mixed before. The mayor's daughter wants to paint the baby's room a particular shade of pink, and they don't have it on their paint chips, so they're creating it for her. It's going to be called Penelope Pink. That's the baby's name, Penelope."

"That sounds like a color pic on the front page," Roger said.

"Is anyone doing a story?" Kurt asked.

"Now you're the one who's kidding," Joy said, examining her fingernails.

"No, it would make a good feature," Kurt said. "People like to read things like that."

"You could put it in the leisure section Saturday," Terry suggested.

"Great." Kurt made a note. "Were you volunteering?"

"Me?" Terry asked with a grimace.

"I'll do it," Dave said.

Kurt looked up and frowned at him. "Are you sure you have time?"

"Yeah, that won't take long."

Kurt nodded and wrote it down. It was getting harder and harder to fill all the pages these days. With Mick gone, the reporters were stretched to their limits.

"Hey, boss," Wally said, "maybe they'd create a new color for you, and you could redecorate your office. Borden Blue."

"I'll keep that in mind when I get tired of the Boring Beige."

When the meeting broke up a few minutes later, Kurt pulled Dave aside.

"Are you sure you're not overloading yourself?"

"Everyone's busy this week."

"I know. But you need to have a fresh outlook on the Jacobs story every day. I don't want you to burn out in the middle of this thing."

Dave nodded. "So far, so good. I'm working up a piece on what happened to his family after he disappeared. The wife's dead now, but I'm hoping to get a phone interview with his daughter. So far no luck, but I'll keep trying to find a way to contact her."

"Good." Kurt hesitated. "You need some R&R time, too."

Dave smiled. "Yes, sir."

"How did things go last night? I know you finished your art story already. I mean the personal end of it."

"Good."

Kurt wasn't sure how much he wanted to know. He didn't want Dave to feel he was prying, or worse, that he wanted to be his buddy. Still, it seemed the time had come to be a little less formal. "I'm glad. Look, Dave, we're going to study together at noon, right?"

"Yes, sir."

Kurt smiled. "Why don't you just call me Kurt? Everyone else does."

Dave nodded, his eyes wide, as if that was a new concept. "All right. In the lunch room?"

"Or my office." Kurt weighed whether they wanted a quiet atmosphere to read the scripture together, or a public declaration that their free time was spent pondering the spiritual.

"It's kind of small in there," Dave said. "Kate Ashe might sit in, if you don't mind."

"No, I don't mind." Kurt was surprised. He'd never heard Kate express an interest in the Bible. "I guess it's the lunch room, then. The conference room might be tied up." They tried to keep the conference room free for the reporters to use as an interview room.

Dave raised his notebook. “I’ll call the paint store and set up an interview with the manager as soon as I’ve called Sergeant Bedard at the Waterville P.D.”

“For your update on Mick?”

“Right. So far, they’ve got nothing.”

Kurt scowled. “There’s got to be something.”

“Bedard’s getting tired of me. And the state police report on the break-in at Fairmonts’ and their interview with William Dunning doesn’t sit well with me.” Dave frowned and shook his head. “But what can I do? I can’t write stories based on conjecture.”

“Let’s do a little digging on Dunning.”

Dave eyed him cautiously. “Do our own background check?”

“Why not?”

“Sure. If the police won’t do it . . .”

Kurt smiled at him. “I’m not saying our state police aren’t doing their job, but they don’t always tell us everything. If there’s anything at all that will help us put a hole in Dunning’s story, or connect him to the senator, we need to find it fast.”

A half hour later Dave knocked on the door frame outside Kurt’s office.

“Come on in. What have you got?” Kurt looked up from the computer screen.

"The sergeant says they don't have any new leads. No activity on Mick's credit cards—they told me that—but the information is really sketchy. It's almost a non-story now, boss. Kurt." Dave's eyes flickered, and Kurt suppressed a smile. "Anyway, they seem to think he's either a suicide or a grownup runaway."

Kurt shook his head. "I'm still not buying it. They might as well say he has amnesia and joined a traveling circus."

Dave smiled. "Not bad. Did you find anything?"

Kurt nodded at his screen. "I've been checking out Dunning and his family. Dunning worked at a paper mill for thirty years. When it closed, he started a small engine repair business. Doesn't make much. His wife works at the vet clinic in Oakland. She's their receptionist and bookkeeper."

"Decent folks?"

"Oh, yeah." Kurt sighed. "Three kids and a dog. The kids are grown up. No red flags."

"Have you searched the paper's archives?" Dave asked.

"Not completely. I found a new business story on the engine repair, and their oldest daughter's wedding." Kurt glanced at his watch. "I've got to meet with the brass in Augusta this afternoon."

"If I have time, I'll do some more looking on Dunning," Dave said.

Kurt nodded. "Guess it's all we can do. Meanwhile, prepare a short statement with a quote from Sergeant Bedard on the credit cards. We need to keep Mick's story alive until he's found and let the readers know somebody's doing something."

It was late afternoon when Kurt got back to the office. The meeting with the publisher and managing editor was grueling. They demanded an efficient use of resources, but Kurt knew his staff was already stretched too thin. Management also wanted more on Senator Jacobs. Keep the public guessing. Grant suggested interviews of local people for their theories on how the senator disappeared. Kurt hated that. It reminded him too much of his own midnight conjectures on Mick.

He'd been tempted to go straight home from Augusta instead of coming all the way out to Waterville again. His house in Belgrade was about midway between the company's two Central Maine locations, and he could use a good dose of Janet. But there were too many details to wrap up, and he knew he would put in another hour at his desk before heading home.

Flowers, he thought. I didn't call the florist.

As soon as he got to his desk, he grabbed the local phone book. He was detailing what he wanted in Janet's bouquet when Dave arrived in the doorway again.

"What's up?" Kurt asked as he hung up the phone.

"I maybe found something in the archives. The oldest Dunning child, Moriah, was an honor student. She took a master's in speech therapy and got married a few years ago."

"Yeah, I saw the wedding announcement."

Dave nodded. "That's where I started. The next kid was a boy. Kenneth Dunning died in Iraq."

"I'm sorry to hear that. What does—"

"Nothing. I'm getting there. The third kid went to KV Community College. He's living in Belgrade, near his folks."

"And?"

"He's an EMT."

"Good, solid profession."

"Yes, sir." Dave didn't seem to realize he'd lapsed in his informality. "But that got me thinking, and I called Mrs. Borden."

"You called Janet?"

"Uh-huh. There's your red flag, sir. Garrett Dunning was on the ambulance the day Elwood Fairmont had his stroke."

Chapter 16

"You want me to visit Elwood again?" Janet asked.

"If you don't mind." Kurt settled down on the couch and leaned his head back.

"I don't mind. Are you sure you want to watch Jeopardy?"

He smiled. "What are my options?"

"Oh, a moonlight canoe ride, followed by a back rub?"

"It's windy tonight, babe. The lake's pretty choppy."

"Mm. You're right."

"But I'd take the back rub."

"With Jeopardy?"

"Sure." He stretched out on the sofa, and Janet clicked the remote.

"You think Garrett Dunning has something to do with this, don't you?" she asked.

"I don't know. But he was there the day you found Elwood, and he would have heard what Elwood said to you."

"Yes, he did."

Kurt yawned. "Chances are he told his father about it."

"Isn't there some confidentiality law about things like that?"

"Sure, but family is family."

Janet sat on the edge of the couch and began to knead his back muscles. "But what Elwood told me was so vague!"

"Yeah, but if Garrett already knew something we don't, he could have put together the pieces that, to us, were just a jumble."

"All right, I'll go and see Elwood. If he's alert, I'll ask him about the Dunnings."

"Mmm."

Janet leaned down and kissed the back of his neck, then started rubbing his tight shoulder muscles. "You're so tense! Who did this to you?"

"The world at large."

"That's God's territory."

He sighed. "You're right. Oh, I meant to tell you." Kurt raised his head and looked at her. "Dave wants to use the canoe Saturday, to take Tory out paddling. If it's calm, that is."

She smiled. "Do you think this relationship has potential?"

"Scads of it. Dave's crazy about her."

"Tory's infatuated, too, but she's being cautious, I think. Sharon hinted that Tory had a bad experience."

"I don't think she has to worry about Dave."

"Rock solid?"

"The better I get to know him, the more I think

so. In fact, if I had any unmarried daughters left, I'd try to set him up with one."

Janet purposely set the time of her visit for late afternoon. She didn't want to tire Elwood with too much company, and she knew Sharon and Andrew were meeting with a social worker across town, to sort out the options for their father's long-term care.

The old man was sitting up in bed when she arrived. He had been shaved, and his eyes glittered with recognition when she stepped into the room.

He struggled for a more upright position.

"Here, let me help you." Janet raised the head of the bed a bit more, and Elwood reached out and seized her wrist.

"You!"

"Yes, Elwood, it's me, Janet." She studied his features and was sure he recognized her, but she didn't understand why he seemed so agitated.

"I did wrong . . . Janet. I . . . kept . . . it all."

She swallowed hard. He was as distressed as he had been when she found him on the floor of his living room nearly two weeks ago.

"Elwood, dear friend, what is it that's bothering you so?"

Elwood's gaze darted about the room, as though searching for someone, then settled back on Janet's face. It struck her that he was making sure they were alone. "He told . . . me . . ."

He halted, breathing fast.

"Relax, Elwood. Just relax. There's time to tell me everything." Uneasily she reached for her tote bag, pulled out her cell phone, and punched in Kurt's number at work.

Elwood seemed to be resting for the moment, and she leaned back. When Kurt answered, she murmured. "It's me. I'm at the hospital. Can you come over here?"

"What's the matter?" Kurt asked.

"I'm not sure. He's upset again. Like the first day."

"I'm coming."

Elwood's eyelids flew wide open, and he struggled once more to sit straighter. "No! You! . . . You can . . . help."

"How can I help you?" Janet wondered if she ought to call the nurse.

"I . . . confess."

She stared at him, not sure she had heard correctly. "Confess? Did you say confess?"

He nodded. "I kept it. You help me."

"Help you how, dear?" She stroked the dry, creased skin on the back of his hand.

"Tell . . . God."

She was glad the newspaper office was only moments away from the hospital. Janet reached once more into her bag and took out her New Testament.

"Don't fret, now, Elwood. Let me read to you what God says. It's here, in 1 John 1:9." She turned the pages. "If we confess our sins, He is faithful and just and will forgive us our sins and purify us from all unrighteousness."

Elwood stared at her, but he said nothing.

"Is that what you mean?" she asked. "Do you have something to confess to God? Because He will hear you, even if you say it in your heart. Tell Him you're sorry, and you know that you sinned. He will forgive you, Elwood."

The nurse poked her head in at the doorway.

"How are we doing?"

"Fine," Janet said, holding the Bible low in her lap.

The nurse came forward and peered at the monitor. "His heart rate went up pretty fast. Is he talking?"

"Yes, a little. I was just reading to him. I think he's calm now."

The nurse nodded, but Janet thought she looked a bit suspicious. "It's not time for his meds yet. Call us if anything's abnormal."

Janet nodded, and the nurse left. She looked at Elwood, but his eyes seemed to focus on the far wall.

"Elwood," she said softly. He didn't respond, so she said it louder. "Elwood."

Slowly he turned his head to look at her. “I never . . . should have . . . kept . . .”

“You’re sure?” Dave Carpenter jotted on his notepad and listened carefully as the elderly woman went on.

“Oh, yes, of course I’m sure. He’s my cousin.”

Dave nodded. “Thank you, Mrs. Ladd.” He needed to get back to the office. He’d spent most of the afternoon talking to old people, asking them if they remembered the Jacobs family, gathering color and data for a new story.

“Would you like some coffee?” Mrs. Ladd asked. Her eyes had a hopeful glint.

“Oh, I’m sorry, ma’am. I need to get back to my desk and type this up.”

He all but ran to his car and pushed the speed limit all the way to Waterville.

It was nearly five o’clock. The clerks and sports writers were gathering their things to leave for the day. Dave circled around to Kurt’s small private office, but that was empty, too. He went to his own desk and put a call through to the Bordens’ house, but there was no answer.

Dave took a deep breath. He had never called the boss’s cell phone. He supposed he could, but he didn’t feel comfortable about it. He decided to write up his rough draft and try Kurt again after a while. The question was, should he include this new information or not?

He sat down and opened a new file. At the top he typed, "I remember the senator."

Kurt walked into the room, and Janet jumped up.

"I'm so glad you're here!"

He hugged her. "What's going on?"

"Elwood says he wants to confess something to God. He kept something."

Kurt frowned and sat down in the chair she had vacated. "Elwood? Elwood, it's me, Kurt."

The old man blinked at him and said, "Janet."

"She's right here."

Janet moved in closer. "I'm here. Elwood, we both love you. Tell us what's bothering you so." His breathing seemed labored, and she whispered to Kurt, "If he gets upset again, the nurse will toss us out."

At last Elwood croaked out, "You . . . pray."

"Yes," Kurt assured him. "We're praying for you, and if you tell us what's got you upset, we'll pray about that."

Elwood gave a deep sigh. "I kept . . . his . . . things. . . . I shouldn't have . . . He told . . . me . . . not to."

Kurt looked up at Janet, puzzled. "Who's he talking about?"

"I don't know."

"Did you ask him about Dunning?"

"No, I didn't have a chance."

Kurt turned to Elwood. "Was it . . . was it something that you stole?"

"No! No! He gave . . ." Elwood broke off, gasping.

"We'd better let him rest," Janet said.

"But he's so agitated. It's keeping him upset."

"I think he wanted to tell me when no one else was here, but I was afraid," Janet said.

The nurse strode into the room. "Why didn't you call me?"

"I'm sorry," Janet said automatically.

Kurt said, "He's trying to tell us something important."

The nurse went to the monitor, then took Elwood's hand in hers, feeling his pulse. "I'll have to ask you to leave. He can't be upset like this."

"But . . ." Janet began.

"Whatever it is, it will have to wait."

Kurt stood, and they went into the hallway. Janet was near tears, he could see.

"I feel awful," she whispered.

Kurt put his arm around her and gave her a squeeze. The elevator opened, and they got on with several other people. Not until they reached the parking lot did they speak again.

"He's so distressed," Janet said, a catch in her voice.

Kurt steered her toward her car. "I know."

"He begged me to help him confess, Kurt."

"You're the one who's told him the most about God. He needed your assurance."

"I tried. I told him God will forgive him. And I gave him 1 John 1:9. But I couldn't tell what it was that was bothering him so."

"Except that he kept something he shouldn't have."

"Yes." She stopped beside the car and looked up at him. "Do you need to go back to the office?"

"No, I'll follow you home."

She clicked the remote on her key ring to unlock the door. She jerked her chin toward him. "The pen and the card case."

"I did think of that, but Sharon says they're not valuable."

"What if there was more?" Janet asked. "He said, 'I kept his things, but he told me not to.' "

"Something like that," Kurt agreed. "*His things*. It could be Jacobs."

She frowned. "Yes. Or it could be Andrew or Paul or Dunning or . . . Oh, Kurt, what if we never know what he's talking about?"

"Easy, now. He's made progress. If he's moved to a nursing home, there may be more opportunity to talk to him."

"You think we'll have to wait that long?"

Kurt shrugged. "We can continue visiting him here, but if he keeps getting so worked up about it, the nurses might keep us out."

“Sharon,” Janet said suddenly. “We need to talk to Sharon. Kurt, if she tells Elwood she knows the Lord and will pray with him, maybe he’ll confide in her.”

“He might.”

Kurt’s cell phone rang. He took it out and punched the talk button.

“Hello?”

“I told you, take that reporter off the Jacobs story!”

“No,” Kurt said without thinking about it. “Who—”

“No more stories about Jacobs, or you’ll be sorry!”

The connection broke, and he sighed.

Janet stared at him, her gray eyes large in her pale face. “What was that about?”

Kurt bit his lip. “It was nothing.”

She only looked worse. “It was another threat.”

He couldn’t deny it. She reached toward him, and he gathered her into his arms. They stood for half a minute like that in the parking lot, until she slowly pulled away.

“Can you drive?” he asked.

She nodded.

He hated to let go of her, but he had to. “I’ll be right behind you.”

Chapter 17

Sharon answered Janet's call and readily agreed that she and Tory could share supper with the Bordens.

"I was just starting to make spaghetti, though. Why don't you and Kurt come over here?"

"Do you have plenty?"

"Yes, Tory's staying in tonight. I guess Dave had to work late. And Andrew's here. Anyway, I always make too much."

"I'll bring salad and . . ." Janet opened her freezer and looked over the contents. ". . . and homemade bread."

"Perfect," Sharon said. "I've got ice cream."

Over the salad, Kurt told them about his and Janet's visit to Elwood and how Elwood had pleaded with her to help him.

"This sort of ties in with what Dad told me last week," Sharon said. "He told me, 'I hid it.' None of us could make sense of that, but . . ." She looked around at them all. "Tory was going through some old papers we found in the attic while I started supper. Tell them, Tory."

Tory took a deep breath. "It seems Grandpa

came up with some money a long time ago that . . . well, I found bank statements from four or five different banks, and he made large deposits over a period of several years."

"It was much more than Dad was making at the time," Sharon confirmed.

"Why didn't you tell me?" Andrew asked. He was clearly angry to have been left out of the loop.

"We just found out," Sharon said. "I was going to tell you, but you were out poking around the barn. I decided to tell you at supper."

"It was a lot of money," Tory said.

"How much?" Kurt asked.

"If you don't mind us asking," Janet added quickly.

"I'm not sure yet," Tory said, "but at least fifty thousand dollars. Maybe a lot more."

"It was during the time we kids were in college." Sharon addressed Andrew in soft, pleading tones. "I always wondered if I'd need to take student loans. I mean, I was the last child, and tuition kept going up. But Dad always told me not to worry about it, that he and Mom would figure something out."

Andrew's eyebrows nearly met as he frowned at her. "I worked at school."

"Yes, but . . ." Sharon shook her head, and Tory took over.

"Uncle Andrew, I don't think your campus job

was enough to pay the full bill, was it? Brown is pretty expensive."

"No, but . . ."

She nodded. "Grandpa made the first questionable deposit toward the end of Geneva's freshman year."

"She worked, too," Andrew said. "She waitressed all four years."

"That's so," Sharon agreed, "but even with us kids working, Mom and Dad couldn't have paid our total tuition. Our college careers overlapped. We should have realized that long ago."

"So . . . where did the money come from?" Andrew asked.

They sat in silence until Kurt said, "I'm thinking that's what has your father so worked up now. He realizes that whatever it was he did—however he got the money—wasn't right. He said today he wanted to confess something to God."

Sharon smiled, with tears shining in her eyes. "Put that together with *I shouldn't have done it,* and *I hid it,* and I think we have a pretty good idea of what's bothering Dad. He got that money dishonestly, and now he's repentant."

"That may be why the burglar has been coming here," Kurt said. "He may be looking for evidence of your father's crime."

"If it was a crime," Janet said. They all looked at her, and she shrugged. "Kurt asked Elwood today if he stole something, and he definitely said no. He said, 'I kept his things, but I shouldn't have.' "

"You think he got hold of something someone lost, like picking up a wallet or something, and didn't return it?" Andrew asked.

"Could be," Janet said.

Kurt grimaced. "I don't know. Fifty k is a lot of bills to find in a wallet."

"There was the money that disappeared with Senator Jacobs," Tory said, and Janet glanced at Kurt. It was what they had discussed but didn't want to say to the family. "Hey, it's public knowledge," Tory said. "It was on the front page of yesterday's paper in Dave's story."

"You think Dad somehow got hold of the missing government money?" Sharon's voice squeaked.

"This beats all," Andrew muttered.

"It couldn't be," Sharon insisted. "Could it?"

"I don't know," Kurt said, "but someone lost a large sum of money at that time, and someone seems to have found a large sum."

"And someone's upset that we're digging up the past," Janet said.

"That's right," Kurt told them. "I've received a couple of phone calls I'd say were threatening. Someone wants me to take Dave off the Jacobs story."

"But if Grandpa had the money and they didn't

know it . . ." Tory shrugged. "Why do they care now?"

"Maybe the money was split several ways," Andrew suggested. "Whoever's been breaking in here may be afraid Dad will tell someone and implicate them in the crime, too."

"It's true that the unexplained money your father had is far less than the missing federal money," Janet said.

Geneva frowned at her. "Maybe he was blackmailing someone, and that was hush money in his accounts."

"Well, whatever happened in 1968, you all need to be careful," Kurt advised. "Don't come home alone, and don't walk out to your car in the hospital parking lot alone after dark. Ask for a security guard to escort you."

"You'd better warn Dave, too," Tory said. "By the sound of things, he's the one this maniac is mad at. He's writing the stories."

Kurt nodded. "Dave and me. Somehow the caller knows I'm behind this. He's calling me, not the publisher, not the reporter. But I'll speak to Dave tonight."

"This is what happened to Mick!" Andrew's glare frightened Janet. It was as though he was accusing Kurt of causing Mick's disappearance. "Someone found out what he was looking into and stopped him."

Kurt looked down at his plate. "We don't

know for sure that anything like that happened."

Andrew threw down his napkin and pushed his chair back in one motion. "Go on saying that if you want, but we all know something has happened. Mick is probably dead."

There was an awful silence, and Janet didn't know where to look.

"I should have listened to Mick last week. He knew something! I'm going to the hospital and get some answers." Andrew stalked out the door before anyone could react.

"Andrew, no!" Sharon ran after him. "You can't charge into the hospital and upset Dad again."

Janet looked at Kurt. His blue eyes were sad, but he stayed in his chair. "I'm sorry, babe," he whispered.

They heard Andrew's car start and roll quickly out of the driveway.

"Should we call the hospital and warn them at the nurses' desk?" Tory asked.

Kurt stood up. "I'll follow him in." He couldn't help feeling a little bit responsible for Andrew's outburst.

He kissed Janet good-bye and drove toward Waterville. So much for a quiet evening with Janet. No Jeopardy tonight. *Wednesday! It's prayer meeting night.* He sighed. It would have done him good to sit through the tranquil service and pray with other men of faith.

When he reached the hospital, he saw Andrew's rental car parked in a handicapped spot near the doors. It took Kurt a minute to find a spot and park, much farther from the building. He hurried inside and up to the Intensive Care Unit.

As he entered the ICU, he could hear Andrew shouting.

"This is your fault, Dad! You stole that money somehow, didn't you? Didn't you? And Mick found out. That's what got Mick in trouble. It was something you did!"

Kurt dashed past the desk where a nurse was frantically punching buttons on her telephone. She stared at him with her mouth gaping.

He opened the door to Elwood's room. Andrew leaned over the bed, screaming at his father. The nurse who had evicted him and Janet stood beside Andrew, tugging at his arm and gasping, "Stop it! You have to stop it."

"Andrew," Kurt said, but before he could get any more out, two uniformed guards, an intern, and an EMT rushed into the room and tackled Andrew.

They had him on the floor in seconds, and one of guards handcuffed him. The second one stood up, panting, and hit the button on his radio. "Subject is subdued. Get Waterville P.D. in here to collect him."

The nurse bent over Elwood and felt his pulse.

"Mr. Fairmont, can you hear me?" The nurse who had been at the station outside peeked in at the door.

"Rachel?" Her voice quavered.

The nurse at the bed glanced at her. "Call Dr. Ridge." She sized up Kurt in a fraction of a second. "You, sir, have to leave. Goodnight."

Kurt looked helplessly toward Andrew, but he was face down on the tile floor. Kurt sighed and went out into the hallway. He started to take out his cell phone, but a large sign glared at him. *No cellular phones may be used in this unit.* Security guards and medical staff rushed past him, converging on the ICU.

"The police station?" Janet asked.

"Yeah, they're bringing him over here." Kurt's voice was faint. "The sergeant says someone will have to bail Andrew out, unless they want him to go to Augusta and cool down overnight in the Kennebec County Jail."

"How much?"

"They don't know yet. Maybe five hundred."

"I'll ask Sharon," Janet said.

"Great. I'm heading over to the office. If Sharon decides to let him stew overnight, call me. And if she's going to the police station—"

"Don't worry," Janet said. "I won't let her go alone."

"I'm sorry, Jan."

"It's not your fault."

"Are you sure? Maybe I shouldn't have told Andrew what his father said today."

"Sharon and Tory are the ones who found out about the money and the extra bank accounts. I think that's what really made Andrew mad."

The phone crackled, and she caught the words, ". . . so bad about this."

"You're breaking up, sweetheart. I'll talk to you later." She replaced Sharon's receiver and put the best smile she could muster on her face before going into the kitchen to answer Tory and Sharon's questions.

"Well, girls, how would you like a ride to the police station?" she asked.

Sharon's face fell. "He didn't."

"I'm afraid he did. Security was very firm, and he's being booked now."

"Is Dad okay?"

"Kurt thinks so, but they wouldn't let him stay to find out."

"This is terrible," Sharon moaned.

"Oh, I don't know," Tory said. "It was totally stupid of Uncle Andrew, but I've never bailed anyone out before. It could be interesting. Come on, Mom, get your purse and your jacket."

Janet put her arm around Sharon. "I don't think we need to hurry. Let's sit down and pray first. Maybe we should even stop by the hospital first and check on your father before we go to the police station. Andrew will still be there."

Sharon hugged her. "Thank you!"

When Kurt walked into the newsroom, he was surprised to see Dave typing away at his computer terminal. He waved at Hilda, the night editor, and called, "Dave! You're still here."

"Hey, Mr. Borden. Yeah, I've been trying to reach you, but I guess you weren't home." He made a wry face. "Tory called and told me just now what happened at the hospital. Too bad."

Kurt walked over to Dave's side and lowered his voice. "Did she also tell you about the unexplained extra money in the Fairmonts' bank accounts?"

"Yeah, but I can't put that in my story."

"Not yet. We need to do a lot of investigating. I think we also need to talk to the police. But anyway, we'll let them take care of Andrew first. What's in your story tonight?"

Dave grinned. "You're gonna love this. I talked to all the old folks in the neighborhood, like you said. I wasn't getting too far, though, down in Belgrade Lakes. Too many new people. So then I thought, why not go up to North Belgrade, where William Dunning lives, and guess what."

"What?"

"I met William Dunning's cousin, Marie Ladd. She told me something very interesting."

"I'm waiting."

“William Dunning worked for Senator Jacobs back in the early ’60s.”

“Well, I’ll be. Do the police know this?”

“I’m guessing not. Might put a different light on the burglary the other night.”

“Yes.” Kurt sat down on the corner of Dave’s desk. “So much is happening, we’ve got to sort out what we can publish and what we can’t.”

Dave glanced at the clock. “Two hours max ’til deadline.”

“Okay, then go easy on Jacobs tonight. You’ll have to write the story about Andrew first.”

“Andrew? You mean him getting arrested?”

“Yes. A lot of people witnessed the fracas, so we have to print something. Something short. Open a new file, and I’ll give you the details. Just say he had a disagreement with his father, who was a patient. Don’t say what it was about. And say in the lead that no one was hurt. That’s important.”

Dave cocked his head to one side. “No offense, boss, but you were there. You’re a fast typist, too. Why don’t you just write it up yourself and put *compiled by staff* in the byline?”

It made sense. Kurt nodded. “All right, but don’t file your Jacobs story until I have a chance to read it. We’ll have to talk to Detective Robbins tomorrow, and maybe Sergeant Bedard, too, and sort out what’s publishable. Oh, and Dave.”

The young man looked up at him, and Kurt

felt a sudden twist in his stomach. What was he getting people into? He shrugged it off. "Be careful."

"You got another call."

"Yeah. On my cell this time."

Dave made a wry face. "How would he know your cell number?"

Kurt shrugged. "I don't keep it secret. It's on the list that everyone here at the office can access. But you're right. Not just anyone could find it easily."

"Did you check your received calls?"

"Yeah. The number was blocked."

"That rots."

Kurt nodded. "So, remember, watch your back, huh?"

"You, too, Mr. Borden."

Chapter 18

"Sharon, I'm sorry," Andrew said. "I don't know what else to say."

Janet kept her attention on her driving, but she couldn't help hearing Andrew's remorse. He sat in the back seat of her Mazda with Sharon, and Tory had the passenger seat up front.

Sharon sighed. "Well, as Tory said, it was totally stupid of you. I'm just glad the doctor says Dad will be all right."

"I really messed up," Andrew said. "Dad will never want to see me again."

"Well, we know the nurses don't," Tory quipped, and Janet smiled.

"I'll stay out of the hospital from now on." Andrew sounded almost humble.

"You have to," Sharon noted. "If you go back, they'll have you arrested again."

Andrew was quiet for a long moment before he said, "I shouldn't have come back to Maine. You were handling things just fine, and there's nothing I can do to help."

"I don't know about that," Janet said. "Kurt intends to talk to the police again tomorrow about

Mick Tyler. They might even want to hear your story firsthand. The things you remember may help them discover what Mick was up to when he vanished."

"I hope so. I really, really hope so."

"Stay over a couple more days, Uncle Andrew," Tory said. "It's always fun when you're around."

"Sure. Arguing, fighting, trips to jail. Guess I've got to stick around for my court hearing, whether I want to or not." He leaned forward suddenly. "Say, Mrs. Borden, is the marina closed for the season?"

"I think so. Not much business after Labor Day."

Andrew sank back against his seat cushion. "Too bad."

"Did you want to rent a boat?" Tory asked eagerly.

"I was thinking we might do a little fishing. Of course, I'd have to have a license. You would, too."

"You could use our canoe," Janet offered. "It's down by the dock. Kurt was leaving it out for . . . well, for whoever wants to use it." She glanced at Tory. If Dave's planned outing was a surprise, she didn't want to ruin that.

"Sure, Uncle Andrew, let's do it," Tory said.

"You want to?"

"Yes. While Mom's at the hospital tomorrow, you and I will go catch some fish."

"All right, I guess so," Andrew said. "I booked my return flight for Saturday, so you're stuck with me for a while."

"Can your business get along without you all week?" Sharon asked.

"I asked myself that when I heard about Mick, and I knew I wanted to be here. I mean, he was my friend. I've messed up a lot of relationships in my life, and it just seemed right to do everything I can for an old friend. And you know what?"

"What?" Sharon asked.

"Carol told me to come. When I told her how upset I was about Mick, she didn't hesitate. She said, 'You know you've got vacation coming, and you never use it. Now's the time.' "

"She's a keeper," Sharon said softly. Janet remembered Sharon telling her about Andrew's second wife, Carol, the sister-in-law Sharon had only met once.

"Yes. I appreciate her more every day."

"You should bring her out to visit us," Sharon said. "I'd like to get to know her."

Janet pulled in at the Fairmonts' driveway, and they all looked toward the dark house.

"It's getting so I hate to go into the house again," Sharon said. "If someone's been in there, I'll—"

"You'll come stay with me and let your brother handle it this time," Janet said.

"Let me take a look inside." Andrew got out

of the car, and the three women waited while he unlocked the door, went into the farmhouse, and turned on several lights.

He came out to the car again. "All clear."

"Terrific." Tory unbuckled her seat belt. "Let's have that ice cream I heard rumors of earlier."

On Thursday morning Kurt glanced through the briefs in the upcoming events section of the paper. There was a poetry reading at the public library. Would Janet enjoy that? She'd probably prefer his original plan: an amateur production of *The Importance of Being Earnest* at the Waterville Opera House.

It was only a day away. He had to quit second-guessing himself and realize that the evening wouldn't be perfect, but Janet would be enthralled, no matter where he took her. And she loved theater. He ran down his mental list. Flowers, check. Dinner reservation, check. Play tickets, check.

He opened his e-mail and sent her a quick message: *See you later, beautiful. Looking forward to tomorrow night.*

Time to get down to work. Out of the corner of his eye, he saw Wally come in the back door of the office. Kurt got up and walked toward the photographers' area, intercepting Wally in the aisle.

"Howdy, Kurt."

"So, Wally, are we going to the Red Sox game together?"

Wally swallowed and didn't quite look at him. "Yeah, well, I'm pretty busy."

Kurt sighed. "Come on, don't give me that. I was counting on you."

Wally shrugged. "You want me to lie about it? Things got really hectic yesterday, and I just . . . couldn't do it. I'm addicted, okay?"

Kurt nodded. Voicing his disappointment was unnecessary. Wally knew. "Well, good pictures for the new paint color story."

"Thanks. It's a cute baby."

"Yeah."

"Excuse me, Kurt?"

He turned around. Molly was at his elbow. "That man wants to talk to you."

He looked toward the receptionist's desk and saw Detective Robbins waiting there.

"Excuse me, Wally." On the way, he tapped Dave on the shoulder. Dave was on the phone but looked up.

"Conference room." Kurt jerked his head toward the visitor.

Dave nodded.

"So, detective, how can I help you this morning?" Kurt asked when they were seated. Dave came in carrying his notebook and closed the door.

Robbins said, "Your tip on Mr. Dunning

prompted us to question him again this morning. He admits he was employed by Senator Jacobs in 1967 and '68. He did maintenance for the senator, ran errands, and drove him sometimes. His wife also worked for the Jacobs family, cooking and cleaning at their summer home."

"Did you ask him about the senator's disappearance?" Kurt asked.

"Yes, and he gave us his version. It was the standard, I'm afraid. He said Jacobs vanished from his Washington office and never came back to Maine. Mrs. Jacobs and the daughter were in Belgrade at the time, and Dunning said they were distraught when Jacobs disappeared. The senator's family stayed only a couple of days after the news broke, then they flew to Washington, or at least that's what Dunning remembers. They still had the house in Portland at that time, so maybe they went there. But Dunning and his wife helped them pack, and later Dunning took the real estate agent out to see the cottage and gave him the keys Mrs. Jacobs left in his care."

"When was that?"

"The next spring."

"Did he say anything that would connect him to this more recent chicanery?" Kurt asked.

Robbins shook his head. "He still denies being in Fairmont's house the other night, if that's what you mean. It seems like a dead end."

"It can't be," Kurt said. "My ace reporter

disappeared after he started investigating the Jacobs story. We've learned that the reporter and his friend, Andrew Fairmont, heard and saw some suspicious things at the Jacobs house in May, 1968. And now the Fairmont house has been broken into twice."

"What's this? I didn't know about the Fairmont fellow."

"He was eleven years old when Jacobs disappeared," Kurt said, "but he and my reporter, Mick Tyler, who vanished last week, saw something going on there a few weeks after the senator's disappearance. Now we find that Dunning, whose car was parked near Fairmont's father's house the night of the last burglary, was an employee of the senator's, and I've also learned that his son is an EMT."

"What does that have to do with it?" Robbins asked.

"Garrett Dunning was on the ambulance when Andrew Fairmont's father had a stroke September sixth. He heard Elwood Fairmont tell my wife there was something he'd done in the past that he was sorry for. The elder Mr. Fairmont wanted to make amends with his children for past differences, but it seemed there was something more to it than that. And then last night, Garrett Dunning was at the hospital when Andrew Fairmont was arrested for criminal threatening."

"How's that?"

Kurt ran a hand through his hair. “Garrett Dunning heard Andrew Fairmont accusing his father of stealing some money back in 1968—money that turned up in his bank account about the same time Senator Jacobs disappeared.”

“Did he do it?”

“I don’t know. Look, detective, I think it’s time you talked to Sergeant Bedard at the Waterville P.D. He’s in charge of the missing persons case on my reporter, Mick Tyler. These two cases are one, I’m sure of it. One of his men also booked Andrew Fairmont last night.”

“Mick Tyler . . . I read about that case. You’re saying it’s connected to the alleged burglaries on Pine Lane?”

“Andrew Fairmont is the connection, although I don’t think he’s criminally involved. He was an unwitting bystander.” Kurt saw that Dave was scribbling rapid notes. “Last night Andrew went to the hospital here in Waterville, where his father is a patient. He wanted to confront his father about the unexplained money his folks seemed to have a few decades ago, and about the things Andrew saw in 1968. Back then, his father told Andrew it was nothing, just a boy’s overactive imagination. Now Andrew thinks differently, and he was angry with his father. Unfortunately, he got quite loud about it in the ICU, and hospital security had him removed. His sister bailed him out, and he has a hearing tomorrow.”

Robbins exhaled in a puff. “And this William Dunning who owns the car from the Pine Lane incident, his son is in it somehow, too?”

Kurt slapped the table. “All I’m saying is, he was in a position to hear things. Last night he may have heard Andrew accuse his father of somehow causing Mick Tyler’s disappearance, which I don’t think is true, but if Garrett Dunning did hear it, and if he told his father, who was the former lackey of the senator, well, then, who knows what that meant to him? And someone wants this Senator Jacobs thing hushed up. I’ve received two threatening calls this week, telling me to take Dave Carpenter here off the story.” He stopped for breath.

“You should have informed me.”

Kurt sighed. “We weren’t sure that the burglaries had anything to do with the Jacobs story, but it’s all coming together now. Don’t you see?”

Robbins eyed him thoughtfully. Kurt wondered if he did see, or if he ever would see. Did his brain make those kinds of connections? But he was a detective, after all, and probably had been one for twenty or thirty years. Maybe this would be his last big case. Kurt considered hinting that Robbins could end his career with a bang if he solved both the Jacobs and Tyler cases.

“I’ll go around and see this Sergeant Bedard.”

“Good,” Kurt said. “And maybe you should talk to the Hillman family, too. They own the

Jacobs house now. If you could get permission to search it—"

"What's the point of that?" Robbins asked. He took out his notebook. "The Jacobs family sold the property more than forty years ago. It sounds like I'd learn more if I talked to this Andrew Fairmont. Let's see, he must be Mrs. Schlesser's brother?"

"That's right." Kurt bit his lip. His frustration was overwhelming, and he could hardly wait to go home and talk this all out with Janet. But it was only 9 a.m., and he had a long day of drudgery ahead of him. "We have a taped interview Andrew Fairmont made in this room three days ago. I can give you a copy if you want."

As soon as Robbins left with the tape, Kurt looked at Dave and smiled. "Well, that didn't go very well, did it?"

"You're very passionate, Mr. Borden."

"I'm supposed to be objective. But at least the police know all the angles now. Whether they're quick enough to put them together, I don't know."

"I'd better get back to my computer," Dave said.

"You've been putting in a lot of overtime," Kurt observed, knowing it was his own fault for pushing Dave. "Take this afternoon off, why don't you?"

Dave eyes sparkled. "Do you think I could? I've got three stories to write today."

Kurt shrugged. “Well, maybe you can get them done and leave a couple of hours early, anyway.”

Sharon was hurrying out of the house after lunch when a car drove up the driveway. She hovered on the porch steps, watching it anxiously, then drew a breath of relief when her second brother got out.

“Paul! What brings you back?”

“Dad.”

She smiled and stepped down onto the path to meet him. “He’ll be pleased. He’s doing much better. In fact, I’m on my way to Waterville now. The doctor is signing him out, and he’s going to a rehab facility.”

“Now? Today?”

“Yes. Do you want to come? We can see him settled in the new place, and then this evening we can go back with Tory and Andrew.”

“Andrew’s here?”

“Yes, he came back Monday. He and Tory have gone fishing.”

Paul frowned. “Why isn’t he going to the hospital with you?”

She sighed. She had hoped not to have to deal with this. “It’s a long story. Andrew’s not allowed in the hospital.”

“Not allowed?” Paul’s voice rose, and Sharon winced.

"Calm down. Just get in my car, and I'll explain everything on the way. Dad is doing much better. In fact, his speech has improved dramatically. This morning he was talking in full sentences." She unlocked her car and smiled at him over the roof. "Are you hungry? We can stop on the way."

"So, Dad, we were wondering if you could tell us anything about these things." Sharon showed her father the printout of a digital picture Tory had taken of the silver pen and card case before Sharon put them in the safe deposit box.

Elwood stared at the picture for a long while, and Paul gave Sharon a nervous glance.

"Geneva and the others didn't know anything about them," Sharon went on with a smile, trying to make it all seem casual. "I didn't know if it was something Mom inherited, or what."

Elwood sighed and lowered the paper. "No."

"It's all right." The last thing Sharon wanted was to make him feel guilty or put him in a panic again, but the doctor was delayed. Showing her father the picture had seemed like an innocent way to fill the time until he was discharged and perhaps unravel a bit of the mystery.

Elwood turned his head slowly in her direction until he looked intently into her eyes. "You know."

"I do?"

He nodded. "Andrew knew. He came here . . . shouting."

Paul's teeth showed in a grimace, and Sharon said soothingly, "He's so sorry about that, Dad. He asked me to apologize for him. It was inappropriate of him to come in here like that last night."

Elwood's eyes were watering again, and she dabbed at his tears.

"The guards . . . took him."

Sharon nodded. "They thought they needed to protect you, Dad. But Andrew calmed down, and he's hoping you'll let him come to visit you later, after you're settled in at Maple Heights."

He nodded. "Tell him . . . that money . . ."

Paul leaned forward, and Sharon said, "Dad, you don't have to talk about that if you don't want to."

His tremulous smile pierced her heart. "I . . . need to."

She stroked his hand. "All right, Dad."

"Senator Jacobs."

Sharon gulped. "Senator Jacobs? Did . . . did these things come from him?" She picked up the sheet of paper.

Elwood nodded. "He gave me . . . some things. Two boxes . . . briefcase . . . papers."

Sharon looked over at Paul to be sure he heard it all. He nodded and said, "The senator gave you some stuff, Dad?"

Again Elwood nodded. "It was . . . after they said . . . he was missing . . . two weeks after."

Sharon's heart raced. "You saw him *after* he was reported missing?"

Elwood swallowed hard. "He hit my car. He told me not to tell . . . anyone. Gave me . . . the briefcase . . . That's where those were."

"The pen and the card case?"

He nodded. "We didn't open it for a long time . . . I said we ought to destroy everything, but . . ." He sighed.

"But what happened to the Senator?" Paul stood and bent low over his father. "Dad, if you know what became of him—"

"Thirty days," Elwood whispered.

"What?" Sharon looked at Paul in confusion, then back at her father. "Thirty days, what?"

"Destroy the stuff in . . . thirty days."

"But . . . you didn't," Sharon said, thinking of the silver items in the chocolate tin and the unexplained bank deposits.

"No." Elwood drooped and whispered, "He never came back."

Dr. Ridge breezed in through the doorway. "Well, good afternoon, folks. Sorry to keep you waiting. Had an emergency. Elwood, how are you doing?"

Elwood focused on the doctor. "Better."

"That's great. Let me just do a quick exam here, and if everything looks good we'll sign you out and have the ambulance take you over to Maple Heights." Dr. Ridge reached to pull the curtain around the bed, and Sharon and Paul stepped out.

Chapter 19

"Janet, thank you for coming." Sharon led her into a bright, sunny sitting room off the corridor at Maple Heights and sat down with her on a sofa.

"This seems like a pleasant place," Janet said, looking around at the colorful upholstery and curtains, the light wallpaper and well-executed landscapes.

"Yes, I'm told the care is very good, and I hope Dad will be happy here for a while."

"A while?" Janet asked.

Sharon was ill at ease, that was plain. She scrunched up her face before answering. "Vic wants me to come home. He thinks I've neglected him far too long. Now that I've got Dad settled here, he thinks I ought to leave."

"That's understandable," Janet said. Kurt would never stand for a separation this long.

"Well, it's difficult with Dad in the condition he's in."

"Yes. Of course you want to be close enough to visit."

Sharon nodded. "So I thought I'd look into the

long-term care options in our area, and Vic even helped me out with that. He located three this morning that are within ten miles of our house and have good ratings."

"So, you're thinking of moving your father down there?" That might be the best solution, Janet thought, but Sharon looked discouraged.

"When I mentioned it to Dad, he got all upset again."

"Oh, dear."

"Yes. See, Paul and Andrew think that if we move him we ought to sell his house. But Dad didn't like that idea. That's when I called to see if you could come. I'm sorry to keep bothering you like this."

Janet patted her arm. "It's no problem, Sharon. Kurt and I will help you any way we can."

"I know. And Dad thinks a lot of you both. That's why I called you. Thanks." Sharon sniffed. "It's great to have found such a good friend up here."

Janet smiled. "I've enjoyed getting to know you, too, and the fellowship."

"Exactly." Sharon opened her purse and rummaged in it, bringing out a tissue. "I left Paul with Dad so I could talk to you now. I hope he's keeping his promise to remain calm and not talk about sensitive topics."

"Maybe you'd better go back in his room," Janet said.

Sharon nodded. "There's one other thing I wanted to tell you first. Dad told Paul and me quite a tale this morning, before we left the hospital."

Janet entered Elwood's new room five minutes later. Paul was reading an article about lake conservation aloud from the *Sentinel*, and Elwood seemed to be enjoying it.

"Janet," he said when he saw her, and Janet smiled. She hadn't seen him this animated since his stroke.

She went to the bed and took his hand. "You look well, Elwood."

He seemed to struggle to get his thoughts out, but his words were clear. "You tell Sharon . . . don't sell the house."

Janet chuckled. "I see you feel strongly about that."

"Don't . . . sell yet," he said.

She nodded and looked at Sharon. "Is there any hurry?"

"Well, no," Sharon said. "Just concerns about maintenance and all that."

"And vandalism," Paul said, and Sharon glared at him. Janet guessed that Sharon hoped to keep the news of the two break-ins from him.

"How do you feel about moving closer to Sharon?" Janet asked Elwood.

There was a pause, and then he nodded. "Okay."

Janet sat down and looked at Sharon and Paul. "Well, maybe it would be possible to wait until spring and see how everyone feels about it then."

"We could do that," Sharon agreed. "I'll call Geneva. She's in real estate, and she can tell us everything we need to do to get ready. I just hate to leave the place empty all winter."

"Maybe you could rent it," Janet suggested.

Sharon frowned. "But then we'd have to move all of Dad's stuff out."

Elwood sighed. "Go ahead, then. Do what you want."

"No, Dad. I want to do what *you* want. If you think you want to keep the house, then we'll wait."

Janet squeezed his hand gently. "You don't have to make that decision today. But I can see that you're feeling better than you were yesterday."

Elwood looked at Sharon and Paul. "You go away."

Sharon laughed. "What, Dad, you want us to leave?"

"I . . . talk to Janet."

Paul stood up and smiled. "Come on, Sharon, we're persona non grata."

"Just give us a few minutes," Janet said. "Get some coffee or something, then come back." When Sharon and Paul had left, she turned to the old man. "What is it, friend?"

He smiled, and she thought his face looked more natural today than it had the last few times she'd seen him.

"I don't really care . . . about the house. I can't live there anymore."

She nodded. "I expect that's so. I'm sorry."

He inhaled deeply. "You helped me."

"I did?"

"Yes. God forgives."

"Yes, He does." Her heart warmed, and she squeezed his hand gently.

Elwood looked up at her and smiled. "I felt so much guilt. All these years. I carried it around."

"I'm so sorry you lived with that. Is it all gone now?"

He nodded. "The things you told me. It helped. You know?"

"About what?"

"Jacobs. The money."

Janet hesitated. "I know that your children think you got some extra money somewhere, but they don't know where. And they think Senator Jacobs possibly had something to do with it."

Elwood lay back on the pillow. "The police need to know."

"Need to know what, Elwood?"

"I kept the money he gave me."

"Senator Jacobs gave you money?"

"Yes. In a briefcase. And papers. Lots of papers. I hid it all."

Janet swallowed hard. She was tempted to call Kurt again, but she determined that nothing would interrupt the story this time.

"Where did you hide it?"

"At home. For a while." He blinked at her, and tears rolled down his cheeks. Janet took a tissue from the box on the nightstand.

"Then what?" she asked gently.

"He didn't come back." He sighed and was quiet for a long time, then he stirred. "He told me . . . thirty days. He would come back. If he didn't . . . I was supposed to get rid of it."

"But you didn't."

"No. That's when I told Olivia. Andrew thought he saw some trouble over there."

"At the Jacobs house?" Janet asked. She held her breath, anticipating his confirmation.

Elwood nodded. "I told him he was nuts." His cackle of laughter startled Janet. "But when Jacobs didn't come back . . . I knew Andrew was right."

"You think the boys did see something significant that night."

"They must have. Something bad happened. And all this time I knew. I kept quiet."

"You told Olivia," Janet hazarded, and he closed his eyes.

"Not for a long time. But then she found the briefcase." He lay silent, and Janet wondered if the telling had exhausted him. At last he opened his brown eyes and met her gaze. "We opened it. It was . . . full of cash."

"The money for the pesticide study."

"It must have been. Part of it."

"And you used it."

"Not then. But when Geneva went to school . . . we were so broke. We opened a new account and put a thousand dollars in it. God forgive me . . . we used it all over the next few years. The kids . . . Tell them to call the police. I won't hide it anymore."

His eyelids fluttered down. Janet sat beside him in silence, holding his hand, and he slept.

Chapter 20

"He wants to tell the police," Janet said to Kurt over the phone.

"That's probably a good idea. Andrew should tell them his story, too, although Detective Robbins may have already listened to the tape of our interview from Monday."

"I'm going home," Janet told him. "I'm going to call Andrew in off the lake, if he's still out there, and send him to the nursing home. Sharon says they'll call the police when Andrew gets there, and if you want to be there, you can go, too."

"Wonderful! Oops."

"Kurt, what's wrong?"

He sighed. "I let Dave take some time off. He left half an hour ago. I doubt the police would let me tape the session."

"You could ask Elwood," Janet said. "Could they object if he says it's okay?"

"I don't know. They might object to me even being there, if they consider it an official interrogation."

Janet gasped. "You don't think they would

arrest Elwood, do you? He's a sick old man."

There was a pause before Kurt said, "I don't know, babe. Receiving stolen property. We're talking about a huge amount of money here. And what about the documents? Did he say what he did with the papers Jacobs gave him?"

"No. He may even be too tired to talk to the police today," Janet said. "I hope they won't badger him."

"I'll go over there now," Kurt said. "Unless . . ." His voice trailed off.

"Call me." She had the distinct feeling that she was going to miss something important.

Tory and Andrew were walking across the road when Dave arrived at the Fairmonts' house. He slowed his Jeep and rolled down the window.

"Hey! Whatcha doing?"

"Hi," Tory cried with a smile that made his stomach lurch. "We just took the canoe out of the water."

"Been fishing most all day," her uncle said, holding up a string of trout.

"You've sunburned your nose," Dave told him.

Tory shook her head in mock despair. "I told him forty-seven times to put on more sun screen. But does he listen?"

Dave laughed. "I'm guessing not."

"Not more than half the time," she confirmed.

"So, what are you doing out here at three o'clock in the afternoon? Playing hooky?"

"Sort of. Mr. Borden told me to take some comp time, so I thought I'd buzz out here and take another look at the Jacobs house." He hesitated, hoping she would invite herself along, and she didn't disappoint him.

"Can I come?"

"Sure!"

She turned to Andrew and held out her fishing rod. "Do you mind, Uncle Andrew?"

"Oh, skipping out and making me clean the fish. I should have known!"

Tory laughed. "You clean them, and I'll fry them up later. You won't be sorry."

"All right, kiddo." Andrew rearranged his gear and managed to add her rod to his load. "I'll see you later, alligator."

"After a while, crocodile," Tory sang. She hopped around the Jeep and climbed into the passenger seat. "Where's my seat belt?"

Dave laughed. "We're only going fifty more feet down the road."

"You can't be too careful."

He smiled and nodded, glancing over at her before he turned in at the Hillmans' driveway. Tory was the girl next door today, but would she morph into the sophisticated city girl tomorrow? She seemed to be everything he could ask for in a woman, but he was aware that getting to know each other could be a process of disenchantment.

You see a pretty girl, and she looks great, his father had told him once. So you assume everything else about her is great, too.

Dave's experiences in the world of dating had taught him that his father's insight was accurate. Would Tory disappoint him, too?

She had fit in so well with the intellectual crowd at the art exhibit Monday night that it scared him a little. In her print silk skirt and sleeveless top, with upswept hair, she'd looked like a fashion model. Simon, the *Sentinel*'s photographer assigned to the event, had thought so, too. Dave had caught him setting up for a photo of Tory.

"You can't use a picture of her," Dave hissed at him. "She's my date!"

"Lucky you," Simon said. The next day he'd e-mailed three shots of Tory to Dave's computer, with the message, "Let me know if you want any printouts." So far Dave hadn't decided whether to chew him out or ask for the pictures.

But he wanted to know Tory better and to spend more time with her, no matter what the outcome. He turned the engine off and looked over at her. She was watching him from under the brim of her sun visor, smiling and wriggling a bit, as though she was bursting with energy.

"So, what did you want to see?" she asked.

He shrugged. "Just the house. The neighborhood."

"It's still there."

"Yeah." He picked up his digital camera and got out. By the time he reached her door, she had climbed out. "Ever been inside?"

"I don't think so." Tory walked beside him as he circled the cottage and the garage, taking in the weathered shingles, the double sash windows, and the new back deck. He snapped a few shots and then looked down at the lake.

Tory jumped along a row of rocks that lined the cleared path to the shore, where the owners could launch their boat with ease. Dave watched her. She was like an antelope, lean and quick. Her ponytail flipped behind her as she hopped to the next boulder.

She looked back at him and waved. She was just a kid. Her sneakers, cutoff jeans, and hooded, long-sleeved T-shirt added to the image. Dave sauntered down the path to join her. "How was it on the water today?"

"Intense. Hot sun, fidgety uncle, but pretty good fishing this morning. We didn't have one nibble since noon, so we finally gave up. Got some nice brookies earlier, though."

Dave nodded and adjusted the camera settings. "Hold it." She struck an Egyptian goddess pose, and he clicked a picture of her balancing on the rock.

"You done looking at the cottage?" she asked.

"I guess so." He didn't want to leave yet, though.

"We've got cold root beer in the fridge."

He grinned. "Let's go."

When they reached the Jeep, they saw Andrew's car pulling out of the Fairmonts' driveway and heading toward the paved road.

"That's odd," Dave said. "But I suppose if it were an emergency, he would have told us."

"Some people will do anything to get out of cleaning fish," Tory said.

Dave drove up to her grandfather's house. Andrew had left the front door unlocked, and they went into the kitchen.

Tory opened the refrigerator and grimaced at the whole fish. "What did I tell you?" She took out a bottle of root beer and got two glasses from a cupboard. "Ice?"

"Of course."

They took their drinks out on the porch and sat companionably in two rocking chairs. Dave set his camera on the railing and tried to put Mick Tyler and Senator Jacobs out of his mind.

"I wonder if Mom's coming home for supper." Tory swirled the ice in her glass.

"Maybe I should clean those fish for you."

"Nah, it's your afternoon off."

Dave took a long sip of root beer. It would be worth cleaning the trout if she invited him for supper. He looked out across the lake. The air was warm, but there was a stiff breeze, too, troubling the gray water with small waves.

"This is a great place to live," he said.

"Yeah, every time I come up here, I start envying Mom her childhood. But she tells me it wasn't so idyllic. The family was anything but peaceful."

"You wouldn't know it," Dave said.

"Yeah, the dirt road and the lake kind of fool you."

"Where does the road go?" he asked suddenly.

"Right over there."

He laughed. "Smarty pants."

She wrinkled her face at him and drained her glass. "It kind of peters out at the last cottage. But there used to be a woods road. You can still follow it for a ways. I think they did some logging in there once, or something. Grandpa could tell you."

Dave looked down Pine Lane as far as he could see, to where it curved around toward the lake. One cottage beyond the Hillmans' was visible from the porch. The mix of pines and hardwoods, flaming now in vibrant hues, blocked out the others. "That guy, Dunning, says—"

"You mean that lying burglar?"

"Yeah, he's the one. He says he was walking down the road to check one of the cottages."

"I heard, and I don't believe it," Tory said.

"Want to walk down there?"

Her eyes narrowed, and he thought she would refuse. But instead she said, “Sure.” He hung the camera strap around his neck, and they walked down the driveway together, then turned away from the Bordens’ and civilization.

“What do you expect to find?” she asked.

“No idea.” He looked over at her, and she frowned at him just a little. He chuckled.

“What’s funny?”

“When you scowl, your eyebrows almost meet, like your Uncle Andrew’s.”

“Is that an insult?” she asked.

“I didn’t mean it to be.”

“Well, I’m told I look like my father, not the Fairmonts.”

Dave shrugged. “The Fairmonts aren’t bad looking.”

“I suppose not.”

“Not as good as the Schlessers,” he murmured, looking straight ahead.

“Hmm.”

He glanced at her then, and she was smiling. He decided to take a risk. “You know the photographer, Simon Davenport, who was at the reception the other night?”

“I saw him.”

“He saw you, too. He took some shots of you. Do you want to see the pictures?”

“What, they’re leftovers that the paper didn’t use?”

"Something like that. They look pretty good. I can ask him to make a set for you."

"Can you delete them from the system?"

He stared at her, unsure at first whether or not she was serious.

She laughed then. "I'm kidding. I'd put them in my scrapbook. I had lots of fun at the art museum."

"Me, too."

They had reached the end of the road, and Tory stopped. Dave stood beside her, looking down the overgrown path that stretched before them into the woods. Tree limbs hung low overhead, but the track was clearly discernible, and probably still navigable for a ways, he decided. There were even old tire tracks faintly visible.

"Let's follow it for a bit."

She shrugged. "All right."

Dave reached for her hand, and she smiled up at him. The teasing demeanor was gone. He stood still, not wanting to change a thing. After a moment, she whispered, "Come on."

They walked slowly into the dim, cool woods. Dave inhaled deeply, savoring the scents of pine and earth.

"I wonder who owns this," Tory said.

"I guess we could look at the property maps at the town office and find out."

A sudden movement caught his eye. "Shh."

She stopped beside him, and they watched a gray squirrel on a maple limb above them. It chattered at them, then ran out along the limb and leaped to a branch of another tree.

"Do you have squirrels in Providence?" Dave asked.

"Everywhere. They're pests."

He nodded, watching her closely. Her pupils were huge in her hazel irises.

"When are you leaving?" As soon as he asked, he wasn't sure he wanted to know.

"Sunday. I'm due back at work Monday morning."

"Too bad."

"I'll miss you," she said.

"Really?"

She nodded. Her face was all serious, almost sad.

"Can I call you sometime?"

"You'd better."

He laughed. "I was hoping we could do something Saturday."

"Like what?"

"Kurt said we can use their canoe, but maybe you're canoed out after today."

"I'm sure paddling around the lake with you will be entirely different from sitting becalmed with Uncle Andrew and two fishing poles for hours."

"Let's hope so," he said.

"At least we took a lunch."

"Why'd you do it?"

"Spend the day with him, you mean?"

Dave nodded.

"To keep him away from the hospital."

"Ah."

"It worked. Mom and Uncle Paul had the whole day to get Grandpa moved to the nursing home. I just hope Uncle Paul hasn't started a fight and been arrested."

"Now you're kidding, right?"

"Sort of. But Uncle Paul can be as grouchy as Uncle Andrew."

Dave shook his head. "It's a wonder your mother's as good-natured as she is."

"She lives with us Schlessers, remember?"

"Oh, so you're not just good looking, you're good tempered, too?"

"What do you think?"

Dave reached toward her and put his hands on her shoulders. "I think . . ." He swallowed. "I think you're right up therc, on both counts."

Her upper lip twitched, and a slow smile spread across her mouth. "I don't think I've ever liked a man as thoroughly as I do you."

He thought about that. "Do you like your uncles?"

"Not always. But I love them."

He decided it was a remarkable thing to be thoroughly liked by Tory Schlesser.

"Andrew's taking this thing about Mick pretty hard," he noted.

"Yeah, well, he can use that for an excuse for his temper for a while, I guess."

The sun was dropping in the west, beyond the trees and the unseen lake, but a ray stole through the branches and made Tory's eyes glint with flecks of gold.

"Will you come back soon?" he asked.

"I don't know. I guess it depends on Grandpa."

Dave nodded, wondering if this was the moment to kiss her. She wasn't laughing now, but she wasn't moving away from him, either. She watched him keenly, as if her senses were as heightened as his. He wondered if her pulse pounded the way his did. He could feel it in his temple.

He reached up and gently stroked back a tendril of her hair that had escaped her ponytail. "Would you care if I kept copies of the pictures from the art museum?"

"For your dart board?"

He smiled. "Right."

He took hold of her sun visor and pulled it off. She didn't protest, so he let it fall to the ground and bent toward her, conscious of the camera lying against his chest. Their lips met, and he folded her closer anyway. He felt her arms slip around him, warming his back. Her kiss was tentative but sweet, rocking him to his toes.

"Ever been to Providence?" she whispered against his neck.

"No." He lifted the camera strap over his head and bent his knees slightly, gingerly letting it slide to earth beside her visor, then prepared to draw her in for another kiss.

"What's that?" she asked.

He was jerked back from paradise. Tory was staring behind him, along the derelict woods road, and he whirled around. The light was fading, and he couldn't see anything unusual. "What?" he asked, not really caring.

"Over there. Where that bird is. Can't you see metal?"

He saw the flutter that was a warbler settling on a low branch. He squinted and leaned down to her height. A late ray of sunlight gleamed for an instant on something in his line of vision. Just a speck, in the midst of a dark thicket of brush below the bird's perch.

"I see it."

Tory let go of him and walked down the path toward the bushes. He felt chilly as she moved away from him. Why did she have to get the explorer urge now?

He sighed and picked up his camera and her visor. Wouldn't want to step on them in the twilight. As he followed her toward the mass of brush, his adrenaline surged again. It wasn't bushes. It was an artfully constructed pile of evergreen branches. The needles clung to the twigs, but they were turning orange.

Tory reached it first and pulled away a large bough. She turned and stared at him with the branch in her hands. He shivered, knowing what it was, before she spoke in that incredulous, uncomprehending voice.

"Dave, it's a car."

Chapter 21

"Think hard, Mr. Fairmont," said the sergeant.

Andrew closed his eyes and leaned back in his chair. "One of them came out of the garage, I think."

"The Jacobses' garage?"

Andrew rubbed his stubbly cheek with his fingers. "It's so long ago, you know? There were two of them, and two cars."

Sgt. Bedard nodded patiently, but Detective Robbins looked bored.

Kurt had arranged the meeting after Janet's call. To his amazement, both police officers had agreed to come to the *Sentinel* office to hear Andrew's story in person. Kurt had approached Bedard and Robbins by saying he was interviewing Andrew Fairmont for the newspaper in a few minutes. Would they like to be present? Andrew had come straight from fishing, not bothering to change or shave when Kurt called him. It had come together so quickly, Kurt was still expecting a glitch. But here they were, sitting in the conference room with a tape recorder running.

The only thing missing was Dave, but Kurt decided not to bother him this time. Andrew had confirmed his hunch that Dave had left the office and gone straight to Tory. Let them have some fun. Kurt would hand Dave a copy of the tape in the morning.

"And what did he do when he came out of the garage?" Bedard asked.

"He, uh . . ." Andrew's expression cleared. "He gave something to the other guy."

Kurt was instantly alert. Andrew hadn't mentioned that in the first interview.

"What was it?" Bedard asked.

"I don't know. It was too dark. Something small."

"I don't see that this is helping much," Robbins said, reaching for his coffee mug.

Bedard ignored him. "Then what?"

Andrew hesitated. "Before they took off, they did something. Mick and I were huddled behind a rock, and I was afraid the guy standing at the back of the car would see us."

"At the back of the car."

"Yes."

Bedard said, "Where was the other man?"

"He was bending down . . . doing something. And then he went to the front and crouched down. It was like the other guy was waiting for him to finish. Then they said, 'See ya later,' that kind of thing, and they left."

"Any idea what it was the second man was doing?"

Andrew shook his head. "Maybe they had trouble with the lights. I told you they didn't turn the lights on, right?"

"Yes. Did you by any chance hear a car trunk close, anything like that?"

"No. We heard that sound we thought was a gun, and when we got over there . . . I don't think the trunk was open."

Robbins shook his head and looked at Kurt. "If you're planning to run a so-called hot news story with this drivel in tomorrow's paper, I don't see the point."

"You don't see any significance in Mr. Fairmont's memories in connection to Mick Tyler's disappearance?" Kurt asked.

"Frankly, no," Robbins said.

Bedard flipped back through his notebook. "I know you think Tyler's disappearance has to do with this old incident, Mr. Borden, but unless we can document that it had something to do with an actual crime . . ."

"It does," Andrew said fiercely, and they all focused on him. "Senator Jacobs disappeared in early May that year. This thing I'm telling you about happened two or three weeks later, at his cottage in Belgrade. Please make the leap and look into that again."

Bedard sighed. "That's difficult, Mr. Fairmont.

You can't tell us who these two men were, and the only other witness, Mick Tyler, has been missing for ten days."

"My father knows something about it," Andrew said quietly, and Kurt saw desperation in his eyes. "Please. I don't want my father to be hurt. He's very ill, and he's almost eighty years old, but it's time we all had some answers."

"You threatened your father at the hospital last night," Bedard said.

"I didn't threaten him, but it's true I was angry." Andrew covered his face with his hands for a moment. "I should have come to you and let you question him, instead of storming in there. It was wrong of me to do that. But you can still get his statement."

Bedard looked at Robbins. "Might be a good idea. But I'm thinking it's time we at the Waterville P.D. assigned one of our detectives to this case. It's taking too much of my time, and it's not really my beat."

Kurt felt an urgency to act. He liked Bedard. He seemed thoughtful and wise, and he had all the background information on the case. If a new officer took it on, he would have to wade through all the Fairmont family squabbles, Mick's lapses, the burglaries, and Elwood's reticence.

"Please, Sergeant," Kurt said. "I'm asking you to take one more hour on this thing yourself. Please. Elwood Fairmont has been transferred to

Maple Heights. If you could just speak to him. I know he knows something about Senator Jacobs. Maybe not what happened to him, but he does have information, and he's sat on it for more than forty years. But he's ready to talk about it now. He wants to clear things up before he dies. Please, Sergeant."

"But a lot of these things happened in Belgrade," Bedard said.

"That's right." Robbins seemed more interested than he had been for the past half hour. "If anyone's going to be digging up stuff out there, it has to be the state police. I don't know why Waterville's involved, anyway."

"Because of the reporter," Bedard said patiently. "The reporter who didn't show up for work. That's where it started."

"In Belgrade," Robbins noted. "He missed an appointment in Belgrade."

Kurt was afraid the case would degenerate into a territorial dispute between the two law enforcement agencies and Bedard would lose his taste for the investigation.

"Gentlemen, please." Kurt held out his hands in supplication. "What matters here is finding out the truth. I know this is hearsay, but today Elwood Fairmont told my wife and his daughter, Sharon Schlesser, that he saw Senator Jacobs alive two weeks after he disappeared from Washington, D.C. Saw him here in Maine. Now,

Thomas Jacobs's daughter deserves to know what happened to her father. Mick Tyler's wife deserves to know what happened to her husband. And Andrew Fairmont deserves to know that what he saw and heard in 1968 was real."

"There were two cars," Andrew said. "One of them could have been Senator Jacobs's car; I don't know for sure. But his car was never found. You'd think, as long as it's been, it would have turned up."

Bedard scratched his head. "You think it's in the lake? Did they drag it back then?"

"No, nobody ever knew he came back to Maine," Kurt said. "They didn't look for him here."

Robbins rolled his eyes. "That lake has been dragged dozens of times in the past forty-five years. Do you know how many drowning victims we get in Belgrade? Ask any game warden. Swimmers in summer, snowmobilers in winter."

Andrew raised his chin as if about to speak, but at that moment Kurt's cell phone trilled.

Kurt bit his lip and considered not answering it. But no, Janet might be wondering if Andrew was going to get over to the nursing home where the others were waiting.

"Excuse me." He got up and went out into the hall and pushed the talk button.

"Kurt Borden."

"Boss, it's Dave. I need you to get the State Police out here to Pine Lane."

Either the connection was weak, or Dave's voice shook.

"I've got Detective Robbins right here," Kurt said. "What is it?"

"Tory and I went for a walk in the woods, Mr. B. We found Mick Tyler's car."

"Don't touch anything," Dave said. "It will take them at least twenty minutes to get here, maybe thirty."

"But should we look to see if . . ." Tory gestured vaguely toward the brush-covered car.

"No! Don't touch it." Dave felt a bit nauseated by the thought of what Tory might see if she looked in the car windows.

"You know it's Uncle Andrew's friend's car for sure?"

"I've been typing up the description every day for a week. That's his plate number."

She nodded. Her face was pale in the twilight.

"Come on," Dave said. "We'd better get out to the road so we can show them where it is."

They walked in silence to the end of Pine Lane. Dave breathed deeply as they emerged from the woods, trying to make his heart stop hammering.

"Dave, I'm sorry."

"Me, too. I'm sorry you had to be here, but I'm

glad you found it. At least we'll know something now."

"He's in there, isn't he?"

Dave shrugged. "Maybe he hid it and skipped town."

She shook her head. "Someone went to a lot of trouble to hide that car."

He met her direct gaze and then looked away. She was right, and he knew it. "Mick and I weren't close," he said. "I was the new kid, and he was the old lion. He was a good writer, but he was prickly. I'd hardly gotten to know him."

Tory took his hand, and Dave clenched his fingers around hers, not wanting to let go of her ever again.

They stood in silence, waiting. All sorts of practical thoughts started coming to Dave's mind. He should have taken a picture, but it was probably too dark in the woods now. If he said that, Tory might think he was callous, but everyone at the paper would want to know why he hadn't. And he'd have to write the story, no matter how late he got to his computer. He couldn't step aside now and let someone else take over the file.

"You could go up to your house and wait," he said.

"I'm not leaving."

He squeezed her hand. "This is the biggest

story I've ever had. Maybe ever will have. And it feels awful."

She was in his arms again. She pushed the camera aside and rested her head against his chest. He clung to her, feeling her sharp breathing.

"Tory, I may be really busy for the next couple of days. If I can't make it Saturday, it doesn't mean I'm ignoring you."

"I understand."

"I'll call you, no matter how stressed I get."

"Thanks."

"I don't want this to be over Sunday," he whispered.

"Me either."

He took hold of her ponytail and let it slide through his fingers, cool and silky, then tugged it gently until she lifted her head and looked up at him.

"Listen, when the police get here, they'll want to take our statements."

"Will they want to see the car first?" she asked.

"I don't know. But we'll probably have to stand around for a long time waiting. That's how it usually goes. Of course, your house is close by. If they're going to do a lot of measuring and photographing and all that, I'll ask them if you can go home. They can come to the house to get your statement when they're ready."

"Okay." She pressed her lips together and then asked, "Will you be with me?"

"Maybe part of the time. But I'll need to be professional about it. In fact, why don't we walk up to my Jeep now, so I can get a notebook?"

They walked slowly up the dirt lane.

"I'm glad you were with me," she said when they reached his Jeep. He got his notebook and decided to keep the camera with him, though darkness was falling fast. He closed the door and reached for Tory's hand, walking back out the driveway toward the lane.

"I'm glad I didn't just up and take a walk in the forest alone one day and . . ."

He halted at the edge of the road. "Me, too."

"Because I would have kept throwing those branches off it for sure. And then I'd have looked inside." Her voice caught, and he put his arm around her, pulling her close against his side.

"It's okay." He kissed her forehead, just below her hairline, and she sighed and leaned against him.

"Do you believe . . ."

"What?" he asked.

"Do you believe God has a reason for everything that happens? Even things like this?"

He tightened his hold on her. "Absolutely."

"I . . . guess I do, too." She sighed. "I never thought much about God until this week. But Mom and Janet talk about Him all the time, and they read the Bible and pray together."

"Really?" Dave asked. "That's great."

"Yeah. Mom seems so much more peaceful. She's concerned about Grandpa, but she's not all tied up in knots now. Uncle Andrew and Uncle Paul used to make her so tense she couldn't be around them much. But these last few days, she's seemed much more relaxed."

"And you think that has to do with her talking to God."

"I do. And . . ."

Tory hesitated, and Dave tipped her chin up so he could see into her eyes. "What?"

"She's changed so much, and it's a good change. I've started going with them in the morning to pray and read the Bible."

Dave smiled. "I'm glad. Do you believe it?"

"Which part?"

"All of it, but mostly about Jesus, I guess. Do you believe He died for our sins?"

She nodded slowly. "It's a little scary. So different from anything I've thought was important before. But . . . yes, I do. I know I don't understand it all, but . . ."

A car came down Pine Lane from the main road. The headlights were on, but there was no flashing light or siren.

"An unmarked car?" Tory asked.

Dave waited a second to be sure. "No, it's Janet."

Tory pulled in a quick breath. "Should we tell her?"

He shrugged. "Kurt knows anyway. And if we tell Janet, she'll start making coffee and cookies for everyone."

"Who's everyone?"

"The cops, the photographers, the medical examiner if they need one, the TV reporters and cameramen, the drivers of the tow truck and the hearse . . ."

Tory gulped. "Right."

"She'll pray, too," Dave said. "Let's go tell her. Maybe there's time for us to pray with her about all this before the police get here."

Chapter 22

Kurt stood just behind the yellow tape barrier with Dave beside him, watching the investigators work. Tory stayed farther back, with Sharon and her two brothers. Sharon had brought a warm jacket out for her, and Tory stood with her hands shoved in the pockets, staring toward the woods. A few other residents drove down the lane to see what all the ruckus was about.

Policemen went back and forth from the car in the woods to their official vehicles, parked along the edge of Pine Lane and in the driveways of the empty cottages. Sergeant Bedard had come along, following Detective Robbins and Kurt, and the state police had extended him the courtesy of letting him go to the crime scene and view thc car in the woods.

Three state troopers had arrived within the first hour, and Robbins had detailed one of them to take statements from Dave and Tory. Kurt hovered and was not chased away. It was short and straightforward. The kids had strolled down the old woods road at dusk, talking and laughing. Tory had notice a metallic gleam in the sunset rays that pierced the canopy. As soon as they determined that a vehicle was hidden there, Dave had called Kurt on his cell phone, leaving him to notify the authorities.

The state's mobile crime lab rolled down the lane, closely followed by the medical examiner's SUV. Two men got out of the crime lab van and were ushered into the woods by one of the troopers, along with the dour medical examiner.

"Bet he hates getting called out this time of night," Dave said.

"He probably gets ninety percent of his calls at night," Kurt guessed. He pushed the button to illuminate his watch. "You sure you're good for this story?"

"Of course."

"You're pretty close to it," Kurt said.

Dave swung and looked at him anxiously. "Please, Mr. Borden. You won't give it to someone else now, will you?"

"No," Kurt said, "but I should. You're part of the story, and you shouldn't be writing it."

"I can leave my name out," Dave pleaded. "I can just say two people found the car, no names. Or Tory Schlesser and her . . . friend."

Kurt couldn't help smiling. "If the TV crews get wind of it, they'll plaster her name and face all over the late news."

Dave swallowed hard and turned toward where

Tory stood, looking small and vulnerable. “Well, she’s very photogenic.”

“Yes, well, try to keep your face out of camera range, all right? If Tory wants to do TV interviews, that’s okay, but I don’t want you compromising our journalism.”

“There aren’t any TV crews here yet,” Dave said.

“There will be.”

Dave nodded. “I figured.”

“What have you got that they can’t get?” Kurt asked him, drawing him a little aside from the other spectators.

“Well, I can describe the scene perfectly, right down to the rutted woods road and the yellow warbler.”

“Good, that’s good. What else?”

“Well, it’s definitely Mick’s car. I saw the plate. If the police don’t release that, can we still use it?”

“I don’t see why not.” Kurt clapped him on the shoulder. “We’ll scoop everybody else. What else can you tell our readers?”

Dave rubbed his ear lobe. “Well, the branches were mostly pine, I think, and they’d been cut a while.”

“Not fresh.”

“Right.”

“Excellent. So we can deduce that the car has been there a while.”

Dave nodded. "If I get a chance to talk to Robbins later, I'll mention that to him. Of course, the car's probably been sitting there since the day Mick dropped out of sight, but they'll want to have a lengthy autopsy before they post a time of death."

"You got that right. At least they can't deny finding the body. The fact that they called in the M.E. is your confirmation of that."

"The car must have been sealed pretty tight," Dave said. "We didn't notice any . . . odor. We would have, wouldn't we?"

"I'm not good at these things," Kurt said. "I'm guessing you would if, say, the windows were open."

"We haven't had a frost yet," Dave noted.

"No. I expect that decay has started."

They stood in silence for a minute. They could hear voices in the distance and see the beams of powerful spotlights beyond the trees, but the path curved, denying them the sight of the policemen at work.

Wally Reed came hurrying down the road carrying his camera gear. "Kurt! They made me park clear up by your house. What's my best shot?"

"They won't let you in where Mick's car is. Get some generic shots of the cops at work."

Wally nodded. "Who's in charge?"

"Robbins. You know him?"

"Yeah, I know him."

"All right," Kurt said. "And I want you to stay here until they either bring the body out or tow the car with him in it."

"Gotcha." Wally began assembling his flash equipment as he scoped the scene.

"How long do you need to write the story?" Kurt asked Dave.

"Well, say half an hour to get back to the office—"

"You can use my computer at home and e-mail it. I've already got Hilda clearing space on page one. We're bumping the president's trip to Taiwan below the fold and giving you all but one column at the top."

"Great. Then I'd say, maybe an hour."

"You can organize your notes and write it up that fast?"

"I'm planning the lead now, while we wait."

Kurt smiled. "Terrific. So, be at my house within an hour. I'll call Hilda and suggest a headline. How's *Reporter found dead in Belgrade*?"

A man came walking out the woods road carrying a flashlight. When he was almost up to the barrier, Kurt recognized Bedard.

"Sergeant," he called, and Bedard joined him and Dave.

"It's your reporter, all right," Bedard said in a low voice, "but you didn't get that from me."

"Are they doing a decent job?" Kurt asked.

"Oh, yes, the crime lab guys are good, but Robbins . . ." Bedard turned and spat in the grass.

"What's the matter?" Dave's voice was strained.

"Off the record?" Bedard asked.

"Sure," Kurt said.

"He's dragging his feet. It's like he was hoping one of the other SP detectives would beat him here."

"Does he faint at the sight of blood?" Kurt asked.

"Nah, I think he's just slow. Maybe he's lost his edge. I heard he's retiring soon." Bedard looked up the road. A hearse was coming down the lane, stirring up the dust. "Listen, you guys just keep your eyes and ears open."

"Are you leaving?" Dave asked.

"Might as well. Robbins made it clear that it's the state's case. I'm to send him a copy of my file on Tyler by 8 a.m."

He stalked toward his Waterville cruiser, and Dave ran after him. "Can I quote you on that, sir? That you have to hand your case to them now, since it didn't happen in Waterville? I mean, that's on the record, right? And did you see anything else that might . . ."

Wally was shadowing one of the crime lab technicians as he returned to the van for a moment, then left it again. Kurt walked over to where the Fairmonts stood.

"How are you doing?" he asked them generally.

Sharon said, "As well as can be expected. How about you?"

"I'm okay. I guess I sort of expected this."

Tory sniffed. "It's him, isn't it?"

Kurt looked at her, then at Andrew. "The police haven't released that information yet."

"But you know," Andrew said.

Kurt took a deep breath. "I'm sorry, Andrew. They brought in the medical examiner, which tells us there is a body. And . . . well, every indication so far leads me to believe Mick's body is in the car."

Andrew nodded, and Paul swore under his breath.

Sharon shivered. "I think I'll go and help Janet. She's baking frozen cookie dough and making a big pot of coffee." She put her arm around Tory. "Why don't you come, honey?"

Tory shook her head. "I want to stay here a while longer, Mom."

"I'll walk you up there," Paul said. He and Sharon turned and went up the lane.

Tory eyed Kurt. "Is Dave all right?"

"He's doing fine."

"He's good at his job, isn't he?"

Kurt nodded. "He's got the makings of a first-class reporter."

They watched two men get out of the hearse and unload a wheeled stretcher, then roll it toward the yellow police tape. A state trooper stepped forward to talk to them. As Bedard drove away, Dave hurried back toward the barrier, to catch what the trooper was saying to the driver of the hearse. Kurt watched him, feeling detached and old. Dave was him twenty-five years ago, but maybe a little smarter.

"Looks like they're going to bring him out," Andrew said. He was shivering with cold but made no move to leave. Tory leaned up against him and slipped her arm around his waist.

"It could be a while yet," Kurt said. "It depends on how thorough the M.E. wants to be here, and . . . well, it depends on a lot of things."

"They'll take the body to Augusta?" Andrew asked.

"Yes. For sure. And it could be weeks before they release the autopsy results."

"Who will contact his family?"

"The state police. They may have already sent someone to Callie's."

"Mick's mother lives in Palermo," Andrew said.

"I didn't know that."

"His first wife is still in the area, too, I think. He had a boy by his first marriage. The kid's got to be thirty or more now." Andrew shook his head. "Time flies."

Kurt said nothing, but reflected on how little he knew about Mick, even after reading Dave's articles. He'd met Callie, and he knew the couple had two children, both in their early twenties, but that was about it. He sent up a silent prayer for the family.

The men with the gurney headed into the woods. Kurt ambled toward where Dave was questioning the trooper.

Kurt had just poured his second cup of coffee the next morning and was skimming the stories inside Section A when the doorbell rang. He had already reread Dave's story and the other front page articles.

"I'm sorry, Kurt," Sharon said as he opened the door.

"No problem. Come on in." He pulled out a chair in the kitchen so she could join him at the table.

"Dad is being insistent, but I'm not sure the police will go along with having you there when they talk to him."

"Well, if they tell me I can't go in, Elwood will have to understand, but I'd be glad to sit in if the police have no objection," Kurt said.

Janet offered Sharon coffee, but she shook her head. "I've got to get back to the house. Andrew dashed off early for his hearing, and he mentioned last night that he plans to hire a lawyer for Dad today. Paul says he's going with me to the nursing home."

"How about Tory?" Janet asked.

"No, she's staying here and doing laundry at the Fairmont Hotel." Sharon gave a wry smile. "Geneva's coming back up this weekend, just for a couple of days. Paul has to go home again Sunday. I hope we can get things settled as far as the police and Dad's care go."

Kurt dropped by the office first, as Sharon had set the appointment with the police detectives for nine o'clock at Maple Heights. Molly handed him fifteen phone messages as he walked past her desk.

"I have the feeling today's going to be a zinger," Kurt told her.

"Right. I've only been here ten minutes." The phone was ringing again, and Molly picked it up. "Yes, he just walked in. One moment please." She looked up at Kurt expectantly.

"In my office," Kurt said and headed down the hall.

While he was returning the most urgent of the messages, Kendra, the librarian, ducked in and laid a stack of newspapers on his desk. He nodded at her without breaking the phone conversation. Kendra's delivery was his usual morning fare: other newspapers. Tory Schlesser's troubled but beautiful face stared up at him from the front page of the Lewiston *Sun Journal*.

He signed off as quickly as he could. Every major newspaper but the *Sentinel* had run a photo of Tory on the front page—the lovely young woman who had discovered the body.

Kurt rang Dave's extension, and Dave picked up immediately.

"Seen the *Sun Journal* or the *Press Herald* yet?"

"I like the *Bangor Daily News*," Dave replied, a lilt in his voice. "Did you catch Channel 5 this morning?"

"I never do TV news in the morning."

Dave laughed. "She told their reporter that she and her boyfriend were out walking when they found the car."

"Interesting," Kurt said.

"Very."

"You don't sound unhappy."

"Would you be?"

Kurt chuckled. "If I were in your situation, I suppose not."

He called an early news meeting and assigned Joy Liston to help Dave run down the list of contacts they needed to make that day in relation to the Tyler-Jacobs case.

"I expect to see Robbins at the nursing home," Kurt said. "I'll try to bring you a tape of the interview, Dave. That's if they continue to treat Elwood as a witness, not a criminal suspect."

"Can I call Robbins later for an update on Mick?" Dave asked.

"Absolutely. Call the medical examiner's

office, too, although I'm sure they won't have much for you yet." Kurt turned to Joy. "You find out where they took the car. Dave has the name of the towing company and the driver. Talk to him if you can, and then see if you can get anything from the family."

"Got it," Joy said, smiling as she made a note on her reporter's pad.

"Discretion, Joy," Kurt said, and she nodded, as though that was her strong suit.

Terry Fallon's glum face told Kurt his staff was not all happy about the choice he had made for the follow-up assignments, but Kurt couldn't think about that now. His style was to make a decision, then move on.

"Dave, try again to get hold of the Hillman family."

"Detective Robbins said last night he's tried, but they're away for an extended trip."

Kurt frowned. "Anything on Jacobs's daughter?"

Dave winced. "I haven't had time the last couple of days, Mr. Borden. I'm sorry."

"It's all right. Maybe Joy can help you with that angle."

Joy's face beamed.

Kurt consulted his notepad. "Roger, you've got the Common Ground Fair . . ."

"I'm all over it," Roger assured him.

"Good. Terry, this thing with the parking

problems downtown. Any follow-up on that?"

"Yeah, sure." Terry frowned. "My biggest gig today is on the new school plans in Oakland, and there's a planning board meeting tonight."

Kurt nodded and made more notes. "Be on the lookout for local religion features, too," he said. "Lately I've felt we haven't been balanced. Lots of government and education stories, not enough community service and religion."

When he dismissed the staff, Wally was one of the last to leave the room. "Hey, Wally," Kurt said as the photographer passed him.

"Yeah, boss?"

"How you doing?"

"You mean . . . ?"

"I mean in general."

"Not bad."

"The offer for lunch stands. Anytime you go forty-eight hours, okay?"

Wally grimaced. "Hey, I can quit anytime I want."

"I know you can." Kurt decided it would do no good to point out Wally's self-contradictions. "Just let me know when."

Wally walked out, and Kurt realized Terry had not left his seat. Kurt started to pick up his papers and coffee mug, but Terry said, "Talk to you, Kurt?"

Kurt pushed his chair back. "If it's about Mick's desk, I'm not ready to think about that."

Terry looked away. "It's not. It's just . . . How come you didn't pick me for this?"

"I thought Joy would have a gentler touch with the family. No offense intended, Terry. Sometimes widows and bereaved mothers respond better to a woman."

"No, I'm talking about the whole thing. Why is Dave Carpenter doing the big story?"

Kurt looked at his watch. He needed to leave within ten minutes to be sure Robbins didn't get to the nursing home before he did and start questioning Elwood in his absence.

"Terry, this was a choice I had to make the day I reported Mick missing. I looked at the staff I had available. I decided to keep you on the city beat, and you've done well. You've been handling your usual work load and a lot of what Mick would have done. We need people who can do that until we hire another reporter. This other thing is big, but it's temporary. You're holding the ordinary news down while Dave covers the aberration."

Terry didn't seem satisfied. "Is it because he's young and will do whatever you want, the way you want it?"

"You're out of line, Terry." Kurt stood up. "Dave is teachable, yes, but the main reasons I picked him are that he's smart and he's fast." He looked Terry in the eye. "Do you realize Dave put out a sensitive, major article in less than an hour last night? He'd already done a follow-up on the Jacobs case and two local stories earlier in the day. I went over the story on Mick personally before it went to press, and I couldn't find a single content error. I'm not sure you could do that."

"I work hard," Terry said.

"I know you do. I'm not saying you don't. The truth is, some people are born with it. Dave is gifted. I wouldn't say that to his face, but it's true. Get used to it. If he sticks with this business, he'll be taking home awards soon. That's the way it is, and that's why I chose him. I'm not putting down what you do. You're consistent and dependable, and that's crucial to a daily newspaper. Now, excuse me. I have a very important meeting across town."

Chapter 23

Things were a bit tense at the nursing home when he arrived. Sharon and Paul were waiting in the lobby.

"Are the detectives here yet?" Kurt asked.

"No. Andrew's in Dad's room with him and the lawyer," Sharon said.

"How do you feel about that?"

Sharon pressed her lips together. "Pretty good, I guess. He seems competent, and I do think Dad needs legal advice at this point."

Paul nodded. "It's long overdue, if you ask me. I can't believe Dad got mixed up in this crazy thing. You've heard the story, Kurt. What's your take?"

Kurt shook his head. "Hard to say. None of us knows how we would react if we were in your father's place that day Senator Jacobs rammed his car."

Detective Robbins and another man came in, and Robbins introduced Detective Hewitt. Paul went to his father's room and returned with Andrew and the attorney, Edward Stone.

"My father has requested Mr. Stone's presence,

as well as Kurt Borden's," Andrew said, shaking hands with Robbins and Hewitt. "We family members will wait out here. Otherwise it would be very crowded in Dad's room."

Robbins frowned, but Hewitt said, "Thank you, Mr. Fairmont. We're ready to take your father's statement now."

Elwood sat in a wheelchair near the window when they entered. His eyes were bright, and his hearing aids were in place in his ears. He was neatly dressed in khaki pants, a plaid shirt, and a brown cardigan.

Kurt shook his hand. "You're looking well, Elwood."

"Thank you. I see you're getting this on tape?"

"If you don't mind."

Stone stepped forward. "Mr. Fairmont, I'm not sure that's a good idea, to give the media access to this conversation."

Elwood waved his hand at Stone. "I want to get this over with and get it out in the open. I trust Kurt. He won't use it to hurt me."

Stone frowned. "But sometimes media exposure is harmful to people, sir."

"I'm going to tell the truth," Elwood said. "What's the harm in that?"

Stone looked uneasily at Kurt. "As your attorney . . ."

"Hogwash," said Elwood. "I hear what you're

saying, but I'm telling you, I've lived with this long enough. Lying, secrets, all of it."

Kurt said nothing but set up the tape recorder on Elwood's nightstand and took a chair in a corner. He avoided making eye contact with Stone and tried to be as quiet as possible as Hewitt set up his own recorder. The police officers settled in vinyl covered chairs, and Elwood began his tale once more.

Ten minutes later, he reached the end. "I didn't want to use the money, but I couldn't just get rid of it. He'd said to destroy the papers, but he didn't really say anything about the briefcase—what to do with it if he didn't come claim it. I couldn't burn it . . . a brief-case full of cash like that! What would you do? I ask you." Elwood looked around at all of them, his brown eyes glittering in his weary face.

Detective Hewitt shook his head. "But the money was stolen, Mr. Fairmont."

"You don't know that," Stone objected.

"True, but it seems likely that money was stolen from the government."

"I didn't know it," Elwood said. "Not for sure. At the time I thought it was all a put-up job. Someone who didn't like Tom Jacobs put out a rumor that he'd made off with some money belonging to the Agriculture Department. Could be true, could be a lie."

"Why didn't you turn it over to the authorities?" Robbins asked.

Elwood sighed. "Believe me or not, we didn't know what was in the briefcase for a long, long time. I hid it and the boxes of papers up in the attic, behind some other stuff, and didn't tell a soul. When Jacobs didn't come back for them, I just left them there."

"How long?" Robbins asked.

Elwood grimaced. "Years. One day while I was at work, Olivia went on a cleaning jag. When I got home that evening, she had the briefcase down in the kitchen. It was still locked. *What's this,* she says." He drew in a deep breath and exhaled slowly. "I hemmed and I hawed, but eventually she got it out of me. She couldn't believe I'd never opened it. *Senator Jacobs has been gone more than three years,* she says. *Don't you think it's time?*" Elwood looked around at them all, breathing raggedly.

"Take your time, sir," Hewitt said gently.

Elwood nodded. "We forced the lock later that night, after the kids were all in bed."

"What was in it?" Robbins asked.

"Money. You know that."

"How much?"

Elwood peered at him with what Kurt interpreted as distaste. "A lot. About seventy thousand. We were stunned. There were a few other things, too. His silver pen and a couple of letters." He looked toward the attorney. “Olivia and I talked it over, but the amount of the money wasn’t right. It didn’t agree with what they said was missing. So we discussed it over and over; was it the Aggie Department money, or wasn’t it? If it was, it sure wasn’t the whole of it. We just didn’t know what to think.”

“But you didn’t use the money right away,” Hewitt said.

“No.” Elwood reached for his water glass and took a sip. Kurt wondered if the old man was taxing his strength too much, but Elwood went on. “For several years, we just kept quiet. Once or twice we talked about it. Should we leave that money sitting there? What if one of the kids found it? Or what if there was a fire?”

“What prompted you to use the money?” Hewitt asked.

“Geneva started college. It was a real struggle to meet her bills, and Andrew was coming right along after her. Olivia suggested we just take a few hundred out of the briefcase to help pay off Geneva’s tuition for the year.” He shook his head. “I didn’t want to at first. I was very nervous about it, in case it was marked or something. But she kept saying, ‘He gave it to you.’ ”

“Did you think that meant the money belonged to you?” Hewitt asked.

Elwood frowned. “I . . . don’t know. I was confused. I figured he didn’t mean for me to keep it forever. He was planning to come back for it. One time I told Olivia that maybe we should try to give it to Mrs. Jacobs, but she didn't want to do that. She said, 'No one knows we have it, Elwood. It's a gift.'" He lowered his head into his hands and sat immobile in the wheelchair.

"Mr. Fairmont," came Hewitt's quiet, patient voice, "what became of the two boxes of documents Jacobs gave you? Are they still in your attic?"

"No, oh, no. I . . . I wasn't sure if they were important or not, but . . ." Elwood drew a deep breath. "After Olivia found the briefcase, I shipped the papers to my cousin in Nova Scotia and asked her to store them for me. So far as I know, she still has them."

The other men looked at each other.

Stone leaned forward. "Mr. Fairmont, can you supply the name and address of this cousin?"

"Sharon can tell you." The fatigue was showing now in Elwood's voice, and he slumped lower in his chair. "Mildred Orkney. I don't remember the address. It's in my address book at the house. She's getting on in years, but she still lives at the same place."

Stone stood up. "Gentlemen, I think Mr. Fairmont has had enough of an ordeal this morning."

"Oh, you're such a dear!" Marguerite Vaughn swung the door wide and beckoned Janet into her modest kitchen. “I was just wishing for some company.”

Janet carried a covered plate to the table. “I brought you some cookies.”

“Let me put the teakettle on,” her hostess said.

“I’d love a cup of tea, but let me do it.” Janet unzipped her jacket.

“All right. You know where everything is.” Marguerite settled into an old pressed-back oak chair. “I see in the paper you had some doings in your neighborhood last night.”

“Yes, lots of traffic.” Janet took the teakettle to the sink and filled it. “I made lots of cookies for the policemen, but as usual I had a lot left, so I brought you some.”

“Peanut butter?”

“Yes, and snickerdoodles.”

“You cook ’most as good as my mother.”

Janet laughed. “I take that as high praise.” She kissed Marguerite’s wrinkled cheek.

As Janet got out the bone china cups and two silver spoons, Marguerite took the foil off Janet’s plate. “So sad about Michael Tyler,” Marguerite said.

“Did you know him?” Janet asked.

“I knew his parents. He was always a strange boy. But he was a good writer, I’ll give him that.”

“Yes,” Janet murmured.

“Been with the paper a long time. I always look

for his articles. He has a way of saying things." Marguerite shook her head. "And he was poking into the old Jacobs scandal. Has the Jacobs family said anything?"

"I don't think so."

"Mm. Of course, it's pretty much just Charlotte now. Her mother died some time back."

"You knew Charlotte Jacobs?" Janet asked.

"Oh, yes. Knew her when she was Charlotte Jacobs, and when she was Charlotte Kenney. Now she's Charlotte Hyde."

"Really?" Janet asked. She was sure Kurt had mentioned the name Kenney in one of their discussions.

"Yes, the Hydes go way back."

"Oh?"

"Almost as far as the Jacobses."

Janet smiled. "How far is that?"

"Oh, Charlotte belongs to the DAR. That's how I know her so well. Ordinarily, she wouldn't socialize with the likes of me, but after I joined the DAR, she started speaking to me. Of course, she lived in Portland, and I mostly saw her at our state meetings. Then she moved out of state. But we have the same patriot ancestor. She's not so bad, really. But the local people all think she's a snob."

"Who's your common ancestor?" Janet asked.

"Caleb Packard," Marguerite said with pride. "On my mother's side."

The teakettle began to whistle, and Janet jumped to take it off the burner.

"Of course, Charlotte has two others all researched and documented, too, but that's all right. I'm happy knowing I have Caleb. I go down to Augusta every Memorial Day and put a posy on his grave."

Janet poured the hot water carefully over the tea bags. "Marguerite, Kurt and his staff have been trying to reach Charlotte to ask her a few questions about the family, but they haven't been able to get hold of her."

"Hmph," the elderly woman said. "Probably because she remarried. She was Kenney for a long time, but now she's married Albert Hyde, and they've moved into a condominium down in Palm Beach. I was invited to the wedding, but there was no way I could drag my old bones down there."

"Your arthritis bothers you a lot, doesn't it?" Janet asked.

Marguerite reached for a cookie. "Yes, it does. Mm, mm, peanut butter cookies. I don't suppose Charlotte would mind if I gave your husband her new address and telephone number. She doesn't get up here much anymore, but we keep in touch."

Janet took a deep breath. "Are you sure? I wouldn't want to upset her, having people start asking about her father's trouble after all these years."

"I think she'd be glad." Marguerite nodded. "Yes, I'm sure she would. Her father was maligned for years. She'd be happy to know anything that would shed light on that business. As a matter of fact, I clipped the article this morning and was going to send it to her. She was just a girl when it happened, you know. Seventeen, I think."

"How sad."

"Yes, well . . ." Marguerite took another cookie. "She took it hard when her father disappeared. She never believed the things they said about him."

"What kind of things?"

"Well, he was a charmer. All the ladies loved him. Some said he probably ran off to Tahiti or Martinique or some such place with one of his secretaries."

"Really?"

The old woman shrugged. "I'm not saying he did. A powerful man like that wouldn't give up his position for some college girl clerk. Although he was a Democrat." Her eyes glittered. "But the GOP isn't immune to that disease either."

Janet smiled.

"Still, he seemed like a good, solid family man, and he liked being in government," Marguerite went on. "I don't think he'd have just dropped out of sight. Politicians don't like to be anonymous. No, he's been dead these forty years and more."

Chapter 24

When he got back to the newspaper building, Kurt and Dave holed up in Kurt's office.

"The police don't want us releasing what he did with the documents until they find out if they still exist," Kurt said.

Dave nodded. "What about the fact that they found money in the briefcase?"

"Robbins says no. It's touchy, and they aren't charging him with anything at this point, but I think for once Robbins is right. I'd hate to see people bothering Elwood about it. I told the detective we'll do a cautious version. Mr. Fairmont told the police he saw Thomas Jacobs two weeks after the senator's disappearance. You can put in the part about the car collision, and also the part about how the boys saw two cars at Jacobs's cottage several days later."

"You mean we can finally release Mick and Andrew's full story?"

"Yes. Mick was killed over this. The police aren't saying so, but we can. We've got Andrew's statement, and he okayed using it. Let's blow this thing open."

He traded the tape of Elwood's interview for Dave's file on Jacobs and left the reporter in his private office to listen to the cassette. Kurt sank into the chair at Dave's desk in the newsroom. It was late morning, and two of the reporters were at their desks, working on articles. The others were out of the office, presumably on assignments. One copy editor was working, but the sports writers hadn't come in yet, and the photographers' area was empty. Across the aisle diagonally from Kurt was Mick's old desk. The computer was on, with the screen saver placidly going through its paces.

Kurt got up and walked over to the desk. To one side was a row of reference and telephone books. On the other side was a jumbled pile of folders and papers. Kurt decided he'd better go through it and see if there was anything important.

He leafed through the stack and realized most of it was hopelessly out of date. Press releases, notes, copies of memoranda. Kurt sighed and sat down, forcing himself to evaluate each item. At the end of five minutes, the entire stack of papers was in the trash. He eyed the row of books and then glanced toward the receptionist's desk. She wasn't on the phone, which was rare, and appeared to be sorting the day's mail.

"Molly," he called softly.

She looked up, her eyebrows raised, and her

face softened as she noticed where he was sitting. "What can I do for you?"

"Bring me a box or one of those mail bins."

She got up and left the room, returning a moment later with an empty carton that had held copy paper.

"Thanks." Kurt pulled the dictionaries, style manual, and thesaurus from the row and placed them in the box. The phone books would stay here for the next occupant of the desk.

He opened the flat desk drawer. A photo frame lay upside down on top of the collection of office supplies. Kurt turned it over. It was a photo from Mick and Callie's wedding. They stood in a flower-bedecked archway holding hands, wearing their nuptial finery. They were so young!

"They look happy," Molly said, and Kurt realized she was hovering, looking down over his shoulder at the picture.

"Yeah." He sighed and placed it in the box. "Listen, Molly, can you put the rest of his stuff in here?"

"Sure, Kurt. What are you going to do with it?"

"Take it to Callie, I guess."

"Do you think she wants it?"

"I don't know." He ran his hand through his hair, wishing he'd been closer to Mick. *Lord,* he prayed silently, *help me to be a better boss. Help me to know my staff well enough to realize when they're hurting, and give me wisdom as to how I can help them. Most of all, please help me to be better about sharing the Gospel with them.*

How could he witness to the people he worked with if he didn't know their needs beyond the walls of the newsroom? The Bible study on Tuesdays was a start, but it was easy. He liked Dave and Tim, and they had initiated it. It was easy to talk about spiritual things with people who were interested. But he wanted to get to know those he didn't like as well, too. The ones who openly rejected God and scorned Christianity were the ones who most needed the light of the Gospel. Terry, for instance. If he wanted Terry to listen to anything remotely religious, Kurt would have to gain his respect and trust.

He felt Molly's hand, tentative on his shoulder, and he looked up at her.

"I can do this, Kurt," she said.

He nodded and stood up. "Thank you, Molly. I'll call Callie and see if she wants Mick's things."

Molly crinkled up her face. "Maybe you should wait a few days. Let the news sink in."

Kurt nodded. "You're right. That's very sensitive of you."

"Thank you." Her smile was brilliant, and Kurt thought she seemed much more mature and competent without the wad of bubble gum.

"No, thank *you* for your help. Just put the box in the mail room, and I'll wait until after the memorial service."

He went back to Dave's desk, sat down, and flipped open the manila folder Dave had given him. A phone number and "Belgrade town office" were scrawled on the top sheet. Beneath it was the address of Edward and Rita Hillman, in New Jersey. Kurt dialed information and asked for the Hillmans' number.

A feminine voice responded after three rings. Startled, Kurt asked, "Mrs. Hillman?"

"Yes."

Kurt introduced himself as her summer neighbor in Belgrade, Maine.

"Oh, yes, Mr. Borden. I remember you. You have the house just above us."

"That's right. Mrs. Hillman—"

"Rita."

"Rita, were you aware that the Maine State Police have been trying to contact you recently?"

"No, why? Has there been vandalism at the cottage?"

It was a prime fear of vacation home owners, and Kurt hastened to put her at ease on that score. "No, nothing like that. It has to do with a previous owner of your lakefront property."

"You mean Senator Jacobs?"

"Well, yes."

"We saw something about it on the news this

morning. A reporter was killed up there or something."

"That's right."

"Was it near the house?"

"His car was found down below, in the woods at the end of the lane."

"Dear me," Mrs. Hillman said.

"The police said they tried to reach you, but you were away," Kurt went on.

"That's the first I've heard of it. We've been right here since we left Maine a month ago."

Kurt chatted for a few more minutes. Yes, the foliage was starting to turn. It looked as if this would be a good year for leaf peepers. The Hillmans thought they might run up for a weekend soon.

Finally Kurt got around to the real purpose of his call.

"Rita, did you know that I'm city editor at the *Morning Sentinel* in Waterville?"

"Oh, that's right. I was thinking you were retired."

Kurt smiled. "Not yet."

"But that means you knew that reporter who was killed."

"Yes. He was our best writer."

"Oh, I'm so sorry."

Quickly Kurt explained to her what Mick's last assignment had been, and why he'd been poking around on Pine Lane when he met his death.

"You sent him out to our house?" Her voice held a tone of incredulity.

"Well, yes. I didn't know at first that the house Jacobs owned was your house, but Mick found out. There's probably nothing significant to be found there after all these years, but I wondered if there's any possibility you'd give permission for me and one of my staff to tour the house. Now, if that's too big an imposition . . ."

"Well, sure, I don't see a problem with that. I mean, you'd be there, right?"

"Yes, if you want, and my wife, Janet, could go along, too."

"Oh, I know Janet. She makes the most divine mint iced tea."

Kurt smiled. "Does she ever. We'd just like for the reporter to be able to get a feel for the layout of the house and picture what it was like when the Jacobs family lived there."

"I'll ask Ed, but I don't think he'll mind. If he says it's all right, I'll call you back and tell you where to get the keys."

Kurt gave her his number and hung up. Molly was just leaving the room with the carton of Mick's possessions, and Kurt got up and followed her to the door of the mail room.

"Molly, have you heard about the Bible study some of us have at noon on Tuesdays?"

"Sure, I heard about it." She eyed him uncertainly.

Kurt shrugged. "Well, I just wanted you to know that anyone who wants to come is welcome."

She set the box down. "Well, thanks, but it's not really my thing."

Kurt nodded. "Okay."

"It's not that I'm anti-God or anything." She cocked her head to one side, and her eyes were wide open and earnest. "I believe in God. I just don't think you have to . . . do God things all the time, you know?"

"Uh-huh." Kurt wondered what "God things" consisted of.

"Besides, Tuesday is the day Joy and I go to lunch together."

"It's okay. I just wanted to invite you."

"Sure. That's cool. If I have any questions about the Bible, I'll know who to ask."

He smiled. "That's fine, but you can let me know if you need help on other things, too."

"Are you all right?" she asked, frowning at him.

"I'm fine. It's just . . . well, I realized that I didn't know much about Mick until a few days before he disappeared. I was paying attention to his work, but maybe if I'd paid a little more attention to his personal needs, I could have helped him out. I don't know."

"Guilt?" Molly asked. "I guess that's not uncommon, but it's not like he killed himself. The police are sure he didn't, right?"

"Oh, absolutely."

"So, you couldn't have saved his life or anything."

"No, that's not what I mean. I was thinking more of . . . maybe just talking to him about his problems and showing more sympathy. I believe God has solutions for every hard spot we're going through. I'm not saying I could have changed things for Mick, but maybe I could have given him some direction and encouraged him."

Her puzzled frown told Kurt she was thinking hard about what he had said. She looked up at him again. "And this Bible club has something to do with that?"

"Well, we read the Bible and talk about what God says in it, and how that applies to our everyday lives. Because the Bible isn't just an ancient story. It's relevant to us today."

She nodded. "I'll tell Joy. She says she has an 'inquiring mind.' Maybe some Tuesday we'll surprise you."

Janet vacuumed the living room drapes and cleaned all the windows on the front of the house, so she could watch the driveway as she worked. When Kurt drove in, she snatched a key ring from the coffee table and ran outside. Dave and one of the young photographers from the newspaper were getting out of Kurt's car, too.

"Did you get them?" Kurt asked.

"The keys or the flowers?"

He laughed. "I meant the Hillmans' keys, but if you got the flowers, that's good."

"They came right after you called. They're beautiful."

He smiled and gave her a quick kiss. "What about the keys?"

"All set." She dangled them in front of him. "That's the front door, and that's the garage. Rita had called her niece at the grill and told her I was coming for them."

"The things you learn." Kurt shook his head.

"Indeed. Wait until you see what else I have for you."

"Oh?"

She grinned and held out the rose-sprinkled slip of paper Marguerite had given her. Kurt squinted at it, then whooped.

"Charlotte Jacobs Hyde! Dave, look at this! Janet found the senator's daughter. She has a new name." He scooped Janet into his arms.

"Happy anniversary," she murmured.

He smiled down at her. "Don't forget our big date tonight."

"I won't. I'll be ready at six." She glanced at her watch. "Come on, we've only got seven hours to investigate the Hillmans' house."

A Channel 8 television truck rolled down the lane, and a state police cruiser came out from the direction of the crime scene.

"Pretty busy here today?" Kurt asked.

"Some traffic. Not too bad. The crime lab guys are still at it."

"At least the TV people aren't swarming the Hillmans' house yet," Dave said.

"Let's leave the car here," Kurt suggested. "Then we won't draw their attention to it."

They walked down the lane to the next driveway and approached the shingled cottage. Kurt fitted the key into the lock on the porch door. Janet felt a bit out of place as they entered the empty house. She caught herself tiptoeing.

"Looks like they've remodeled since the Jacobs family owned it," Kurt said, noting the sheetrocked walls and modern kitchen appliances. The living room was dominated by a fieldstone fireplace. The chairs and sagging sofa were definitely "camp" furniture—family discards and yard sale finds. A bedroom opened to the side, and a bathroom with a shower jutted out beside the back deck. Upstairs the walls were not finished, and there was no ceiling. The underside of the roof could be seen in each of the three small bedrooms and the bathroom. The partitions between the rooms went only about a foot higher than Kurt's head.

"You'd have thought they would have had something fancier," Janet said.

"Back then people lived simpler," Dave suggested.

Kurt nodded. "The Jacobses bought this when they were just ordinary folks. They liked the location, so they kept it."

The rooms were bare of amenities. They found linens wrapped in plastic in a closet. The mattresses were covered with plain sheets. Joe, the photographer, snapped a few pictures.

"Wonder which room the senator used," Dave said, looking out a window over the back deck.

"Probably the downstairs." Kurt went to stand beside him.

Janet nodded. "That one's bigger and more private, and it's got a great view. Definitely the master bedroom."

They found nothing significant in the cottage, and after observing each room they went out and locked the door.

"Want to look in the garage?" Kurt asked.

"Sure," Dave said, but without much eagerness.

Kurt undid the padlock and rolled the door open. The small building held a push lawnmower, a gas grill, tools, water skis, and life jackets. Overhead a canoe hung from the rafters, and the back wall was covered with old Maine license plates. Janet wandered around, looking at the collection of summer paraphernalia.

"Some of those license plates go back before the senator's day," she said. A plate for nearly every year hung on the wall, starting in 1927, up until 1966.

"1943 is missing," Kurt said, eyeing the wall.

Janet checked, and he was right. "There's no space for it."

"I'm sure it's nothing," Kurt said.

Dave frowned. "My dad's a collector. I seem to remember they didn't make plates in 1943. I'll look into it."

Joe clicked several photos of the license plate display and the other items inside the garage, and they went out into the sunshine. Kurt locked the door and took Janet's hand. "Well, I guess it's back to the old grind."

"Say, Mrs. Borden, maybe you should call the senator's daughter first," Dave said as they walked up the lane.

Janet frowned. "Do you think so? I can if you want."

Dave looked at Kurt. "I've got to call all those cops again this afternoon, and the M.E.'s office. Joy is up to her ears in the story on Mick's family and the memorial arrangements."

Kurt nodded. "All right. Mrs. Hyde might take it better if a concerned neighbor calls than if a reporter tracks her down and starts asking personal questions."

"I'll ask her if she'd mind talking to you," Janet said, "but what if she says she would mind?"

"You'll charm her into giving a phone interview, I'm sure," Kurt said.

• • •

It was nearly quarter past five, and Kurt knew he had to get free of the office somehow. Tonight had to be perfect for Janet. Thirty years of faithfulness was nothing to be sneezed at, but they were celebrating much more than that. Kurt intended to show her tonight how deeply he loved her and appreciated her. He didn't want to imagine what his life would have been like without Janet.

Take today, for instance. In the middle of the chaos, she had cheered an elderly friend, helped him investigate the cottage, and tracked down Charlotte Jacobs Hyde. Her excitement when she'd phoned him at the office just before three o'clock was so vivid, he smiled remembering it.

Charlotte was willing to talk to Janet. In fact, she'd revealed that she had possession of some of the senator's old records—not his official papers, but the old household records. After he disappeared, his widow remarried, and Charlotte didn't like her new stepfather. She'd never lived with him and her mother, but had roomed with a girlfriend until her first marriage. Her mother let her have whatever she wanted out of the Washington house and the summer cottage as mementos, however. So Charlotte kept a lot of things, including a household account book.

"She's going to express mail some things to me. What do you think of that?" Janet's voice had risen with animation.

"And you asked her if you could share it with your husband, the newspaper editor, and the world at large?" Kurt had asked.

"I sure did. And she said Dave can call her Monday. Honey, she's so happy you're trying to find out what happened to her father, I think she'd deliver the records in person if she weren't attending her granddaughter's wedding tomorrow. Oh, and she told me to wish you a happy anniversary."

Kurt grinned. Leave it to Janet. He rubbed his scratchy jaw. Better shave before he went home. He glanced at his watch. No time. Ah, well, it wouldn't be the first time he shaved in the car.

He stopped by Dave's desk.

"I'm wrapping up the police update," Dave said.

"Great. We'll run that and Joy's story on Mick's memorial service on page one, with the fire in Sidney and the bridge repair photo. The feature on the Jacobs house will be on the front of the local section with two of Joe's pictures of the interior of the cottage."

Dave nodded. "I can't wait to talk to the senator's daughter. That ought to be a great story."

"I'm sure it will be. Maybe more than one. Charlotte sounds like a character. She's probably got a million stories."

"Memories of her father and summers in Belgrade," Dave said, a dreamy look settling in his eyes. "Statesmen she's met . . . high society parties . . ."

Kurt glanced at the clock on the wall. "Listen, I've got to run. Hilda seems to have everything under control."

Dave looked over at the night editor's desk and nodded. "I'll be leaving soon, too. Oh, and Kurt, Detective Hewitt is much more cooperative than Robbins. He told me they'll take a closer look at William Dunning."

"Great. Of course, we can't print that."

"No, but if they get results we can. Now that they have Mick's body, they need to find the motive and the weapon."

"Cause of death yet?"

Dave shook his head. "Not officially, though Hewitt told me there was no weapon in the car. That implies there's a weapon somewhere, right?"

"He must have been shot."

"Probably," Dave agreed, "but they're not saying so. The M.E.'s office says don't expect anything until the middle of next week."

Kurt drove toward Belgrade as quickly as he could. That wasn't very fast, since he had to drive through town in Waterville, then the small town of Oakland before he finally hit a rural road with a 50-mile-per-hour speed limit to Belgrade. Once he reached that point, he put the cruise control on and reached for the electric razor he'd laid on the passenger seat. It was getting dark, but that didn't matter. If he could get the whiskers off during his last ten miles of road, he'd have time to take a quick shower and change his clothes before he and Janet left for the restaurant.

He slowed for the intersection with Route 27 and headed toward Belgrade Lakes. Pine Lane branched off the main road a few miles out, along the lake shore. He eased the car back up to 50 and pushed the cruise button again.

Her gift. What did I do with her gift?

He swiveled to look quickly at the back seat. *Whew.* It was there, professionally wrapped at the store and ready. His mind drifted back to Mick Tyler and the lack of a weapon at the crime scene. Maybe he was stabbed or clubbed to death. It didn't have to be a gun.

Suddenly Kurt realized the car behind him was zooming up on his left. *Guess he's in a hurry.* He held the wheel steady with his left hand while he continued shaving with his right. The light car in the other lane was beside his but didn't seem to be gaining. It was a four-door sedan. A Saturn, he thought. Kurt braked slightly, hoping to drop behind and get the car past him, when suddenly it swerved toward him.

He dropped his razor and grabbed the steering wheel with both hands, but it was too late. The tires on the passenger side hit the gravel, and Kurt's car lurched. He tried to correct, but the other car was still there, too close.

Chapter 25

Kurt clutched his forehead and gasped for breath. The car had stopped spinning, and the air bag had deflated. He must have lived through the crash. He inhaled carefully, and pain lanced his right side. He swallowed, tasting blood. His fingers shook as he fumbled to unfasten his seat belt, not finding the button at first.

A rap on the glass near his ear made him jump, and he gasped at the pain again. Someone stood beside the car. Now the person was trying to open the door; he could hear the door handle being worked. But of course it was locked. Kurt reached along the door panel, searching for the inside lever. At last he pulled the release, sending another wave of nauseating pain through his body.

"Are you all right?" A woman opened the door wide and stooped toward him.

"I . . ." Kurt frowned up at her.

"I saw you go off the road," she said. "Do you need help?"

"Thanks. I . . ." Kurt gulped. "There was

another car. A Saturn, I think. White or beige. Did you see it?"

She looked down the road, and Kurt realized his car had landed pointing back toward Belgrade Village and Augusta.

"I saw him," the woman said. "He kept going. I was back a ways behind you, and I saw everything. Are you hurt?"

"I . . . maybe . . . yes. Thanks for stopping," Kurt said. It hurt to move his arm. He wondered if he would be able to get out of the car. Maybe he should try to get back on the road and just drive home. Janet would do whatever was needed.

"Sir, your head is bleeding," the woman said.

Kurt took a couple of ragged breaths and knew he should see a doctor. "Can you call the police?"

"Why don't I just take you to the hospital?" She placed her hand under his elbow. "Come on, it will be faster. I'll take you right to MaineGeneral."

"Can't you call . . ."

"I don't have a cell phone," she said.

"I do . . . somewhere." Kurt patted his breast pocket, but the phone wasn't there, and he couldn't remember where it was. Had he left it on the dashboard? Or the passenger seat? No, that was his razor.

"Come on," she said again.

"My house is . . ." Kurt swallowed, again

tasting blood. He closed his eyes for a moment. "Can you just go call an ambulance, please? I think I need it." He opened his eyes and stared in numb disbelief at the barrel of a pistol.

"I said come with me." Her voice was hard as flint.

Kurt drew as deep a breath as he could and tried to move his leg out the door. He gasped at the pain that sliced through his side once more. A beam of light swept over the woman and became a glare. She wore a short wool jacket and dark pants. Kurt tried to see her face, but looking up sent knives of pain through his neck, and he lowered his gaze to her hands again. The gun was gone. Another vehicle drew up on the shoulder of the road behind Kurt's car, and the light disappeared. He heard a car door close, but it sounded far away. Leaning back against the seat, he closed his eyes again.

"Sir, are you all right?" a man's voice said, close to him.

Kurt opened his eyes once more, but the effort it took was exhausting. "No, I'm not. My side. And my—my arm. I guess I bumped my head, too."

"I'm a fireman, and I have first aid training. I'm off duty, but I've got my cell here. Let me call an ambulance, and I'll try to make you more comfortable."

"Thanks," Kurt managed. The woman was

gone. Had he imagined it? No, she was real. But the gun? He wasn't sure.

Janet! She'll be so scared! He tried to send up a prayer, but the words wouldn't form in his mind. Suddenly he remembered that it was their anniversary, and Janet was waiting for him to take her to dinner.

"My wife," he choked.

"Take it easy, sir," the man beside him said. "We'll contact her. Just relax. The ambulance is on the way."

Kurt let himself slip into the warm darkness.

Paul Fairmont drove his rental car up Route 27, probably too fast, but traffic was light and the road had recently been rebuilt. He hoped Andrew was at the house and could fill him in on everything the lawyer had said about their father's situation. They needed to get Dad settled in Massachusetts near Sharon. That would be the best solution—get him away from all this craziness.

Just before the entrance to Pine Lane, a tow truck with its yellow bubble light flashing was backing up on the left shoulder. Paul slowed and peered at the vehicle the driver was preparing to tow. His pulse took a dive, and he flipped on his signal, pulled into the dirt road and stopped.

The tow truck's driver leaned out his window, looking behind him as his assistant directed him in backing closer to a dark Toyota sedan. The driver's side front fender and door panel were crumpled.

Paul swallowed hard. "Hey!" The two men stared at him. "Is that Kurt Borden's car?"

"Dunno," the driver said. "An ambulance was leaving when we got here, and a trooper told us to tow this car to the garage. Said he'd stop by with the paperwork later."

"Where'd the cop go?"

The second man pointed toward where Paul had left his own car. "Down there."

Paul hurried back to his compact and spun gravel as he headed down Pine Lane. Sure enough, a police car was sitting in the Bordens' driveway. Paul parked at the edge of the lawn and rushed to the door. It was slightly open, and he could see a uniformed officer inside. Janet stood talking to him, her face pale. She was dressed in an elegant amethyst dress of lace and chiffon. Paul had never seen her so lavishly turned out. She wore more makeup than was her custom, but it wasn't overdone, just . . . classy, he decided. Kurt was a lucky man. Except that . . .

Janet saw him and caught her breath. "Paul!"

He stepped into the hallway and glanced at the officer. "I'm sorry, Janet. I didn't mean to intrude, but I saw Kurt's car being towed. I thought perhaps I could help you out."

"Thank you." She clasped his hand. "Officer

Tilton just told me about it." She looked at the policeman and said, "This is Paul Fairmont, a friend of the family."

"Is Kurt going to be all right?" Paul asked.

"He had some injuries, and the ambulance took him to MaineGeneral in Waterville," Tilton said.

"Can I take you there, Janet?"

She threw him a grateful glance. "Thank you. I'm a little shaky right now. I'm not sure I could drive myself."

"I'd be happy to take you," Paul said. "I'll wait outside."

She nodded. "I'll just be a moment."

Paul stood leaning against his car. The trooper came out a moment later, and Paul approached him as he opened the door of his cruiser.

"How bad is it, officer?"

Tilton shrugged. "Hard to say. Head injury. They always bleed a lot. But he was conscious when they put him in the bus. They had him on a spinal board. Might be some neck damage and internal injuries. Mr. Borden was in a lot of pain."

Paul winced. "Thank you. Do you think Mrs. Borden is all right? Is there anything else I should know?"

"No, she seems like a level-headed lady."

The officer got into the car and drove off. Janet came out of the house and paused on the steps to be sure the door was locked. She had put a black sweater over her dress, and she carried a small, black clutch purse.

Paul opened the car door for her. "If you don't mind my saying so, you look stunning, Janet."

She smiled as she climbed in. "Thank you. I thought of changing to jeans, but I didn't want to take the time. I do feel a bit overdressed for the ER."

Paul closed the door and went around to the driver's side. "Just relax, Janet. I'll get you there quickly and safely." He reached over and squeezed her hand, then started the engine.

"I've got my phone," she said. "Do you want me to call someone so they'll know where you are?"

"I left Sharon at the nursing home with Dad. Is Andrew at the house?"

"I don't think so. And Tory's off on the lake with Dave."

"Let's wait until we know something, then," Paul said. "When they tell us Kurt's going to be okay, we'll tell everyone the good news."

She nodded. "I figured I'd wait a bit before telling my children. They've all called today to wish us a happy anniversary."

"It's your anniversary?" No wonder she was so dressed up. This was a big night.

"Thirty years," she said with a nod. "But the children all live out of state, so I'll wait to call them back with this news. No sense getting them all worked up until I know how bad it is."

They reached the corner, and Paul noted that Kurt's car and the tow truck were gone. Janet fell silent, and Paul glanced over at her as he turned onto the paved road. She squeezed her lips into a flat line, but her eyes were serene. She must be worried to pieces. From what the policeman said, Kurt's condition sounded serious, and Paul knew head injuries weren't to be taken lightly.

"Officer Tilton said someone forced Kurt off the road," Janet told him.

"I saw that his car had hit something," Paul said, "but there was no other vehicle there, at least not that I saw. Just the tow truck."

"They drove off. Hit and run."

"Do you think it was deliberate?"

She caught a breath. "The officer didn't say so, but I told him about . . ." She turned to face him squarely. "Kurt's had some threatening phone calls lately. It's this thing with Mick and your father and Senator Jacobs. Someone doesn't want it to come out."

"I'm sorry," Paul said. "Janet, if there's anything else I can do to help you, please don't hesitate to ask."

"Thank you." She smiled and squared her shoulders. "God is in charge. I'm trusting Him in all of this. But I know He uses people—people like you, Paul, to comfort and aid His children."

Paul thought about that. He wasn't even sure he believed God was real. Even so, he wanted to fulfill Janet's trust in him and make sure she was taken care of while Kurt was unable to be at her side. If somehow that was part of God's game plan, he guessed he didn't mind.

Andrew drove slowly down Pine Lane. He was tired, very tired. Arranging for his father's care and his legal defense, if needed, enervated him. He was beginning to appreciate all Sharon had done.

The Bordens' porch light was the only illumination at their house. *That's right. Tonight is Kurt and Janet's anniversary.* Kurt had mentioned their date to him this morning before he left the nursing home. Andrew envied Kurt his long, secure marriage. The Bordens seemed genuinely devoted to each other. It made him think of Carol with a flicker of longing. As he turned in at the driveway to the farmhouse, he decided to call her first thing and tell her that he missed her. He wouldn't mess up this marriage like he had the first one. It was worth making the effort.

The kitchen light was on, and Tory's car and Dave's Jeep were in the yard. He mounted the porch steps and tried the door, but it was locked. With a sigh, he pulled out his key ring. Where was Tory, anyway? He'd hoped she'd be here and have supper ready. Probably out rambling with Dave again, but they ought to be back. It was dark. Had Tory said something about going out in the boat? He'd about decided the reporter was good enough for his niece. Maybe. Dave had better behave himself.

Andrew smiled. Just look at him, getting all protective over Tory. It wasn't like she was his daughter. He wondered what Vic Schlesser would think of Dave.

He turned to face the driveway, hoping to get more light to help him select the right key. Someone stepped out of the shadow of the rose bush to the left of the steps.

"Good evening, Mr. Fairmont."

Andrew's heart raced. He blinked at the man. "Hello. Do I know you?"

"Not yet. Please get back in the car."

Andrew stiffened. "Why should I?"

The man raised his hand, and Andrew saw the gun. He gulped.

"On the contrary," the man said, "why shouldn't you?"

Chapter 26

Janet followed the intern into the examining room off the ER. She schooled herself to keep her face from showing any shock or dismay. The doctor had warned her that Kurt was hooked to an IV and several monitoring devices. The cut on his scalp had been stitched and bandaged, and he was wearing a neck brace and support for his cracked ribs. She could see him for a few minutes before he was admitted and transferred upstairs.

Even with the preparation, she had to pause for a moment before approaching the bed. They had cleaned him up, she was sure, but there were still traces of blood on his cheek and forehead, and a few splotches on his shirt. His face was gray. She had never acknowledged that Kurt was middle-aged, but he seemed to have gained fifteen years since she and Dave toured the Hillmans' cottage with him that morning. For the first time she noticed the fine lines at the corners of his eyes, and his hair seemed to have faded a shade.

"Are you all right, Mrs. Borden?" The intern pulled a chair into place for her.

“Yes.” She stepped forward, and Kurt opened his eyes. His face lit up when he saw her, and at once his youthful demeanor returned.

“Jan!”

She grabbed his hand, careful not to touch the intravenous line. “Honey, you look awful!”

He laughed and then winced. “Kiss me anyway. I was so worried about you.”

“You were worried about me?” She shook her head and bent to kiss him. “The doctor says you’re going to make it.”

“Was there any doubt?”

“I don’t think so. I just didn’t know much until I got here. It was hard not to worry. I had to trust the Lord to take care of you.”

He smiled and reached up with his free hand to stroke her hair. “Was that hard? You’ve taken such good care of me, you probably didn’t want Someone Else doing that.”

“Aw, you.” She kissed him again and settled into the chair.

“You look gorgeous,” he said.

Janet smiled and squeezed his hand. “Thanks.”

“Scared you pretty good, didn’t I?” he asked.

She nodded. “It’s every woman’s nightmare. You’re all dolled up for a big night with your sweetie, and the doorbell rings. You look through the peep hole, and there’s this clean-cut man in a Smokey Bear hat waiting to drop the bomb.”

"I'm sorry I did that to you."

"You didn't do it. The guy who ran you off the road did. The officer said someone forced you off the road and left you there bleeding."

Kurt frowned. "There was another car. It happened really fast." He yawned. "I'm sorry, babe. They gave me something, and I'm groggy. Are they keeping me here tonight?"

"At least. It's all right, honey. You can sleep. I'll be right here."

He smiled, and she wondered why she'd thought he had aged. He was the same man she'd married, only better.

"I'm sorry about tonight. My timing is horrible." His eyelids were drooping.

"It's all right. Paul's calling the restaurant to cancel the reservation. I told him to pick Sharon up and use the theater tickets."

"Paul Fairmont?" Kurt seemed to be making an effort to focus.

"He brought me to the hospital. You don't mind if they use the tickets, do you?"

"No." He rubbed his chin and scowled. "I only shaved one side. You said you got the flowers, right?"

"Yes, honey. They're perfect." She was going to say that they must have cost a fortune, but she thought better of it. Instead, she said, "I love you."

He pulled in a deep breath and his eyes closed.

• • •

Dave pulled the canoe up on the sand. Tory grabbed the two life jackets and her backpack.

"Looks like the Bordens are gone," she said, glancing toward the dark house.

"Yeah, Janet told me to just leave everything on the deck if they left before we got back." He took the two paddles out, and they walked up the path.

"Come on over to my house," Tory said. "We'll get something to eat."

"Your house." Dave laughed and set the paddles down.

"Yeah, yeah. Grandpa's house, okay?"

"Okay. What have you got?"

"What do you care? It's free."

He pulled her close and kissed her. He'd been wanting to do that for the last hour, but canoes weren't conducive to romance, he'd decided. The idea was fine, gliding over the still water together in the moonlight and all that, but when it came down to logistics, climbing over the thwarts to get close to the lady could be downright dangerous.

Tory clung to him and stroked his back gently, encouraging him to extend the moment. Tonight was perfect. Absolutely sublime.

She snuggled down against his chest with a soft sigh.

"What are you thinking?" he whispered.

"It's like we're Janet and Kurt, standing here on

their deck. Did you know they've been married thirty years?"

Dave smiled. "I think the boss mentioned it twenty or thirty times this week."

"Thirty years."

"Yeah." He looked over her head, across the glittering water. "Tory, I hope I'm with you thirty years from now."

She straightened slowly and peered at him. "I should probably say something about how it's awfully soon to be thinking like that, shouldn't I?"

"Should you?" He bent and kissed her again, sliding his fingers through her hair. She squeezed him, and Dave wondered why he'd thought dating was so complicated. It was simple with Tory. He sent up a swift, silent word of gratitude to God for bringing her into his life.

When he released her, she held him close for a moment and then pushed away. "Come on. Aren't you hungry?"

He let her lead him by the hand down the steps and around to the driveway, then down the dirt road toward the Fairmonts' house. Had he rushed things? The prospect of a lifetime together might have scared her a little, but Dave knew he was ready. Every moment he spent with her made him long to be with her always. Everything he learned about her made him want to know more, to immerse himself in Toryology.

They cut through the grove of pines where he and Janet had investigated the car the week before, coming toward the driveway from the side. Dave heard voices. He stopped, pulling Tory's hand to make her stop, too, at the edge of the pines.

"Get in," a man said. "You're driving."

"That's the car Uncle Andrew rented this time," Tory whispered.

Dave stared at the two men getting into the car. The moonlight illuminated the front yard. He didn't recognize the man opening the passenger door, but he had an impression of a large, older man. Was it his posture, or the way the moonlight gleamed on his glasses?

A gun!

The stranger held a pistol, Dave was certain. He pulled Tory back into the shadows.

"Don't let them see us! That guy's got a gun."

Tory gasped. "Are you sure?"

"Yes."

"Then Uncle Andrew's in trouble. Do you have your cell phone?"

"No, I left it in the Jeep so I couldn't drop it in the lake." The car backed around on the grass, then rolled down the drive toward them. Dave turned his face away and leaned against Tory, behind a big tree. "Don't move 'til they're gone."

When the lights of Andrew's car swept out onto Pine Lane, he seized Tory's hand and ran with her to his Jeep.

"Hop in."
"Are we following them?"
"We've got to. Don't we?"
He started the engine and grabbed his phone from the dashboard.
"Cool," Tory said.
He handed her the phone. "Call 911. Tell them what we saw and that it's Andrew's rental. And pray."

"Take a left here." The man shifted on the seat as Andrew slowed to make the turn north onto Route 11.
"Where are we going?" Andrew asked.
"You'll see."
Andrew was silent for several minutes, trying to make sense of his plight.
"Did I do something to you?" He dared to ask.
The man chuckled. "You and your friend."
"My friend?" The back of Andrew's neck tingled. This was what happened to Mick. The certainty was chilling. And yet it was different. When he left his father's driveway, the kidnapper had allowed him to turn toward the highway, not the old woods road where Mick's body was found. Andrew took that as a good sign.
They were headed toward Oakland, he knew that much. Beyond was Waterville, the small city where his father was in the nursing home and Kurt Borden worked at the newspaper. On his

right was Messalonskee Lake, though he couldn't see it in the darkness. It was one of the larger lakes in the cluster that defined the Belgrade region, and stretched nine miles along the road between Belgrade and Oakland.

"Mick Tyler snooped around," the man said. Andrew threw a glance at him, but it was too dark to see much besides his imposing bulk and a faint gleam off the gun barrel.

"Mick was a reporter. That was his job." Andrew tried to keep his voice steady.

"Yeah, well, if he'd kept his mouth shut, he'd still be doing it."

Andrew swallowed hard. The country roads were dark, but another car met them as they came down a hill. In the glare of its headlights, he looked at the man once more. Heavyset, glasses, sixties or older, shortish hair, dark knit sweater with a lighter shirt showing at the neckline. It wasn't much.

"I haven't been snooping," he said. "I'm just here to take care of my father. He's very ill."

The man laughed. "Yeah. Right. Too bad he didn't kick off when he had that stroke." He sighed. "One more loose end."

Andrew decided he didn't have much to lose. "Was Mick a loose end?"

"You might say that. I never knew you boys saw us. Never in my life dreamed anyone saw us that night. Then Tyler started sniffing around, asking everyone about the senator. I heard he was out to Belgrade, digging up the past so to speak, so I came out to Pine Lane and let on I was a neighbor. He told me what he saw that night. Big mistake."

Andrew was silent. He didn't need to ask what night the man was talking about. It had to be that night in 1968, when he and Mick had seen the two cars leave the Jacobs cottage.

"He was a good reporter," the man went on, waving the gun a bit too freely, Andrew thought. "He found out too much, and now it seems all the Fairmonts and the Bordens are snooping around, and that kid reporter."

"But . . ." Andrew's heart raced. He was driving rural roads with Mick's killer beside him. His own story about what he and Mick saw and heard that fateful night was published earlier this week. Mick had been dead eight days, he figured, when an abbreviated version of his story ran in the *Sentinel.* If Mick was killed because of what he saw more than forty years ago, then the killer had at least as much reason to do away with Andrew. He not only saw what Mick saw, he'd made it public.

"Are you going to kill us all?" he asked at last. "Because my family won't give up looking for an explanation. Dave Carpenter won't, either, and Janet and Kurt Borden surely won't. We're all in this together, trying to find out what went on back then, and why Senator Jacobs gave my father all that stuff two weeks after he'd disappeared, and what happened to him after that."

"You'll have the FBI up here before we know it," the man sneered. He held the gun up close to Andrew's temple. "They can speculate all they want, but there's no proof. Your father might have had evidence at one time, but it's not there now. You're the only witness left who saw me and my friend that night."

Andrew's heart pounded. *He wouldn't pull the trigger while the car's moving. Would he?*

They were in North Belgrade now, approaching the fork where Routes 8 and 11 separated.

"Go left," the man said, and Andrew signaled and slowed for the turn, then drove on toward Smithfield. There was almost no traffic.

"You broke into my father's house," Andrew hazarded. That was why he was so certain there was no evidence. He'd searched for it twice and come up empty.

The man chuckled and relaxed, lowering the gun to his lap. "I'll never admit it."

This man must be Dunning. But Andrew would never have a chance to testify against him. Dunning was taking care of the possibility right now, and Andrew was driving toward death. "But why . . . ?" Andrew closed his lips firmly. He hadn't meant to voice the thought, but the man turned toward him with a smile.

"We'd thought all this time that the evidence was gone. But all of a sudden, a couple of weeks ago, my son hears an old man making what he thought was a dying confession. That old man was Senator Jacobs's nearest neighbor, and he was telling a friend that he'd kept something he shouldn't have. Well, when my son told me that, I thought, what if he's still got the documents that disappeared in '68? It was unlikely, but I knew I couldn't take the chance on this old guy connecting me to Jacobs's death. What if the old man died and something incriminating was found in that house across the road from Jacobs's camp?"

Andrew swallowed hard.

"Turn left." Dunning gestured with the pistol. "Right up there."

Andrew was surprised. He put on his signal. Was there a road here? He realized it was a driveway. He waited for a pickup truck to pass before he pulled in.

The man lowered the gun as the glare of thc headlights washed over them, but kept it pointed at Andrew's midsection. "You're the only one left who saw us switch the plates that night. With you out of the way . . ."

The truth dawned on Andrew as he pulled slowly into the gravel driveway. The two men he and Mick had seen that night were taking the Congressional license plates off the senator's car. Of course! There was an all-points bulletin out on the senator's car since his disappearance, and the description included his Congressional plate number. The men had to be sure no one recognized Jacobs's car by the special plates before they . . . what? That car had never been found. The lake beside the cottage was too shallow. They must have deep sixed it someplace where it would not be found. The ocean, most likely, or maybe even the Kennebec River. They had to get the car and the senator's body away from the area where people knew him and would instantly recognize that car. And so they took an old plate from the garage and put it on the senator's car for his last journey.

He stopped the rental car before a modest white clapboard house. A figure approached them, and the man rolled down his window. Andrew squinted to see the newcomer, but he could be sure of only one thing. It was a woman.

"Have you got Borden?" Dunning asked.

"Not exactly."

Dunning swore. He turned toward her for a moment in obvious annoyance. Andrew considered his chances of getting away if he jumped out of the car and ran toward the road. But his captor's attention swung back to him almost immediately. "Don't move, Fairmont." To the woman he said, "What happened?"

"We couldn't let him go to his house. It was

like you said. His wife was there. So our friend got him to stop, and I played the kind bystander. Borden was smashed up pretty badly, though. I'd just about convinced him to get in my car and let me take him to the hospital when a genuine good Samaritan stopped."

"Just great."

"Yes," she agreed bitterly. "I had to leave him. The fellow was calling an ambulance."

"So he's hurt pretty bad?"

"There was some blood, but he was conscious and talking to me. A bit fuzzy, but he'll make it."

Dunning swore again. "Follow us."

"Right. Maybe it will be enough if we take care of this one. They'll never be able to prove anything. It was just two boys, you know, and they'll both be gone now."

"Shut up." Dunning rolled up his window and gestured toward the road with his pistol. "Drive."

Andrew swallowed hard. His hands shook as he put the car in gear. By some miracle, Kurt wasn't with him on this grisly odyssey. He was glad of that. But one thing was certain: these people were going to kill him.

Chapter 27

Dave drove conservatively, keeping well back behind Andrew's car. Tory sat beside him, holding the cell phone. He could feel her tension. They rounded a curve, and he saw that a truck was coming toward them from Smithfield. Not only that, but Andrew had braked to a stop and had his turn signal on. Dave slowed the Jeep.

"Now what?"

"It's a house," Tory said. "Drive on past. If you stop, they'll notice."

The truck passed, and Andrew turned his car in at the driveway. Dave drove on down the road.

"Find a place to turn around," Tory said.

There were no side roads for the next quarter mile, and in exasperation, Dave slowed. "Hang on." There was no traffic, and he did a quick U-turn in the road. "What if they drove in there to throw us off and went back the other way?"

"No, you did a good job. They don't suspect a thing."

"Sure, that's what you say." He pulled to the side of the road several yards below the driveway and turned off the lights. Should he turn around again? If Andrew and the other man left the house, would they head for Smithfield, or back toward Belgrade? He decided to wait where he was. But if Andrew's rental came out of the driveway, what would he do?

"Dave," Tory said in a very small voice.

"What?"

"Could we . . . pray together?"

He smiled and pulled in a deep breath. "Of course."

He could see Tory bow her head in the dimness. Dave kept his eyes on the road ahead and prayed out loud. "Dear Lord, please give us wisdom, and keep us safe. And whatever's going on with Andrew, please help him. Amen."

Tory said softly, "Dear God, I don't think Uncle Andrew is a believer, and this doesn't look too good for him. Please keep him alive and give me a chance to tell him about You."

Dave reached for her hand.

"Amen," Tory said.

"Amen." Dave looked over at her. Tears streaming down her face reflected the moonlight. "It's going to be okay," he whispered. "God is in charge."

"Maybe we should get out and take a look," Tory suggested. "We could see if Uncle Andrew's car is in the yard."

"Let me call the police again," Dave said. "At

least we can tell them where the house is." He took the phone.

"Hey!" Tory said.

Dave saw it, too. A car was pulling out of the driveway Andrew had entered, heading back toward Belgrade and Augusta. Dave was glad they hadn't come toward him, or they surely would have noticed the Jeep sitting there on the shoulder.

"You call." He thrust the phone into her hands and put the Jeep in gear.

"Wait."

More headlights shone from the driveway. Dave held his breath. A second car eased out onto the road, following Andrew's rental.

Dave exhaled. "That's the same Mitsubishi that Janet and I saw near your house last week."

"Are you sure? Don't let them get too far ahead."

He eased the Jeep out onto the pavement and turned the lights on. "Get the dispatcher on the line. Tell him we're following them back up Route 8, and there are two cars now. We're about a mile from the merge with 11."

Tory made the call and said to Dave, "They want me to stay on the line and keep them posted as to where we are."

"Good. We're passing the merge now. Still heading south, toward Belgrade Village."

Tory relayed the information and then said,

"Fantastic! Dave, he says there's a state trooper a mile or two ahead, coming this way. He'll pull over now and watch for the two cars."

Dave drove on, letting the other cars lengthen their lead on him, but keeping their taillights in sight on the straight stretches. At last he saw another car pull out from a driveway.

"That's the trooper!" Tory cried, and Dave eased off on the gas.

"Why are you slowing down?" Dunning barked, raising the gun to a level with Andrew's ear.

"There's a police car back there."

The kidnapper looked over his shoulder and swore. "No," he moaned. "No, Alice, no, no, no! Do not stop."

"He's pulling her over," Andrew said. "She has to stop." After a tense moment, he saw in the mirror that the cruiser had passed the stopped sedan and was now directly behind him, blue lights flashing.

"Keep going," Dunning said.

"Are you crazy? I have to stop."

"I'll tell you when to stop," Dunning insisted. "Keep going."

Andrew gritted his teeth and drove. As he topped a rise, he exhaled sharply. "Can I stop now?" Even as he spoke, he applied the brakes. Before him two cars with flashing blue lights were parked at the edges of the road, one facing each way, and between them was an almost flat obstruction.

"What's that?" Dunning gasped.

"Spike mats." The front tires hit the mat, and Andrew fought for control of the vehicle. The pistol went off next to him with a painfully sharp report. He couldn't hear anything after that, but he could see the officers gesturing to him as soon as the car stopped. He put the engine in park, raised his hands above his shoulders, and sat still, waiting for them to come to him.

"Help me, help me," Dunning screamed. At least it must have been a scream, but Andrew's ears were still ringing, and it sounded like a tiny voice echoing in a bucket.

Andrew looked over at him. Dunning had dropped the pistol and was holding his thigh and shrieking, "Help me! It was an accident! Please, please, help me! I didn't mean to shoot!"

Chapter 28

Janet and Sharon sat on the Bordens' couch poring over the contents of a carton that had just been delivered. Kurt was stretched out in his recliner. His bruised face gave him a dangerous air, but he was too groggy to play the role of a desperado. Every time Janet looked at him, his eyelids had drooped a little lower.

"The senator's daughter just sent you all this stuff?" Sharon asked. "She's very trusting."

"I told her my husband is going to see that her father's story is revealed, and she was eager to do anything she could to help. Here, I'll take this packet of letters, and you look through Mrs. Jacobs's household account book."

"All right." Sharon took the battered old notebook from her and opened it. "I barely remember Charlotte. I was little when her father disappeared. But I recall she was pretty. And stuck-up. At least, that's what all the other kids seemed to think. She went swimming with us once."

They were silent for several minutes, reading. Janet wasn't sure what to look for, but the correspondence she was reviewing post-dated the senator's disappearance by several years and seemed irrelevant to the case.

Sharon sat back with a sigh.

"Anything?" Janet asked.

"No. And the handwriting's hard to read."

"Want to swap?"

"Sure."

Janet handed her the sheaf of letters and took the notebook.

"I love your necklace," Sharon said. "It makes your eyes look bluer."

Janet smiled, fingering the sapphire pendant. "Kurt gave it to me for our anniversary. It was in the car when he crashed, all wrapped up fancy. The tow truck driver brought me the package and Kurt's cell phone and razor the next day."

"And Kurt's all right?" Sharon whispered, darting a glance in his direction.

"The doctor says he'll be fine in a few days. They let him come home yesterday, but he's still stiff and achy."

"Those bruises look terrible."

"Yeah, he's on some pretty strong pain meds," Janet conceded.

"Did they find out who ran him off the road yet?"

"No, but they're working on it. The Dunnings are both in jail, but there had to be a third person. From what Andrew said, Mr. and Mrs. Dunning had to be in it with the man who caused Kurt's accident, but we don't know who he is, and they haven't told the police. The three of them hoped to get both Kurt and Andrew and haul them off somewhere and . . ." Janet swallowed hard.

Sharon nodded. "God protected them that night."

"For sure," Janet said.

"Didn't Kurt identify that woman as the one who stopped and tried to get him into her car?"

"Alice—that's Mrs. Dunning—denies she was there, and Kurt was so disoriented he couldn't make a positive ID. But the fireman who called the ambulance identified her car as the one stopped behind Kurt's when he got there."

"Well, that's something."

Janet frowned. "It's been three days."

Sharon reached over and squeezed Janet's hand. "Tory and I have been praying all weekend. She had to be back at work today, so she left last night. I miss her awfully."

Janet smiled. "You and Dave."

Sharon nodded. "I hope that turns out well. He seems like a wonderful guy, and I'd hate to see Tory hurt again."

"I don't think you need to worry about Dave, but Kurt will ride herd on him, once he's able to go back to work."

"I'm going in tomorrow," Kurt said, shifting in the recliner.

"I thought you were asleep!" Janet jumped up and went to his side. "How are you doing?"

He sighed. "Still sore. I think I should get up and walk around."

"Let me help you."

He reached for the lever on the side of the chair and grimaced. "Maybe I'll wait a while."

"If you need to get up . . ."

Kurt looked up at her with a crooked smile. "I said I should, but I didn't say I would."

She laughed and dropped a quick kiss on his forehead. "I'll bring you some lemonade."

"Coffee," he corrected.

"All right."

When she returned a few minutes later with coffee mugs for Kurt and Sharon, Kurt was asleep in the chair.

"Honey?" Janet asked softly, but he didn't stir.

She smiled and went to the couch. "Here, Sharon, this is for you. If Kurt doesn't wake up in five minutes, I'll drink his."

"Thanks." Sharon set the mug on a coaster.

Janet picked up Mrs. Jacobs's account book and scanned through it. Suddenly an item caught her eye, and her pulse picked up speed.

"Sharon, look at this."

"What is it?" Sharon leaned toward the notebook Janet was holding.

"Regular payments in the winter of '67, and I checked back for the two previous years.

William and Alice Dunning worked regularly for the Jacobs family while they were here at the cottage."

Sharon nodded, scanning the list of expenses Mrs. Jacobs had written neatly in the book. "We knew that."

"Yes. William drove for the senator and did maintenance. His wife cooked and cleaned," Janet said. "But I noticed that in the off season, when the Jacobs family was in Portland or Washington, they also paid someone to keep an eye on the place."

Sharon frowned. "Don't most of the camp owners do that?"

"Sure. They get someone to check now and then for break-ins and scoop snow off the roof after heavy storms."

"So, William Dunning didn't do that for them?"

"Apparently they hired another young man for that. Look at this payment in December of 1967, and again in February of 1968."

Sharon looked closely at the notebook. "Is that who I think it is?"

Janet stood up. "Kurt!"

Kurt jumped and blinked, putting his hand to his brow. "What, babe? My coffee ready?"

Janet took the notebook to his chair. "This will wake you up more than the coffee would. Look, honey."

Kurt stretched his legs and reached for the book. “What? Show me.”

“This fellow worked for the Jacobs family in the late sixties.”

Kurt bent over the notebook and squinted. He looked up at Janet, wincing as he raised his chin. “Ow. Is it time for my pill?”

“Yes, I’ll get it.”

“Get me the phone, too.”

“Are you going to call the state police?” Sharon asked eagerly.

“No. I’m still a little fuzzy, so I’m calling Sergeant Bedard at the Waterville P.D. He can decide who else to call.”

Chapter 29

Janet looked around the room with satisfaction. Two weeks had passed since Kurt's accident. Elwood's family and friends had gathered at the retirement home to celebrate his eightieth birthday. The staff of Maple Heights had set up chairs and refreshments in the sunroom so they could all enjoy the afternoon together. Kurt sat beside her in one corner, holding her hand and seemingly content to let the Fairmonts take center stage.

"Well, this is quite a party. Thank you all for coming," Elwood said.

Geneva smiled and patted his hand. "You're welcome, Dad."

"We're all pleased to be here," Sharon added, placing a paper plate in his hand.

"Janet's cheesecake?" Elwood asked, eyeing the confection with anticipation.

"That's right," Sharon said, "and here's your tea, right beside you on the table." She continued serving cheesecake, aided by Tory, then sat down beside her husband, Vic Schlesser. Janet was pleased that Vic had come for the weekend.

It was the first time she had met him. She liked him, and he had agreed to attend church in the morning with his family and the Bordens. Tory wriggled in between Dave and her uncle Paul on the love seat. Janet smiled as she watched Dave's expression. He was in love, no doubt about it, and if Tory's contented smile was any indication, she reciprocated.

"How are you feeling, Kurt?" Elwood asked, looking anxiously toward his friend. Kurt's bruises had started to fade but still cast purple shadows on his face.

"Better every day. I went back to the office last week, and things seem to be almost normal." Kurt squeezed Janet's hand, and she smiled at him, rocking gently in her comfortable chair.

Charlotte Jacobs Hyde sat next to Elwood, sipping her tea and eyeing the cheesecake longingly. She had refused Sharon's offer of a slice, but Janet thought she might be regretting that decision as the Fairmonts exclaimed how good it was.

"Mrs. Hyde, we're so glad you could come," Geneva said.

"It's a pleasure. I didn't want to see the old cottage until now, and whenever I came to visit in Maine, I stayed away from it. My last memories of the place were grim. But now that we know Father wasn't a criminal, and that he didn't abandon Mother and me on purpose, I find that I've some very pleasant reminiscences of Belgrade."

Elwood smiled at her. "It's good to have you here, Charlotte. Haven't seen you since you were a girl."

"That's right," she agreed. "I remember that last summer. Your children were getting big. Geneva was going into eighth grade that fall, I think."

Dave's cell phone trilled, and he jumped up. "Excuse me." He headed out into the hallway.

Just then Andrew came through the door. "Sorry I'm late, Dad. I just came from Augusta."

"What's the word on Detective Robbins?" Paul asked.

"The judge denied bail. You know he's charged with Mick Tyler's murder and attempting to kill Kurt. He's going to stay in custody until trial, and they're investigating his role in Senator Jacobs's disappearance. There may be some conspiracy charges for him and the Dunnings."

Kurt spoke up. "The district attorney told Dave this morning that they're collecting evidence against Robbins and William Dunning in the Jacobs case. He didn't come right out and say it, but we got the impression that Alice Dunning spilled the story—not just on what they did to Mick Tyler, Andrew, and me, but it seems conclusive that Dunning and Robbins were behind Senator Jacobs's death as well."

Sharon shook her head. "The senator's security man and driver."

"Yes," Andrew agreed. "Dunning practically admitted it to me in the car the night he kidnapped me. He came right out and said they'd switched the license plates on the senator's car."

"We went back and looked in the garage," Kurt said. "We think they took the last plate in the series off the wall, the 1967 one. When we looked closely, we found there were nails where it would have hung, but we didn't notice that the first time we were there. They probably took that one since it was the most recent and wouldn't draw attention like an older one would have."

"And the empty spot on the wall wasn't conspicuous," Janet added.

"So why did they kill my father?" Charlotte Hyde asked. "They didn't get the money."

"They thought they would," Andrew said. Geneva scooted her chair over to make room for him between her and their father. "When Senator Jacobs dropped out of sight with the documents, someone pursued him, trying to kill him and get the papers back. He eluded them for a couple of weeks, bringing the papers to Maine. They nearly caught him, and in desperation he gave the documents to Dad."

"But he wasn't caught then," Paul said with a puzzled look. "You told me he was probably still alive until the night you and Mick Tyler saw the men at Jacobs's cottage."

"That's right," Andrew said. "He managed

to outrun them for several more days. But he didn't feel safe enough to contact his family." He smiled apologetically at Charlotte Hyde. "Back then we didn't have cell phones and e-mail. I think your father hid himself well for a while and felt your mother was better off not knowing he was out there. He came back to Maine the day Mick and I saw what we saw. He hoped to get the papers back from Dad and get them into the right hands."

Elwood shook his head. "When you told me what you and Mick saw, I wondered if he would come to our house that night. I waited up, but no one came."

Andrew frowned. "I suspect he was killed that evening. Dunning told the police the senator showed up scared but determined. He asked Dunning and Robbins to help him hide until the next day. He had come back to Belgrade to get the documents and was planning to come out in the open and blow the whistle on several officials in the Department of Agriculture. But someone got to Dunning and Robbins first and bribed them to stop the senator. They accepted a large sum of money to get Jacobs out of the way and retrieve the incriminating papers. Jacobs wouldn't tell them where the documents were, but they figured they were in the cottage. They were pretty frustrated when they couldn't find them."

"Be glad they didn't know you had those boxes, Dad," Geneva said, squeezing Elwood's arm.

"There was plenty of reason for them to stop Mick, and for Robbins to try to stall the investigation into Mick's death," Paul said.

Sharon nodded. "Mick was stirring up the old story of the senator's disappearance, and Mr. Dunning had already heard through his son, the EMT, that Dad said something that sounded like a confession the day he had his stroke."

Dave appeared in the doorway. "That was Detective Hewitt on the phone. Just thought you'd all like to know, William Dunning has confessed that he and Detective Robbins killed Senator Jacobs, on directions from someone higher up. With the help of a couple of his staff, an undersecretary in the Department of Agriculture was embezzling the money from the pesticide study. Jacobs gathered all the evidence against him, and the undersecretary wanted those incriminating papers back."

"Those papers have now been recovered from Nova Scotia," Andrew said. "Dad's cousin kept them safe all these years, not knowing what they were. The FBI is sending two agents to take them to Washington, and to question Robbins and Dunning."

"But the money in the briefcase . . ." Geneva said.

"Yes," Elwood agreed. "If someone else embezzled the money for the agricultural study, how did Senator Jacobs get it?"

"I think I can answer that," Janet said. "It took Sharon, Kurt, and me a while to go through all the Jacobs family's papers Charlotte sent us, but last night we found a very interesting letter." She looked at Kurt.

"Go ahead, sweetheart," he said. "You found it and recognized its importance. Of course, everyone will know about it when they read Dave's story in tomorrow's *Sentinel*."

Janet smiled and faced the eager group. "Well, a month or so after the senator disappeared, his wife contacted his attorney. You see, the senator and Mrs. Jacobs had discussed selling a piece of property they owned in Bar Harbor."

Charlotte Hyde nodded. "They got a steal on that shorefront land, not long after Dad was elected to the Senate."

"The lawyer was surprised when Mrs. Jacobs asked him if the deal would still go through, since her husband was missing," Janet went on. "The attorney wrote back and told her the deal had been made, and he'd delivered the check to Senator Jacobs personally about two months previous to her call."

Elwood's jaw dropped. "You mean . . . the money he gave me wasn't from the Department of Agriculture?"

"No, I'm afraid the embezzler got away with that."

"Because I didn't turn over the papers," Elwood moaned.

"He's dead now," Kurt said. "It's too late to prosecute him, and the money is probably long gone."

"Wait a minute," Paul said. "You're saying the money in the briefcase belonged to Senator and Mrs. Jacobs."

Kurt nodded. "Yes. As nearly as we can make out, the senator deposited the check from the real estate deal—his lawyer checked on that with the Realtor after Mrs. Jacobs wrote to him—and dropped out of sight when he was ready to blow the whistle on the embezzler. We now know that man had mob connections. Elwood, the car you saw drive by after Jacobs gave you the boxes may have been hired killers."

"Dad!" Sharon gasped, and the other Fairmont children stared at their father with amazement and respect.

"Dunning had driven the senator to the bank a couple of weeks earlier," Andrew went on. "He knew the senator had withdrawn a large sum of cash shortly before he disappeared. Jacobs never had any of the Department of Agriculture's missing money, but the man who stole it made it look as though he did. Dunning and Robbins hoped to get the money Thomas Jacobs took from the bank, as well as the documents. They overpowered him the evening Mick and I saw them, but the money wasn't there. Although they didn't know it, Jacobs had already given it to Dad with the papers."

Paul nodded. "Maybe Jacobs was afraid he'd need to hide for a while to be safe, and would need a lot of cash."

Kurt shrugged. "We don't really know why he was carrying so much cash, or why he didn't tell his wife."

"He was always protective of Mother," Charlotte said with a sad smile. "She paid the household bills out of an allowance Father gave her every month, but he always balanced the checkbook and had the tax returns prepared, that sort of thing. He probably handled all of the paperwork on any real estate or stock transactions, too."

"So you think he figured your mother was better off not knowing about this embezzlement thing until everything was settled?" Kurt asked.

Charlotte nodded. "He wouldn't tell her about something like that. She would have worried too much. Attitudes were very different back then from what they are today. Father almost never discussed Senate business at home. Mother occasionally went with him to social events in Washington, but she would never have spoken out on a political issue or anything like that. And it would be like Father to take care of selling the land himself. As to withdrawing the cash, he might have planned to make arrangements for our whole family to get away someplace for a while. He had Mother and me get passports in the spring of 1968, but we hadn't used them yet. I wondered at the time if he was planning a surprise vacation or something, but he wouldn't tell us."

Kurt nodded. "But he knew he was in trouble the day he hit Elwood's car, and he didn't want to take a chance of losing the documents or his own money, so he asked his faithful, dependable neighbor to keep it all for a while."

Elwood sighed. "I should have given that money over to the family. Poor Mrs. Jacobs! I'm so sorry, Charlotte."

"We didn't suffer from losing the money." Charlotte reached over and patted his hand. "We had enough, and losing Father was so much more tragic! But you mustn't trouble yourself about it. My father had a lot of investments by that time, and Mother was comfortable."

"But seventy thousand dollars! It should have gone to you and your mother." Elwood closed his eyes for a moment, then looked at her steadily. "Property values have gone up since then. My farm is worth more than that. I could—"

"Stop it," Charlotte insisted. "You didn't steal it. Father gave it to you, and because of that you were able to educate your children well. By the time you opened that briefcase and realized what you had, I was married, and Mother had remarried as well. We didn't need it."

"But he didn't mean for me to have it."

Dave said, "Probably Mr. Jacobs didn't want to endanger you if the killers got to him, Mr. Fairmont. That's why he said to destroy the papers. But he was distraught. I doubt he wanted you to destroy the money, too. He fully expected to come back for it."

"Even so," said Charlotte, "I don't blame you, Mr. Fairmont."

"I've always felt so guilty."

"You mustn't. It's in the past."

Andrew said, "Maybe my family can talk about this later."

Sharon nodded. "It's a shame, but I'm sure we all need time to think about it."

"Well, if you expect me to sue you for the missing money, forget it." Charlotte picked up her cup and sipped her tea. "Consider it a gift from my father in return for hiding those papers for him."

"Dad," Andrew said. He hesitated, and Elwood looked at him in question. "I just want to say that I never appreciated all you and Mom did for me, and I never really thought about how you paid for college for all of us. I'm sorry. I was ungrateful for a lot of things, and . . . well, I think I understand now why some things were the way they were."

"Me, too," said Geneva. "Thank you."

"And thank you, Mrs. Hyde," Sharon said. "We all appreciate your graciousness. You could have filed charges when you found out about this."

"Nonsense. Life is too short to go about prosecuting an old neighbor."

Elwood's eyes glistened with tears. "Thank you, my dear."

Sharon stood up, holding a canvas tote bag. "Mrs. Hyde, I have something here that my family has agreed we'd like you to have. It's something that was in your father's briefcase when he gave it to Dad way back then."

"Oh?" Charlotte watched with interest as Sharon withdrew an old, square tin from her tote bag and opened it.

"We believe these things belonged to your father, and you and your family ought to have them." She took out the silver pen and card case and passed them to Mrs. Hyde.

Charlotte held them in her hands and looked down at them. She took a deep breath. "Oh, yes." Tears filled her eyes. "Yes. These were Father's. Mother told the police he was carrying them when he disappeared." She looked around at all of them. "Thank you so much, all of you Fairmonts. And thank you, Mr. and Mrs. Borden and Mr. Carpenter, for pushing this investigation until you learned the truth. You all put yourselves at risk for that. I will never forget it."

Geneva took a tissue from her purse and tucked it into Charlotte's hand.

"We're glad we could do it," Kurt said. He squeezed Janet's hand and stood. "Dave and I had better get back to the office now."

"I'm heading for Augusta," Dave corrected him. "Detective Hewitt is holding a press conference in an hour. I'll pick up Wally and be on my way."

"I'll see you later," Tory said, and Dave stooped to whisper something in her ear.

"Have fun, folks." Dave waved to them all and headed for the door.

Sharon stepped up and handed him a plate. "Here! Take some cheesecake with you. We've got tons of it left."

Dave accepted it with a smile. "Thanks! 'Bye, all."

"See you in the funny papers," Elwood called, and they all laughed.

"Mrs. Hyde," Sharon said, "won't you have a piece? It's delectable."

Charlotte's cheeks went pink, and she smiled. "Well, maybe just a sliver. And is there any more tea?"

"I'll get a fresh pot." Geneva stood and reached for the china teapot.

Elwood sighed. "It's good to have all my children here."

"We're glad to be here, Dad," Paul said. "We ought to do this more often."

"How about Thanksgiving?" Sharon asked. "We're hoping to move Dad closer to our house by then, and we'll host a Fairmont family feast like you've never seen before!"

"I suppose we'll have to invite Dave, too," Vic said with a mischievous smile.

"You'd better, or I won't be there," Tory told him.

Kurt and Janet said good-bye to Elwood and all his guests and walked out to the parking lot together.

"Do you need to go back to the office?" Janet asked.

Kurt shook his head. "Not really. It's almost four o'clock, and I'm tired."

"You'd better come home and get some rest," she said. "You're still healing, you know."

"Hm. Right. I need to be well enough to drive down to Boston next week for the game."

"Is Wally going with you?"

"No. I thought I told you."

"You did, but I figured maybe you'd give him another chance. You expected him to go cold turkey for almost a month."

Kurt winced. "Yeah. Wally's not good at delayed gratification. You think I should make him a new offer? You wouldn't mind?"

"No. I'd enjoy going with you, but Wally

would be ecstatic. Why don't you talk to him tomorrow? It's still a week away. If he could go a week without smoking, that would be a huge accomplishment."

Kurt smiled. "All right, I'll do it." He opened the passenger door and stood watching her in surprise as she walked around the front of the car. "Where are you going? I opened the door for you."

Janet laughed. "I thought I was driving."

"I'm not that bad off. I can drive my best girl home."

She smiled and walked back around the car and slid in. When Kurt had climbed in on the driver's side, she leaned over and put her arms around his neck. "That was good teamwork. Solving the senator's murder, I mean."

"Yes, you and I work well together."

She laughed. "I meant you, Dave, Andrew, the police, everybody. Even Mick had a part in it."

"A big part."

"Yes. But you're right about the two of us. We're a super team."

"Of course I'm right. You did almost as much work on this case as Dave and I did. And we've sold more papers this month than ever before. Subscriptions are up eight percent."

"That must make Grant Engstrom happy."

"He's practically purring. So be forewarned: next time a mystery comes up at the paper, I'll put you on the payroll as a consultant." He kissed her, and Janet rested in his arms.

"I love you."

Kurt smiled and drew a deep breath. "So, you want to eat out tonight? I still owe you an anniversary dinner."

Janet shook her head and nestled against his chest. "Let's stay home. One party a day is enough excitement. I'd rather spend a quiet evening at home with you."

"Oh, yeah," Kurt agreed, holding up his key ring and selecting the car key. "My favorite place on earth: fourteen Pine Lane, where nothing ever happens."

Dear Reader,

I am often asked how much in my books is true. This book is pure fiction, but it did have a real-life inspiration.

I grew up in the town in this story, Belgrade, Maine. I worked for the *Central Maine Morning Sentinel* in Waterville as a correspondent for about twenty years, and my husband Jim was a copy editor there and at the *Kennebec Journal* in Augusta. I used the *Sentinel* as the setting for fictional editor Kurt Borden's job.

Several years ago I learned about the disappearance of Judge Joseph Force Crater in 1930. He was one of the most famous missing persons in America for the next fifty years. His fate is still unknown.

What really fascinated me was that Judge Crater had a summer home in my town—Belgrade. His wife, Stella, was there at the time of his disappearance. On August 3, the judge took a call at his cottage, and then immediately started packing to return to New York by train. He didn't tell his wife who called or why. Stella expected him back at the cottage by August 9, which was her birthday, but he never came.

Much has been written about the judge's

disappearance. At first, I considered writing a novel centered on this historical event. But I decided to move forward in time and write about a more recent fictional disappearance—one that local residents would remember. And so, instead of Judge Crater, this story features the disappearance of fictional Senator Thomas Jacobs.

I hope you've enjoyed the story. If you'd like to leave a review on Goodreads, Amazon, or other venues of your choice, that would be much appreciated by the author.

Sincerely,
Susan Page Davis

About the Author

Susan Page Davis is a fiction writer who has published more than eighty novels. Some of her other mystery and romantic suspense books are:

The Maine Justice Series: *The Priority Unit*, *Fort Point*, *Found Art*, *Heartbreaker Hero*, *The House Next Door*, and *The Labor Day Challenge*.

Mainely Mysteries Series: *Homicide at Blue Heron Lake*, *Treasure at Blue Heron Lake*, and *Impostors at Blue Heron Lake*, written with her daughter Megan.

Frasier Island Series: *Frasier Island*, *Finding Marie*, and *Inside Story*.

Also, *The Saboteur*, *Just Cause*, *Witness*, *On a Killer's Trail*, and *Hearts in the Crosshairs*.

Many of her historical novels also include mysteries: *The Crimson Cipher*, *The Sheriff's Surrender*, *The Gunsmith's Gallantry*, *The Blacksmith's Bravery*, and more.

Susan is a native of Maine, now living in Kentucky. She is the mother of six and grandmother of ten. She is a past winner of the Carol Award, the Inspirational Readers' Choice Award, and the Will Rogers Medallion Award for Western

Fiction. She was named Favorite Author of the Year by Heartsong Presents readers for 2010. Visit her website, where you can view all her books and subscribe to her occasional newsletter, at: www.susanpagedavis.com.

Discussion Questions

1. Janet's neighborly efforts put her in the middle of an uncomfortable situation. Have you ever tried to help someone and gotten in deeper than you'd imagined? Were you sorry afterward?

2. Was Kurt right to put Dave on the story when Mick disappeared?

3. Kurt wants to help Wally quit smoking, but his attempts aren't very successful. Should he leave Wally alone? Or is there something he could do differently that might help more?

4. The Fairmont children bicker constantly. Is it too late to reverse this pattern? If you have children, how did you try to prevent this tendency in your own family?

5. Janet has a poor self-image. She gave up her job when she and Kurt moved to Maine. How does she fill the gaps this has left in her life? What else might she do?

6. Dave prompts Kurt to start a Bible study at work. What else does Kurt do to reach out to the people who work under him?

7. Is it too late for Elwood to set things right with his children? What growth do you see in Elwood? Sharon? Paul? Andrew? Geneva?

8. The children don't think much of their mother's paintings. Why do you think Olivia persisted in this hobby? How is it important to the plot? Do you think they will value her art more highly now?

9. Where do you see Dave in ten years? Kurt? Tory? Janet?

Books are produced in the United States using U.S.-based materials

Books are printed using a revolutionary new process called THINKtech™ that lowers energy usage by 70% and increases overall quality

Books are durable and flexible because of Smyth-sewing

Paper is sourced using environmentally responsible foresting methods and the paper is acid-free

Center Point Large Print
600 Brooks Road / PO Box 1
Thorndike, ME 04986-0001 USA

(207) 568-3717

US & Canada:
1 800 929-9108
www.centerpointlargeprint.com